"How I want you, my raven-haired love."

Dan's voice was roughened by desire as he wrapped Chris in his arms. "Tonight, tomorrow, forever...."

An uncontrolled fire swept through her as he kissed her deeply, possessively. Then his fingers slipped under the straps of her nightgown, baring her shoulders.

Chris gasped when his hands moved down to the fullness of her breasts. Arching upward, she met his hunger with her own, wanting, needing all of him.

"Now," she murmured entreatingly. "Please, Dan, love me now...."

THE AUTHOR

Eileen Nauman believes in living life to the fullest. By the age of seventeen she had broken mustangs in Oregon, received her pilot's license and soloed in a Cessna 150. She then joined the Navy as a meteorologist for the Air Wings. Eileen and her husband, David, now live on a small farm in Ohio, where they enjoy raising Arabian horses.

Touch the Heavens is the first romance published under Eileen's own name. She also writes under the pseudonyms Lindsay McKenna and Beth Brookes. The freshness and originality of her writing won her an award as Most Innovative Romance Writer of 1984.

Touch the Heavens

EILEEN NAUMAN

Harlequin Books

TORONTO • NEW YORK • LONDON
AMSTERDAM • PARIS • SYDNEY • HAMBURG
STOCKHOLM • ATHENS • TOKYO • MILAN

Published March 1985

ISBN 0-373-25151-3

Printed in Canada

In Memory
of
Doug Benefield
Test Pilot

When I first met you to interview you, I wondered if you were born part eagle. You lived to fly, flew to live. Your world never consisted of feet on the ground. No, you felt happiest with a stick in your hand and rudders beneath your booted feet, sailing through that vast blue ocean called the sky. And having been a test pilot for such a long time, you had survived longer than almost all of them. There was a natural intimacy between you and the bird you flew, an understanding. You were a natural stick-and-rudder man.

Your ability to share your knowledge of test piloting, with even the uninitiated such as myself forever imprinted you in my heart. On August 29, 1984, you died at the stick of your beloved B-1B bomber; you went out like you came in: flying. And I know from the way your voice grew gruff and your eyes softened when you looked at that bird that you loved what you were doing. And I was privileged to not only see, but feel that fierce pride and satisfaction within you toward your profession, as one of the greatest test pilots in the world.

Doug, you were an eagle and truly, you did *Touch the Heavens*....

DAN MCCORD'S EYES NARROWED as he spotted the woman in a dark-blue Air Force uniform standing near the flight line. So *this* was their woman test-pilot student, Captain Chris Mallory. So intent was she on inspecting the line of jet aircraft parked on the concrete ramp that she hadn't heard him approach. A wry smile tugged at his mouth as he allowed himself to fully enjoy the sight of her.

She was tall for a woman, but not for a test pilot; probably around five-foot-seven, he guessed. Her hair was a luxurious black with blue highlights, like those of a raven's wing gleaming in the early-morning light. Although Dan had met several women Air Force pilots during his career, he was pleasantly surprised: Chris Mallory was decidedly feminine in every respect. Her thick black hair curled softly into a shoulder-length pageboy that barely brushed her shoulders. Small, dainty pearl earrings adorned her earlobes. Nice, he decided. Very nice. There was an air of confidence around her that widened his smile. Even at a distance of twenty feet, she was a woman who would definitely command any male's attention.

As if finally sensing his presence, Chris Mallory turned her head slowly toward him, giving Dan the full impact of her violet gaze. He had never seen anyone with such wide, heather-colored eyes. Her face was square, softened by slightly full lips that curved upward. Overall, he decided, an arrestingly attractive woman—the kind who made him want to stare at her like an eighteen-year-old boy instead of a thirty-two-year-old man. He walked forward, extending his hand.

"You must be Captain Chris Mallory. I'm Major Dan McCord, one of the instructors at the Test Pilot School."

Chris smiled warmly, automatically proferring her own hand. Her slender fingers met and were enclosed by his in a firm grip. She gave a slightly embarrassed laugh, as he continued to hold her hand. Reluctantly, he released it.

"Yes, I am Captain Mallory. How did you know? Or is test-pilot student written all over me?"

He grinned. "Just a lucky guess. Actually, some of the guys think I'm psychic." Nice sense of humor, he thought. Dancing amethyst eyes with a real spark of life in them. Chris Mallory possessed a blend of femininity, confidence and allure, with emphasis on the allure. He felt excited by her presence in the test-pilot curriculum. If her looks were any indication of her skill as a pilot, she was going to do well as the first woman to challenge the male dominion of test piloting for the Air Force.

Chris found herself warming to Dan McCord, missing little in her initial inspection of him. He was a good five inches taller than her, with lean features and eyes the color of the sky she loved to fly in. Deeply tanned by the California sun, he carried himself with easy grace. Yet within him, Chris sensed there was a tightly coiled power. She would have been more on guard if his mouth had been thin or cruel looking. But it was a firm, well-shaped mouth. His walnut-brown hair was neatly trimmed and tapered in typical military style.

"I'd accept the psychic bit if I didn't know that nearly every national newspaper had announced that I'd be arriving today at Edwards Air Force Base to begin processing for Test Pilot School."

"Looks like I've been caught in the act," Dan admitted. "Now I'll have to confess to reading all the publicity anticipating your arrival."

Chris groaned. "Not to mention the television coverage. You'd think I was the first woman astronaut or something."

He liked her ability to remain at ease with him; something that other women military pilots never did accomplish. "You are a first, captain. But I was hoping that all this fanfare wouldn't deter you from looking forward to school."

She found herself beginning to relax. Maybe this new chapter in her life wasn't going to be as tough as she thought. Dan stood before her, one hand resting lazily on his slim hips. His flight cap was edged in silver with the gold major's oak leaf on one side, perched confidently on his head. His one-piece olive flight suit fit his lean, whipcord body to perfection, emphasizing his broad shoulders and well-muscled chest. "What almost stopped me from coming was my car," she admitted ruefully. "It broke down outside of Lancaster, about thirty miles from here."

His brows dipped. "Oh?"

She gave a shake of her head. "I got lucky and found a loose wire on the distributor; otherwise, I'd be hitchhiking onto the base. Somehow, I suspect the other test-pilot students wouldn't think much of that."

Dan became serious, watching her through half-closed eyes. "You're a pilot, not a car mechanic. I don't see why anyone would make fun of you if you hadn't been able to fix it."

"I expect some of the students are going to try and find the least little flaw in me and blow it out of proportion." She forced a smile, realizing the palms of her hands were damp. McCord was affecting her strangely, and suddenly Chris felt nervous around him. And at twenty-nine years old! Still she could see that she was affecting him similarly. Was this chemistry? Had that invisible web snared both of them within its unseen grip? In a characteristic gesture, Chris touched her hair, smoothing several strands back into place from her now rose-flushed cheeks.

"Don't worry about that. We're prepared to deal with any student who might cause you a problem, captain." He looked at his watch. "You were supposed to arrive over at personnel at 0900 this morning."

"How did you know that?"

"Because the commandant ordered me to meet you over there and help you with the processing procedures." Then he gave her an appraising look. "But, like any good student, you're here early."

"I just wanted to come down and take a look," she whispered, keenly aware of his maleness. "Some of these jets I've flown. Most of them I haven't. I just wanted to see...."

"I understand. Once flying gets in your blood, it's there to stay. Look, I have to do some proficiency flying in that F-4 Phantom sitting over there. Why don't you go over to the cafeteria and get some coffee? I'll meet you at personnel at 0900, and then we'll get you settled into the Barracks Officers' Quarters."

A new thrill coursed through her. Dan McCord appeared to be genuinely interested in her welfare. She had been prepared to steel herself against the chauvinism she would be facing because she was breaching the male dominion of test piloting. "You've got a deal, Major McCord."

"When we're alone like this, call me Dan. I only stand on military formality when necessary, Chris."

She felt the caress in his voice as he used her name, and felt a shiver of expectancy ripple through her. "Well—" she began uneasily.

"No argument. Hey, I've earned the honor of escorting you around, I want you to know that."

She tilted her head, confused. "What do you mean?"

Dan grinned boyishly. "Every instructor at TPS wanted to do the honors. We drew cards and I got the queen of hearts."

Chris found herself unnerved by his probing look.

"In more ways than one," he added huskily. Then, gesturing toward the flight line, he said, "And if I have my way about it, I'll be your instructor in three of those combat aircraft."

Before she could think of a glib retort to his flirtatiousness, McCord had gone, moving down the flight line toward the awaiting aircraft. Chris watched him, unraveled by his charm, friendliness and warmth. A silly smile touched her lips, and she shook her head. Normally, after having survived seven years in the military, she could trade teasing retorts with the best of them. But Dan McCord made her feel like a giddy seventeen-year-old girl on her first date.

LATER THAT MORNING, after two hours' worth of paperwork, Chris was officially enrolled as a student for Test Pilot School. She was about to ask where the barracks was when Dan appeared at her side.

"I'll escort you over to the Barracks Officers' Quarters and get you settled in your assigned rooms," he offered, lifting his flight cap in playful imitation of a porter.

"You don't have to do that," Chris spoke quickly. "I'll find my way."

"But I *want* to," he answered, settling the flight cap back on his head. "Come on, I have all the necessary forms filled out so we can whisk you through."

The BOQ was the home for all single officers who wanted to live on base. It was mandatory that all students stay at Edwards simply because of the amount of training and flying that took place. All the married students were assigned to small, stucco, one-story homes on Sharon Street. Dan pointed out that it gave moral support to the families to be with others going through the same grind.

Chris entered the large rooms, looking around. Dan leaned casually against the door and watched as she inspected her new quarters.

"I thought you might like some lunch before you start unpacking," he offered when she had finished. "I—"

"What's this? The Air Force's finest woman pilot at a loss for an answer?"

She gave him a flat look, trying not to smile. "That's happened a few times," she acknowledged lightly.

Dan gave her a boyish grin. "I imagine after being hounded by the media, there's something to be said for silence. Come on, grab your hat and I'll give you a quick tour of the base," he urged. "I'll bet you're tired. You'll probably want to crash after lunch."

A cold chill swept through her. "Please don't use the word 'crash,'" she said, a sobering quality in her voice.

"Poor word choice on my part. Let's think about lunch instead, okay?"

She remained silent in his Corvette on the way over to the Officers' Club. The building sat up on a hill, its white walls gleaming in the pale December sunlight.

"What do you think of our base so far?" he asked, parking the Corvette in the crowded lot.

"It's big. Impressive."

"The base covers three hundred ten thousand acres of Mojave Desert." He rested his hands on the steering wheel for a moment, looking over at her.

"And speaking of impressive, I understand you have some pretty distinguished qualifications yourself."

Chris squirmed beneath his admiring gaze. Every time he looked at her it was as if he had reached out and touched her bodily. The sensual tension seemed to vibrate between them. It was a disturbing chemistry that made her feel suddenly shy. "I met the requirements for TPS," she responded modestly, wanting to avoid bragging about her credentials. She climbed out of the sports car.

Dan checked his stride, aware of her new coolness. Why had she become reserved with him?

"How was your flight today?" Chris finally asked, trying to break the uncomfortable silence.

Dan ushered her into the spacious lobby, adorned with paintings and photographs of Edwards's colorful history. "It was beautiful. You'll find that you'll want to fly early in the morning before everyone else gets up there. The air's calmer."

"I can hardly wait to climb back into the cockpit of a fighter," Chris confided fervently.

Dan smiled, directing her to the dining room and found an empty table. It was the first time since their meeting that she had shown some of her true feelings. "You love flying, eh?" he asked, sitting next to her. "When you were born did your parents think you were part eagle?" he asked teasingly.

Chris compressed her lips, avoiding his warm, interested gaze. "I don't have any parents."

"Both dead?" She was too young to have both mother and father gone. He saw her face grow tense, and Dan realized he had stepped into something larger than he could have possibly anticipated.

"I'm an orphan."

Dan sat back, sensing—no, feeling her carefully shielded anguish. His thoughts acted like a circuit breaker on his emotions. *She had no one? No one at all?*

No wonder she had all the earmarks of a loner. Toying with the fork, he pondered the consequences of her lack of family support. His mouth curved into the semblance of a smile for her benefit. "Just because all of us Air Force pilots are handsome devils, doesn't mean we don't blunder into things at times." He reached forward instinctively, his hand briefly settling on hers. "I'm sorry, Chris."

The instant his hand touched hers, a thrilling pulse sent her heart beating faster. But before Chris could respond, Dan had removed his hand. He was an instructor at TPS. One of *her* instructors. And more than that, he was a major and she was below him in rank. Further, he was a relative stranger to her. There were a hundred reasons why Dan McCord shouldn't have touched her. But her heart... oh, God, her heart surged with an instant's joy at his touch.

"I shouldn't be so defensive," she began. "I'm more tired than I thought from the trip."

Dan grinned easily. "Forget it. I understand."

The waitress came over and interrupted them. Chris ordered a Scotch on the rocks and Dan ordered a beer.

"You're hard to figure out," she told Dan. "You should be anti women pilots like everyone else."

His laugh was low, resonant. "I'm many things but not that. I'll be truthful with you, Chris. I like your company."

"You're coming on strong, major."

"Why do you confuse honesty with a pass?" he parried.

Chris blinked. "This isn't the first time I've been around fighter jocks. You're all alike. Real hotshots with a male ego a mile wide. You all think you have something to prove. Especially to a woman military pilot. I'm not interested in being your latest challenge, Major McCord."

"I'll be the first to admit that I like the way you fill out that uniform." His azure eyes grew dark. "And you're right about me liking a challenge. I wouldn't be in the test-pilot business if I didn't. But you're wrong about my being a fighter jock. I used to fly B-52 bombers. I flew the slower, heavier aircraft just like you did," he said, his voice firm. "I flew the F-4 Phantom during the war. But otherwise, I was weaned on bombers and lived most of my military life in them. Now, does that make you feel a little guarded about me?"

She liked his honesty. It became him. A slight smile edged her full lips. It was common knowledge that fighter jocks were far more aggressive than bomber pilots. "I would never have guessed it. But then, you are a paradox."

"Comes with the territory, Chris. I don't know too many test pilots that aren't like day and night, Jekyll and Hyde. You are too, you know. So be careful of the pot calling the kettle black."

She relaxed within the aura of their parry-riposte conversation. Leaning her elbows on the table, she smiled. "Not me. If there is a set of words to describe me, it's consistent, loyal and responsible."

Dan took a swallow of his beer, his eyes dancing with silent laughter. "I'd prefer to use more complimentary adjectives, such as beautiful, sensitive and shy."

Something happened inside Chris. Her heart raced strongly for a moment and she felt giddy—like a child. But she had never felt like a child in all her life. How had he brought out this hidden side of her—and on less than one day's acquaintance! She couldn't resist a smile. "You're a fighter jock at heart, major. I don't care *how* long you flew bombers. You're long on b.s. and short on sincerity."

Dan grinned wickedly. "Think so? We'll see," was all he said.

CHRIS WAS FINISHING OFF the last coat of polish on her fingernails when she heard a knock at the door.

"Come in." Who could it be? She knew no one on base yet except Dan McCord. A small, blond woman in a dark-blue uniform came in. Chris gasped, rising.

"Karen! I don't believe it."

"Finally, after a year we get to see each other again," her friend laughed, coming forward. Karen was only five-foot-three and reminded all who saw her of a blond, blue-eyed pixie come to life. Careful not to smear the drying nail polish, Chris hugged her. Karen stepped back, taking off her cap and smoothing her short curly hair back into place.

"Come on in the kitchen, Karen. Like some coffee?"

The petite blonde made herself comfortable at the kitchen table. "Love some. I arrived at Edwards a little more than a month ago. I work over at Test Pilot School in Operations. As soon as I heard you were being assigned, I had to let you know you had a friend here."

Chris smiled happily, putting the coffee on. Karen and she had been roommates throughout their four years at the Air Force Academy. Afterward her friend had failed her flight test and gone into a different military career. But it hadn't stopped them from remaining close over the years.

"Right now, I could use a friend," Chris confided.

"Amen. You're really biting off a big chunk by being the first woman in the Air Force to try for test-pilot status."

"Around these guys, I may just decide to clam up or watch my words. It's safer that way, I think."

"I understand. In a sense, I'm glad I flunked out of pilot training, Chris. Watching you as you weather the chauvinism, the dirty looks and even worse verbal insults from the men would make me quit." Karen gave her friend a keen look. "Every newspaper article I've read on you asked why you became the first woman test pilot. And your answer was always the same: you had earned the right to take a shot at the most prestigious job in the Air Force. Level with me. Why did you apply to TPS?"

Chris sipped the coffee. "Maybe a better question would be: what makes Chris Mallory run the way she does?"

"I thought it might be because you were orphaned and you don't have anyone. Test piloting is risky. Maybe you had nothing to lose if you did die. Sounds dumb, I know." And then she shrugged. "I never was good at psychology."

"You almost flunked out on it," Chris agreed. "I love to fly, Karen. It's that simple. I never told the press that because I would come off sounding like some pie-in-the-sky idealistic female." She slowly turned the cup around in her hands. "Flying makes me happy, Karen. Up there, I'm free—free of the past. The sky has no memory. It forgives and forgets who and what you are or are not. I don't have to remember that I'm an orphan. Or that I'm a woman in a very male-dominated business. Up there I'm a woman. And the sky doesn't care. And neither does my aircraft." She smiled sadly. "See, I told you it would sound philosophical and idealistic."

"No," Karen murmured, "it sounds like you. There are a number of instructors over at TPS like you. They just live to fly. It's their full-time mistress. They want nothing more out of life than to climb into the cockpit of a plane and take off for the blue sky."

"I think I just met one of those guys. Major Dan McCord."

Karen's eyes widened. "Ohh, him! He's such a terrific guy, Chris. And he's single, too."

Chris frowned. "No matchmaking," she warned sternly. "By the way, how's your love life?"

"Much better. I'm dating an instructor by the name of Major Mark Hoffman. He's wonderful."

"I can tell by the sound in your voice."

"You'll like him. I know both Mark and Dan were excited about having you at TPS. They know a woman can be a fine test pilot, unlike a lot of other guys over there who think you'll wash out before you set foot in the place."

Chris took a deep breath, then exhaled slowly. "Well, when you consider I've never sat behind a stick of a fighter plane, they could be right. It means having to work twice as hard as any other student in order to make the grade."

"Isn't that the truth? When will women ever get a fair shake? Why do we always have to start from behind and be twice as good as any man at something before we're taken seriously?"

"I don't know. I thought I'd had enough of that pressure and stress when we went through four years of hell at the Academy. But here I am, doing it all over again, breaking new ground." Chris shook her head. "And I'm so tired of wearing flight uniforms all the time with no makeup or jewelry." She touched her shoulder-length hair, now shining with blue highlights after its recent brushing. "I've made up my mind. I might have to dress like a man, but I'm not going to look like one. After the mandatory morning flights, I'm putting my earrings back on and adding a bit of makeup." She held out her hands. "And I'm going to wear nail polish."

Karen laughed. "Good for you! At least I get to wear a skirt and pumps all the time. But you know the flight rule about no jewelry. If you wore a ring on your hand and had to eject, the jewelry might get caught on something and you'd lose that finger."

"Or worse, my whole hand. No, I realize the rules are there for a reason, but I'm determined to keep my femininity intact, regardless."

"Oh, don't worry, Chris. With your looks, you could wear a gunnysack and still turn heads."

Chris laughed with her. "We'll see just how many heads I turn tomorrow morning. And I can guarantee you, not all of them will be admiring ones."

2

CHRIS PROCEEDED UP THE LONG SIDEWALK toward the Test Pilot School building. She touched her hair, now in a chignon at the nape of her neck, in a gesture of nervousness. *Why do I feel as if I'm going in front of a firing squad,* she wondered. *I thought I'd sweated enough for my wings.* Her stomach was tied in knots. She was dressed in her snug one-piece green flight suit that was adorned with all the appropriate patches on each shoulder. The small pearl earrings and pale-pink nail polish and light application of makeup subtly emphasized her femininity. Her blue flight cap rested on her black hair, the double silver bar on the cap shining brightly in the January sunlight.

Chris stifled her anxiety as she climbed the last few steps to the cream-colored building. Whether she wanted to or not, she had thought about Dan McCord off and on throughout the past two days. The image he projected as a playboy pilot out to have a good time was simply a sham, she decided. McCord was made of much more reliable material than the ego-ridden jet jockeys she had worked with throughout her career. Dan possessed a thread of gentleness coupled with incredible sensitivity that threw her completely off guard. Chris had no defense against kindness. Taking a deep, uneven breath, she opened the door, uttering, "Welcome to the real world, Captain Mallory." Chris knew there would be men in her class who would hate her presence. And there would be other pilots who would applaud her efforts based on her flying skills and ignore the fact that she was a woman. Inwardly she drew a small breath. At least one instructor, Dan McCord, was on her side and that made her feel a twinge of relief on an otherwise stressful occasion.

Adrenaline made Chris's heart pound faster as she walked down the highly polished hall to the first classroom. A small knot of pilots stood off to one side, giving Chris a challenging stare. Her mouth went dry, but she didn't let her gaze waver. She was damned if she was going to feel belittled by a bunch of jet jockeys. Their gazes raked over her as she passed. Chris's keen hearing picked up a few stage whispers and then a collective laugh from the group. It wasn't going to be easy to integrate.

From 0800 through noon they heard from many of the instructors explaining curriculum, flight schedules and the school's aims and goals. Chris was attentive throughout the presentations, but never as much so as when Dan McCord stepped to the front of the room. He looked relaxed, breathtakingly handsome in his flight suit and keenly alert. She smiled to herself. Wasn't that something they all shared in common: that "look of the eagles"? She hadn't seen a man here today who didn't possess that characteristic.

"I'm Major McCord, and I'll be your instructor for the first thirteen weeks of flight aerodynamics," he announced. He scanned the room, found Chris, and saw her color fiercely. "The curriculum is drawn up to teach you how to work in a team-oriented environment. In each team there will be a test pilot, a navigator and an engineer. You'll work on gathering data, planning and carrying out what you've discovered and then evaluating it on actual test flights. After that, a written report on your assigned research projects will be handed in." McCord stopped his slow pacing from one side of the room to the other, his eyes narrowing. "I can't stress the importance of teamwork here, ladies and gentlemen. Part of being a test pilot is understanding that you don't work alone." His gaze settled briefly on Chris. "The pilot is only a part of the team. It's true, you will be flying the aircraft. But at times you'll need a navigator in that back seat—more importantly, a test engineer. Without him or her, your job wouldn't exist. This isn't an area where egos can get in the way," he warned. "You set aside your prejudices and your opinions, and stick with the *facts* and only the *facts*," he concluded, his voice growing harder.

McCord had already picked out which pilots would be a problem to Chris. Earlier, Captain Richard Brodie had swaggered up to Chris while she was talking with two other pilots. Dan had just walked into the lounge area when he saw Brodie make a pass at Chris. He had to curb a smile as Chris easily evaded him. Brodie had not expected her to turn him down and departed fuming, his ego decidedly wounded.

Brodie, as he liked to be called, was the typical macho fighter jock who lived, drank and partied hard. He flew like few other pilots dared. If Brodie didn't square off with Chris within the first month, Dan would be surprised. And if Brodie did, it was up to the instructor to put a quick stop to it.

He paused, glancing at his watch. He had ten minutes before lunch. "One more thing before we break for chow," he continued. "Just remember this: you are the best. You've got the confidence, competitiveness and intelligence that can't be matched anywhere else in the world. You are *it*! And you're at the toughest school in the world. What we wring out of you in the next forty-six weeks will be unbelievable. But you were chosen because of your tenacity. You all have what it takes or you wouldn't be here. Okay, let's break," he ordered. "Those of you who don't want to hit the NASA cafeteria up on the road can hang around for the sandwich truck. It's a blue-and-white affair that's got a variety of junk food on board." He allowed a momentary smile. "It's affectionately known as the Roach Coach."

The students laughed with him and they rose, dispersing quickly. He caught up with Chris. "I'd like to see you in private for a few moments," he said.

Her eyes widened, and he chastised himself for sounding so damned official. "Don't worry, it's good news," he added with a persuasive smile.

"Okay."

Chris's heart beat furiously. What was happening to her? Dan always seemed to make her feel shaky and breathless. He took her elbow, guiding her out of the room and down the hall. She put her flight cap on as they swung out the back door to the parking lot. "Where are we going?" she wanted to know.

"O'Club for lunch," he answered casually, escorting her to his Corvette.

Chris slowed, a smile barely touching her mouth. "Is this official business, major?"

He laughed pleasantly, opening the door for her. He leaned closer, his azure eyes disturbingly intense. "Absolutely. After watching you shoot down Captain Brodie, I decided to use a different approach."

Chris climbed in without a retort. She enjoyed Dan's company and looked forward to the lunch. Giving him a wry look she said, "The Captain Brodies of the world will never match your approach, major."

A twinkle came to Dan's eyes. "I've known Brodie off and on throughout my career. He has the tactics of a bull in a china shop, thinking every woman will swoon over him because he's a fighter pilot."

"Well," Chris said, laughing good-naturedly, "I thought he was going to faint from shock when I turned down his invitation for lunch today."

"Wise choice. Besides, you're going out with a better man anyway."

They both laughed in unison. "The only reason I went with you is because you made it sound like an order," she teased.

He pursed his lips. "It was."

Chris knew differently, but she remained silent. McCord would no more use his rank and authority for personal gain than she would. But she let him think that she believed him.

The car was warm, taking the edge off the cold, blustery day. It wasn't unusual for snow to fall in the high desert near Edwards, located one hundred miles northeast of Los Angeles. The Telupachi and San Gabriel mountains that surrounded Antelope Valley were already cloaked in their white raiments of snow for the winter season. She glanced over at Dan as he got in. The Corvette purred to life and he shifted the gears. He probably flew a jet just as smoothly, she thought.

"So far, so good?" he asked her conversationally.

She nodded and smiled. "I'm thrilled, if you want the truth. And by the way, you're a very effective teacher. You had all of us sitting on the edge of our seats."

Dan gave her a sidelong glance. "Coming from you, that's a high compliment. Thanks."

"It's well earned, I must say."

"Who knows, maybe one of these days you'll be teaching there, too."

Chris gave an explosive laugh. "Oh, sure! Let's take one step at a time, shall we? First, I have to learn how to fly combat planes. Next, I have to graduate."

His azure eyes grew warm with admiration. "There wasn't a prettier person in that room this morning than you."

Her heart gave a leap and she pursed her lips.

"There you go again." She colored prettily beneath his look. "Am I going to have to put up with this for forty-six weeks?"

Dan's smile was devastating. "Roger that, my raven-haired beauty. You're just going to have to learn to take compliments with grace and say thank-you."

"Then, thank you," she murmured, her voice growing husky. She thrilled to the words, "raven-haired beauty."

"That's better. Hungry?"

"Starved!"

"Good, we need to get some more meat on your bones. You're too damn skinny for your height."

Chris ordered a steak sandwich, French fries and a garden salad. Over lunch, she relaxed in Dan's soothing presence. The dining room was filled to capacity with Air Force officers and civilians alike. Dan pointed out Chuck Yeager, one of the most famous of all test pilots. Yeager had brought the U.S. into the jet age by riding the Bell X-1 through the sound barrier. Chris stared at the short, wiry man with respect. She looked back over at Dan.

"I'd give my right arm to do something similar to what he's done," she whispered.

"We're all 'golden arms,' so don't be giving your right arm away for anything," he teased. It was the pilot's skill at getting the plane into the air and landing safely that counted. The myth that it took a "golden arm" or the "right stuff" to do it was synonymous with test piloting. "And don't worry, you're going to go on to create a special chapter in the history books for all women who go into testing," Dan said, meaning it.

"I still can't figure out why you have so much confidence in me when I'm behind the eight ball to begin with."

Dan toyed with his fork, a smile lingering on his

mouth. He enjoyed being close to her, and was secretly amazed at how much Chris had relaxed around him. She had lost much of her previous defensiveness. Perhaps it was the adjustment of settling in at a new base. "Why do you always see yourself playing catch-up?" he posed softly, meeting and holding her violet gaze.

Chris squirmed, compressing her lips. "I've always felt like that."

"Could it have to do with your past?" Dan watched her stiffen, her eyes growing hooded, more distant. He reached out, gripping her hand for just a moment and then releasing it. "You're talking to me, Chris. I'm a friend. Don't retreat from me."

"I don't want to discuss it."

"I do."

"My personal life is my own."

Dan's eyes narrowed speculatively on her. "Correction. When I feel it interferes with your attitude, it becomes *my* business. I'm in the habit of extracting the very best of each student's potential. Your attitude of playing catch-up could prevent you from making a quantum leap forward by learning to fly combat jets in a very short period of time." His voice was velvet lined with steel, and it netted the desired result.

Chris had been trained in the military, and responded to his tone. She watched him with new respect. She placed both elbows on the table, staring at him. "I don't happen to agree with your assessment of me, major. But if you think it's going to interfere with my flying, then I'll tell you."

"Good," he encouraged, his voice becoming gentler, less authoritative. "Maybe it will be more painless if I ask you a few key questions." He looked up at Chris and his chest constricted with guilt as he saw hints of pain in her mobile features. This wasn't going to be easy....

"Go ahead."

"Were you always an orphan?"

Chris swallowed. "My mother gave me up when I was born."

"So you were placed in an orphanage. For how long?"

"Not long initially. I went through a series of foster homes like everyone else until I was about eight, and then was sent back to the orphanage."

Dan grimaced, resting his chin on his folded hands. "That must have been hard on you emotionally."

"I don't need your pity!"

"You have my understanding, not my pity," he countered coolly, watching her face lose its lines of tension. "So how did you fare in grade school?"

Chris took a sip of her coffee. "If you want the truth, it was a salvation. I could spend hours hidden away in books of all kinds ranging from math to English." She made a wry face. "Going back to the orphanage every afternoon was always a downer."

Dan wanted to reach out and comfort her to neutralize the hurt that still lingered in her voice. "That's why you enjoy being alone?"

Chris raised her chin, her violet eyes resting on his concerned face. "I don't like it, but I've learned to cope successfully with it."

He gave her a reassuring smile. "Okay, the hard part's over. Now tell me why you feel you're behind everyone else here at TPS."

She shrugged, insecurity evident in her voice. "Not having any fighter experience is going to be my toughest transition. If that isn't catch-up, nothing is. Otherwise, I feel confident in my other abilities."

McCord wanted to reach out and hold her hand, but he couldn't. Not here and not now. "You're a bright, articulate woman with an awesome intelli-

gence, or you wouldn't have been chosen from all
the military pilots in the services combined.''

"You can't understand the feeling unless you've
been there, Dan."

He pursed his lips, his eyes narrowing intently
upon her. Right now, at that instant, she was vulnerable and trusting him. "Hasn't the fact that
you've accrued impressive career credentials im-
pacted on you? Hasn't it made up for your sense of
being something less than what you think you are?''

She shrugged. "Most of the time, yes. But there are
those moments when I feel like a seventh-grader
again, struggling to understand chemistry, or a
ninth-grader, pounding physics into my head." Her
eyes grew worried. "And I feel that way about
learning how to fly the combat jets now, Dan. I feel
so...." She groped to convey her sense of frustration
and anxiety. "So helpless!"

Dan cocked his head, listening to her voice. "That
bothers you, doesn't it? That sense of helplessness?''

She gave him a feeble smile. "Wouldn't it anyone?"

"As long as you can make decisions, you aren't
helpless.''

Her nostrils flared with pent-up frustration. "I
was a puppet for the first eighteen years of my life,
Dan. I was subject to someone else's ideas of what I
should or should not be. And I feel like I'm back in
that role by being here at TPS without proper fighter
experience.''

Dan studied her in the tense silence, assimilating
the depth of her worry. His own childhood flashed
to the front of his memory. Unwanted by his young,
immature mother who preferred globe-trotting with
his millionaire father, he had been foisted upon his
aunt and uncle at the tender age of seven. From then
on, Howard and Melvina McCord had been more

like his mother and father than his real parents, Preston and Vanessa McCord. He could identify with Chris up to a point. He had come out of a sterile household, cared for by a nanny. It was a godsend when he was given to Howard and Melvina. At least he received love and attention, filling that aching gap in his youthful heart.

He studied Chris. Although she had never known the security of love while growing up, it hadn't stopped her from achieving a brilliant career. She had been denied emotional sustenance, but she had respected herself as a unique individual. And in order to protect that core, Chris had learned to put up defensive walls to ensure her survival as the individual she knew she was—despite the years in the orphanage.

"Yes," he answered gently, his voice holding a caressing quality to it, "I think I am beginning to understand." He shook his head. "And lady, you are special," he whispered. "Very special."

She blushed deeply, unable to meet his eyes. Her heart suffused with an incredible warmth. The awkward silence lengthened, and Chris nervously cleared her throat. "I think it's time to get back."

Dan stood, picking up the bill. "If I had my way, we'd take the rest of the day off and just talk," he murmured. Then, flashing her a reassuring smile, he asked, "How about this evening at 1800? How would you like to climb into Double Ugly and take me for a flight?"

Chris gaped at him. "Are you serious?"

He placed his hand beneath her elbow, guiding her out of the dining room. "Is it a date? Meet me on the ramp with your flight gear, and we'll take you up in an F-4."

She gave him an incredulous look. "You are serious."

"Have I ever lied to you?" he asked, opening the front door.

"One of your faultless attributes, Major McCord, is your honesty," she murmured dryly. He walked beside her, his body inches from her own, and Chris gloried in his closeness. He was incredibly masculine. She gazed up at his mouth, tantalized by its shape and sensuality. She nearly lost her scattered thoughts.

"Not to mention being single, handsome, well-off and—"

"Here we go again," Chris griped, tossing him a broad smile.

Dan opened the Corvette's door for her. He loved to see her eyes sparkle with life. And he promised himself he would give her a measure of happiness that was long overdue.

"Then we have a date?" he pressed, sliding into the driver's seat.

"I suppose...."

He feigned wounding by her hesitation. "I ought to get a purple heart for being around you," he taunted.

Chris momentarily placed her hand on his forearm. She felt the steel-corded strength of his muscles beneath her fingertips. "Listen, if you can stand being around me, you deserve more than a purple heart."

Dan pulled out of the driveway. "Raven, you're easy to be around. Believe me." His blue eyes took on a look of merriment. "Besides, I've managed to dodge all the slings and arrows you've thrown at me so far and I'm not wounded in action. We've got nowhere to go but up from here."

Chris gloried in the caressing tone of the nickname he had given her. She leaned back, laughing fully. "You are impossible, Major McCord! I could never have dreamed you up if I tried."

"Just dream about me in your sleep," he said, his voice a roughened whisper.

Dan's reply sent a shiver through Chris, and she had no returning quip. All she could do was stare at him.

3

CHRIS COULD BARELY CONTAIN THE PULSE-POUNDING EXCITE-MENT threading its way through her. But her anxiety was well hidden as she walked toward the light-gray Phantom with its long, bulbous black nose. Dan McCord was already there waiting for her, talking amiably with the crew chief who serviced the plane. McCord flashed her a smile of welcome as she approached.

"Well, ready to become a Phantom Phlyer?" he teased, motioning for her to climb the ladder hooked on the left side of the fuselage. Chris returned the smile, hoisting herself up the steps into the rear seat.

Dan watched her progress as she slipped into the cockpit. She placed her helmet on the console in front of her.

"I thought you called it Double Ugly?"

"We call it that when it's going outside its performance envelope," he said in way of explanation climbing aboard. "We also called it DRUT."

She saw mirth lurking in his eyes when he said it. "Okay, I'll bite. What does DRUT stand for?"

An irrepressible grin tugged at the corner of his mouth. "Turn the word around and you'll see," was all he said. Dan situated himself in the pilot's seat, and the crew chief came up the ladder to help both of them strap into their unwieldy harness system. Straps went over both shoulders and then buckled into a seat belt that went across their laps.

Chris chuckled to herself, noticing the crew chief stealing glances at her. She had grown used to the crews staring. She was an oddity—a woman out of place. She gave the chief a smile as he handed her the green-and-brown camouflaged helmet with "Mallory" printed on the front of it. Thanking him, Chris settled it on her head. God, it felt good to be back in a cockpit again! In less than fifteen minutes she would be airborne, and all the trials and tribulations of her life would slip effortlessly off her shoulders as she rode the jet up into the dark-blue skies.

The flight suit she wore was specially constructed to take the gravity forces created by the combat jet's massive engine power. When going at high speed turns or angles it was easy to black out from high G-forces. The G-suit prevented it from happening. It would automatically push the flow of blood out of her legs and back into her head and upper body.

Plugging in her headphone set she monitored all conversations with Dan, the control tower and other necessary communications. Dan raised his hand, thumb up, giving the signal for the ground crew to step away.

Her heart pounded as Dan inched the throttles forward to start the two huge turbojet engines. Then, the Phantom roared to life. Each engine was mounted halfway down the fuselage directly beside her seat, the semicircular scoop intakes sucking in huge amounts of air. Anticipation mixed with joy. She was sitting in one of the most feared combat fighters in the world.

"You about ready to go?" Dan asked.

Chris snapped the oxygen mask to her face. "Ready, ready now!" she returned, choosing the old B-52 axiom that the Strategic Air Command crews used.

Dan laughed. "Raven, you're a girl after my own heart. I want you to sit back and relax. I'll take Double Ugly up and give you an idea of its capabilities as well as its drawbacks."

"You mean I get the full treatment?"

"Better believe it. Once airborne, I'll turn the stick over to you, and you'll get the feel of this ugly bird. Canopies down," he ordered.

With a double set of flight controls, Chris hit her canopy lever, watching the Plexiglas lids slowly close. There was a soft whoosh as it locked tightly on each separate compartment. Although pilots never flew without their oxygen masks clamped securely to their faces in case of a leak, the cabins were pressurized.

Within minutes the F-4 was trundling heavily along the concrete taxiway. Chris helped Dan by switching radio frequencies and handling other little chores that would make his job less complicated. She watched the flaps lower, the whirring sound shivering through the Phantom. Now, with the flaps down, the lift-off capability of the fifteen-ton fighter was increased. Her pulse beat raced as she heard the engines shrieking as they readied for takeoff.

Dan pushed down on the brakes and rudder system beneath his booted feet. With his left hand, he inched the two throttles forward, watching the *RPM* gauges jump higher. The harnessed power throbbed throughout the aircraft. The day was dying with the inky stains of night tainting the dusk. The F-4, its array of red and white blinking lights situated on tail and wing tips, bellowed furiously on the cold desert, demanding to be released. Smiling to himself, Dan could almost feel Chris's excitement in the rear cockpit. She hadn't said much, but the tremor in her voice gave her away.

"I'm going to request afterburners upon takeoff," he informed her. *Might as well let her experience the raw, awesome power of the F-4,* he thought. He called the tower and received permission. "Let's tempt the gods," he said. "There's an old Air Force myth about

flying so high that we'll anger the mythical gods of
the sky. Are you game?'' he challenged.

She grinned, thumbing the intercom button. "Listen, I tempt fate regularly. The sky gods and goddesses are on good terms with me. Let's go for it."

Chris felt him release the brakes. Instantly she was
pushed back in the seat, her breath momentarily
torn from her by the impact of the aircraft's power.
The F-4 thundered down the runway like a growling
cat running full tilt after its quarry. Suddenly the
afterburners were engaged by shoving the throttles
all the way forward. She could do nothing but sit,
crushed against the seat. The landscape was a blur,
the F-4 shivering with unleashed might as it hurled
itself down the longest runway in the world. Suddenly Dan pulled back on the stick and the fighter
left the earth in a single bound like an unchained
eagle being released to the freedom of its true domain: the sky.

The Phantom's flaps came up on the wings, landing gear tucking neatly beneath its belly, gaining
speed, hitting Mach .9 in only a few seconds. The
angle of climb was breathtaking. The F-4 quickly hit
six hundred knots, and Chris watched the altimeter
unwinding like a broken spring as they streaked to
five, ten, fifteen, twenty and twenty-five thousand
feet. Exhilaration surged through her as she became
a part of this magnificent fighter that raced along the
very edge of the stratosphere.

Dan began to bring the nose back down at thirty-five thousand. At forty thousand the Phantom had
struck Mach 2. He could feel the aircraft sloughing
off the sticky drag of the low subsonic region. The
higher they climbed, the less air there was to slow
them down. At forty-five thousand, he leveled out
the F-4. "Well?" he asked, grinning, "what do
you think?"

Chris gave a shaky laugh. "Things happened so fast that my thinking was way behind the plane! It's wonderful! What a thrill!"

Dan's eyes crinkled with pleasure. Her voice mirrored her happiness. She loved flying as much as he did. That mass of metal, wire and circuitry was a living extension of himself, docile beneath his hand, ready to obey his every command. "Take the stick," he ordered.

Chris slid her gloved fingers around the column. She felt Dan release the stick and rudders to her command and now, she was flying the incredible F-4 Phantom.

For two hours they flew in a restricted flight area over the Mojave. Chris's initial excitement settled down as Dan began to teach her how to handle the Phantom. She was pleased with Dan's technique as an instructor. His explanations and orders were easy to follow, and it made the flight that much more thrilling.

"Just remember," Dan was saying as she reluctantly made the final banking turn that would take them back to Edwards. "Never allow the Phantom to fly at too high an angle of attack."

"What happens if she goes out of her controlled flight envelope?" Chris wanted to know, restlessly scanning the gauges as she flew the fighter.

"First the nose will abruptly yaw from side to side. And almost simultaneously, it will start to pitch up and down and will depart from controlled flight. And if you don't catch it right then, it will go into spin. From there, if you're anywhere around ten thousand feet or less, you eject."

Chris compressed her dry lips. Her mouth always felt cottony after being on one-hundred-percent oxygen for over an hour. She reached up, adjusting the soft rubber mask against her face. Her skin always itched beneath it! And if she had worn makeup, it would have broken the airtight seal of the mask against her skin. If that occurred, she might die of hypoxia, or lack of oxygen. "Is it mandatory if the F-4 is in a spin at ten thousand you automatically bail out?"

She heard Dan's grim chuckle. "You try and pull this ugly bird out of a dive at less than ten thousand, and it'll be a mad race between you and the dirt as to whether or not you can pull it out in time, Raven. Don't chance it. Punch out and live to tell about it."

The past two hours spent with Dan hadn't seemed like an instructor-student relationship. Instead, it had been a wonderful time spent between two adults who both became childlike when they flew in the arms of the sky. Dan's voice was always warm, coaxing and praising her performance. The few times he had had to correct her were done without rebuke and only in a matter-of-fact tone. She never had to be told more than once, either. "But has anyone tried to kick this bird out of a dive below ten and live to tell about it without punching out?" she wanted to know.

"Not many," he returned grimly.

She nodded. "Not very forgiving, is she?"

"No. She can damn well be your coffin if you start messing around with her in flight. This isn't a fighter to play with."

Back on the ground, Chris felt like a shackled eagle once again. Instead of taking the ramp vehicle back to the school, Dan talked her into walking the quarter mile. It was cold and the wind was cutting. Chris zipped up her green flight jacket. She was glad for Dan's closeness beside her as the darkness engulfed them. Her black hair, once in a chignon and plastered down over her skull from wearing the helmet, blew in silky abandon, barely brushing her shoulders. She reached up, pulling several strands from her eyes. Her heart swelled with happiness and her step was buoyant.

Dan glanced over at her, aware of the light and dark shadows playing across her face. How had Chris grown more beautiful? Those violet eyes were wide and lustrous. Her lips were curved softly upward at the corners, as if she was smiling about some happy secret known only to herself. Most of all, he liked her proud, easy carriage. She was all woman—a very confident, competent woman. "You know, Bill Craig was right," he said, catching her gaze.

"Major Craig? The officer who gave me my flight tests to enter TPS?"

"Yes."

A mischievous glint came to her eyes. "And what did he have to say?"

"That you had the best pair of hands he'd ever seen. I agree with him. You're smooth. You fly by the seat of your pants."

Chris blushed fiercely, avoiding his admiring glance. "I'll bet you say that to all your women pilots," she teased, trying to make light of his compliment.

Dan reached over, pulling her to a halt. "No, you don't." His hands settled on her shoulders. "I'm not letting you get away with that."

Chris looked up into his handsome features, her lips parted in response to Dan's unexpected action. A pulse leaped crazily at the base of her slender throat as she felt his gaze linger upon each delicate feature of her face. She swallowed. "What are you talking about?"

A wry smile curved his sensual mouth. "My Raven doesn't know how to take a genuine compliment gracefully and say thank-you." He drank deeply of her widened violet eyes. "I meant what I said. I wasn't idly throwing you a compliment."

He was so close...so dizzyingly masculine. Chris shut her eyes momentarily, trying to hang on to her sense of reality...of logic. *This shouldn't be happening*, her mind screamed. *It was only six months ago! Six months! I hurt too much...I can't go through this again!* But her heart spoke another, more pounding message throughout her tense body. "Please..." she begged, trying to pull out of his grip. Another part of her, the woman drawn to him, wanted his touch, his closeness.

"Don't fight me," Dan whispered gently. He placed his hand beneath her chin, forcing her to meet his eyes. "You've got a special touch with an aircraft, Raven. You can be proud of your skills. Now," he said, his voice becoming more authoritative, "will you believe me when I say you have good hands?"

She nodded convulsively, drawn to his mouth—a firm, well-shaped mouth that smiled often, then drew into a grimace of wry amusement or thinned when he was upset. She felt Dan's fingers follow the curve of her jaw, sending heated prickles of pleasure across her skin. His touch aroused her senses, stirred to life coals of yearning she had thought were dead. Her pulse was pounding wildly in her throat, her breathing became shallow as he cupped her face, drawing her inexorably closer...closer....

"Chris..." Dan reverently whispered her name, his breath moist against her face. Automatically she closed her eyes, lifting her chin, anticipating... waiting.... Then his mouth brushed her lips tentatively, with great tenderness. It shattered her fragile composure. His tongue traced the outline of her, tasting, probing, feeling...beneath his gentle advance, her lips parted, allowing him entrance. A small moan rose in her throat as his mouth pressed more urgently against her own, and she felt as if embers of desire were sparking brightness within her reawakened body. Instinctively she rested against him, enjoying his maleness, wanting to maintain the contact. Her feelings for him warred with the logic in her head. Part of her knew this was right and good. And yet, her mind screamed out in warning.... She felt Dan's arms go around her, drawing her near, fitting her perfectly against his body.

Gradually Dan drew away from her well-kissed lips. Lips that were glistening, parted and full with the invitation to be kissed once again. He groaned inwardly, forcing himself to stop before he lost total control. She trembled perceptibly within his arms, and he was wildly aware of her yielding female softness. He managed a partial smile, pulling several strands of hair away from her cheek, cradling her face within his palm.

Chris inhaled shakily, forcing herself away from Dan. "You—can't...shouldn't," she said weakly, her feeling of euphoria waning. Her eyes mirrored her confusion as she looked up at him. "Is this what you were after?" Chris demanded, taking another step away from him, her voice riddled with hurt. "How many of the jocks did you bet you'd kiss me after the first flight?"

Dan looked at her through narrowed eyes. "What are you talking about, Chris? What bets?"

She shakily touched her lips that throbbed from the virile stamp of his mouth. She was so much jelly, her knees feeling wobbly, her heart pounding. Chris tried to gather her sharded thoughts.

Dan advanced upon her, capturing her arm before she could flee into the darkness. "Hold on just a minute, Chris. This isn't finished." He pulled her around. "Now what's all this paranoia about me betting the guys?"

She drew herself up, chin high, eyes flaring with hurt and anger. Her heart wanted to believe in the honesty of his actions. But her suspicious mind won out. "You know what I'm talking about! Men at the

Academy and at the squadron I flew with tried to pull the same trick! They'd bet to see who could get to me first. I fell for it once. Just once!" Her eyes glittered with tears. "You're no different. I thought you were, but I was wrong."

His lips thinned, and he took a better grip on her wrist. "Now listen to me," he grated softly, his face inches from hers. "I didn't plan to kiss you just then. Hell, it was the farthest thing from my mind." That was a lie. "But when you stood there looking so damn vulnerable and happy, something happened inside me." That was the truth. His voice became more coaxing. "Chris, you're a beautiful woman with heart and incredible sensitivity. You do something to me."

She avoided his burning gaze, feeling suddenly humiliated at having thought the worst about Dan's unpremeditated actions. "Then why did you take me on the F-4 tonight?" she hurled back.

"Because the commandant gave me permission to start training you early so you wouldn't find yourself behind. That's why."

Slowly she looked up. Was he telling the truth? Chris searched his eyes to try and find trickery lodged in their depths. She found none. Grimacing, she muttered, "I overreacted. You can let me go now. I'm not going to run away like some lost child."

Dan eased his grip, sliding his hand up her arm, his fingers caressing her shoulder. "Raven, you aren't lost anymore. You don't have to go through this school alone. I'll be there. I've gotten permission to take you up on evening flights during the week and on weekends." His voice grew more urgent. "No one wants to see you pass this course more than I do. You deserve the chance. And I'm going to make sure you get a fair shot at it. I'm sorry I hadn't told you this earlier." A self-deprecating smile curved his mouth, tearing at her heart. "Maybe then you would have realized I kissed you because you were so damn enticing."

Her eyes glistened with tears as she heard—no, felt—his belief in her. He had volunteered his free time to help her learn to fly the combat aircraft. Dan didn't have to do that. Her lips parted, trembling. "I'm sorry," she offered, "you have every right to—"

"Ssh," he commanded, returning to a more military stance. "If anything, I ought to chew you out for being so damned paranoid. Come on, we'll both freeze to death if we don't get inside soon."

The building was empty with a few lights illuminating the quiet hallways. Dan guided her to his small office. He threw his flight cap on the desk, motioning toward a chair that was stacked with manuals.

"Have a seat—if you can find one. I'm going next door to fix us a pot of coffee. We need something to warm up."

She took off her flight cap and jacket, placing the manuals on the tile floor. Looking around the cramped cubicle of an office, Chris saw many books on aerodynamics, calculus and higher math surrounding her on shelves that sagged beneath their weight. Impressive-looking certificates adorned one wall, attesting to Dan's academic expertise. On another wall were various color photos of him in an F-4 or with his squadron mates in what could only be Vietnam. There was a huge mound of paperwork that demanded his attention in the middle of his desk. Although it was far too small, the office was neat and that said something for the way Dan McCord operated his life on a daily basis.

Unconsciously Chris touched her lips where he had kissed her earlier. When had she ever melted into a man's arms like that? Never, a small voice whispered in her head. One kiss. One gentle kiss had opened the depths of her still-healing heart. And what about the explosions that had rocked her body? Chris took an unsteady breath, trying to logically assess those intangibles. Was Dan sincere when he meant that he would see to it she would not get behind the other students?

She chastised herself for doubting him. Dan had already proven that by requesting permission to take on extra instructing time to help her. Chris looked up when he returned. He handed her a cup.

"You take cream and sugar, right?" Dan asked, settling himself behind the desk.

"How did you know?" she asked, a smile coming to her lips.

"The O'Club the other day. I remember you put in one cream and two sugars." He gave her a devilish look. "Really, Raven, you're sweet enough that you don't need the extra sugar."

Chris laughed freely. "Honey would melt on your tongue, too! You and Dave Haney. I don't know which of you is worse." Haney was a navy pilot student who had said kind words to her on that first day of class.

Dan grinned affably, sipping the steaming coffee. "Just as long as he doesn't have you in his gun sights, he's safe."

She sobered. "Dan, we have to talk."

"I told you—anytime, any place."

"No, I mean seriously."

"I'm always serious where you're concerned, Raven."

"Then quit grinning like the cat that just ate the mouse!"

Contrite, Dan suppressed a laugh. "Okay, what is it?"

She fingered the mug, staring down at the contents. "This isn't right, you know."

"What isn't?"

"Us. You and me."

"Why not? You're a woman and I'm a man."

Chris met his smiling eyes, responding to him easily despite the serious subject she wanted to discuss. "Correction—you are a lecher of the first order."

"Or I'll die trying."

"Dying isn't funny."

He shrugged. "We're all going to die someday, Raven. It's just a question of when and how. Is that what you wanted to discuss so seriously?"

Chris shivered at the mention of death and dying. It brought back sharp, anguished memories. Oh, God, would she ever be able to sleep a night without reliving the events of that horrible day?

"Raven? Hey, where did you fly off to?" Dan kidded, watching her eyes suddenly grow misty and faraway.

"What? Oh—" She paused to gather her thoughts. "No... I wanted to discuss us. I'm a student here and you're an instructor. If any of the other students find out what has happened, there could be jealousy. I don't want anyone to think I didn't earn my way through this school or received preferential treatment."

He started to interrupt, but she held up her hand.

"No, it's true, Dan," she continued earnestly. "Some of the jocks will accuse me of that, regardless. But I don't want the reputation of other women who might follow in my footsteps tarnished because of my... indiscretion."

He pursed his lips. "You have a relevant point," he conceded. "But what we do on our off-hours is no one's business but our own."

Her nostrils flared. "Come on! You know that in a tight little community such as ours, talk gets around. And eventually, it will land right here at TPS. I just can't jeopardize my chances of becoming a test pilot. What would Colonel Martin think of this if he knew?'' she challenged.

Dan leaned back in the chair, enjoying the play of emotions across her features. "Tell me to be discreet. Which I will be.''

"You haven't heard a word I said!''

"Calm down. I'm aware of your feelings and your concern for your reputation. And I don't intend to embarrass you publicly here with the male students.''

She gave him an accusing look. "You've got this all planned, haven't you?''

"I'm a test pilot by nature, Chris. I preplan as much as I can and then carry it through." A grin edged his mouth. "Come on, are you going to sit there and tell me you didn't enjoy that kiss?''

She blushed beautifully, at a loss for words, for once. "You just keep your distance," she warned throatily, her violet eyes golden with fire.

His grin widened. "Is that threat for my benefit or yours?''

"You're impossible, McCord! I've never run into a jock like you in my whole life! Where did they find you?''

He shrugged nonchalantly, taking another sip of the coffee, his eyes filled with laughter. "I'm one of a kind, Raven. Your kind. And don't forget it. Because if you try to, I'll be right there to remind you.''

She stood, infuriated and frustrated with him. "Thanks for the coffee and the flight, major. If you don't mind, I'm going to go study. At least my books won't talk back to me!''

"Hey," he called, sitting back up, reaching for a manual. "Before you storm out of here, take this and read it.''

Chris turned, giving him a black glare. "What is it?''

"The F-4 manual. You might as well eat, drink and sleep this baby until you can recite it forward and backward. I'm going to test you on it next week. So be ready."

She stared at the three-inch-thick manual and then at him. Jerking it from his hand, she muttered, "With you, I'm ready for anything!"

4

"I DON'T CARE if the Joint Chiefs of Staff blessed this affair," Captain Richard Brodie growled, his feet propped up on a desk. "There's no way a broad can be a test pilot." He looked up at his two companions who loitered nearby at their respective desks. It was 1245 and most of their fellow students were filtering in for their afternoon classes, which would start promptly at 1300.

"I dunno, Brodie, it's been almost three weeks and that 'broad' as you call her, isn't looking too bad," Captain Greg Rondo said, a grin on his wide, handsome features. "Take a look at how good Mallory's doing in the F-4. She ain't no slouch at the stick, buddy."

Rondo was quick to recognize from the outset of his assignment to TPS that every student possessed a marked degree of overachieving drive and desire. He was no exception. He thrived on competition—if not with himself, then pitting his skills against another pilot or taming a shrewish jet aircraft. Yes, they were all winners bent on being the best, setting high personal standards and demands for themselves.

Brodie snorted, turning the paper coffee cup around on his desk. "Screw her." He lifted his head, glaring up at Rondo. "She's an icy bitch if I ever saw one."

Rondo sat down next to him. "She's got hands, though," he pointed out, delighting in poking holes in Brodie's opinionated stance. "Take a look at her test scores in Double Ugly. The gal ain't flying extra hours for nothing. And from what I've seen, she handles the jet real well."

"You're only saying that because you want to get close to her," Brodie growled.

Rondo smiled. "I think she's kind'a interesting, myself. Good hands, good in the classroom. I'd like to fly with her." A glint came to his light-blue eyes. "I'll bet that girl could do an inside loop with Ugly and come out smiling."

Brodie shook his head. "*Nobody* puts an F-4 into an inside loop and lives to tell about it, buddy. You know that as well as I do."

Rondo shrugged his thin, wiry shoulders. "Just give me a chance to go up with Mallory, and I'll show her what an F-4 can really do."

"You'll probably scare the hell out of her," Brodie said, chuckling. "Man, she's cold."

"Well, with jocks like you aiming to shoot her down, I don't blame her for not being none too friendly," Rondo challenged.

Brodie returned to dutifully turning the cup around in long slender fingers. Mallory was an enigma. She was the epitome of a grade-*A* student: attentive, serious and worked her rear off on any project assigned to her. A thread of jealousy ate at him. For two weeks he had suffered the ribbing of the other pilots because Mallory had turned him down for a date. There had to be a way to get to her, he finally decided. But what was the key? He had watched in silence as Julio Mendez, the engineering officer from Brazil, had made peace with Mallory. She treated Mendez with deference and politeness, and the Brazilian officer flew as often as he could with Mallory. They were making an impressive team in the standings, gradewise.

He scanned the half-filled classroom of men in green flight suits. Everyone had finished their morning flights by now and was ready to tackle the

arduous afternoon of mathematics, theory and aerodynamics. What made Mallory tick? He pursed his
thin lips, his brows dipping downward. What got to
her? The only time she ever changed was when
Captain Karen Barber came around. They were ob-
viously friends, and that was when Mallory seemed
most at ease. Somebody had to get to her and force
her to screw up. A woman couldn't stand the pressure.

He made a mental note to contact a friend of his
from Reese Air Force Base, where Mallory had been
an instructor pilot. Maybe he could dig up some
juicy gossip to spread around. Brodie was angry because eighty percent of the class accepted the woman
as a bona-fide student. He fumed inwardly. How
could a test pilot evaluate equipment for the military
if she hadn't flown in combat?

Everyone was meandering around, holding their
perennial cups of coffee, textbooks placed dutifully
in front of their desks, talking about the morning's
flights. Brodie saw Karen Barber bounce through the
classroom door. Her hair was in ruffled disarray, her
eyes sparkling and a smile on her lips. Wasn't there
always a quick smile for everyone from Barber?
Often she would drop in to visit with Chris before
class started and then disappear down the hall to her
office.

Brodie roused himself, watching her like a cat
ready to pounce on his next quarry. He checked to
make sure Major Mark Hoffman, her boyfriend and
also an instructor at TPS, was nowhere in sight. It
wasn't a secret that Karen and Mark were involved
with each other, for they were often seen at the
O'Club together after class. Brodie didn't want to
tangle with Hoffman because he might have to fly
with him at some point. Getting Hoffman angry
might also mean the naval officer would deliberately
foul up a test flight that they had to pull together,

making Brodie look bad. And he didn't want any bad marks.

"Hey, Barber," he called. His voice carried across the room, so that everyone automatically looked up from their conversations. "I'm surprised the Air Force lets any women work here at TPS. Everybody knows this is a man's world over here."

Karen looked up, stunned by his accusation. Brodie's tone was both irritating and challenging. Her eyes widened. She swallowed, a myriad of answers forming in the back of her mind. Karen didn't want trouble. But she couldn't afford to allow the brash officer to get away with it, either. She was aware of all eyes upon her and felt heat racing upward from her neck into her face.

She forced herself to remain calm. "I'm not even going to respond to such a question, captain. It doesn't deserve an answer."

Some of the men exchanged nervous glances, then looked toward Brodie and Karen. Brodie grinned confidently. "How did you broads get assigned over here?"

"Hey, ease off," Rondo warned under his breath, glancing around at his fellow classmates. A number of other officers were frowning at Brodie, others seemed shocked and still others waited to see the outcome of the confrontation.

Brodie forced a laugh, slapping Rondo on the back. "Hey! It's okay! We're just having a little fun here. Aren't we, Barber? I mean, if you women want to be one of 'us' you have to learn to stand up and take some locker-room humor every once in a while."

"Captain Brodie, why don't you pick on someone your own size then?" Chris Mallory challenged, her voice cutting like a whip across the room.

There was an abrupt silence as Chris stepped into the room. She still had her helmet and oxygen mask

tucked beneath her right arm, having just gotten off
a flight. The dark-green uniform made it obvious
she was a woman even if she had no makeup on.
Ebony-colored hair swirled around her shoulders,
wispy bangs barely touching her knitted brows. Her
violet eyes were narrowed with intensity as she
glared over at Brodie. She walked in, her movements
calculated to look at ease, as if she weren't concerned
with this meeting. She had heard the conversation as
she walked in the door.

Brodie swung his gaze sharply to Mallory. Dropping his feet from the desk, he smiled like a cat finding a bigger mouse to torment. "What's the matter,
captain, don't you care for my humor?"

Chris halted, no more than three feet from where
he lounged. Her nostrils were flared, her eyes flashing with leashed anger. "No, I don't. I never did like
bullies," she returned in just as soft a tone. "I'm not
about to let you say things like that about Captain
Barber or myself."

Brodie's mouth thinned. His heart began a faster
beat as anger surged through him. Mallory was
exactly the same height as himself, and he felt a moment's intimidation by her challenge. It was immediately replaced with a growing hate. "Do you always
butt in where you're not wanted?" he ground out.

"Brodie!" Rondo begged, getting up and coming
over to stand between the two pilots. He smiled
weakly at both of them. "Come on, ease off—both of
you. It was just a little joke, Chris. Brodie, just tell
Karen you're sorry and we'll call a truce. What do
you say?"

Chris stared at Brodie. "You start something and
I'll finish it. We don't have to put up with this kind
of harassment from you."

Rondo took a deliberate step between them, his
voice hardening. "Both of you knock it off," he
growled quietly, giving them each a warning glare.

"I never apologize for anything I say," Brodie snarled over at Chris. "Just watch your six, Mallory."

Chris drew in a sharp breath. When one pilot warned another to watch his "six," it was as close to throwing a punch as possible. Six was the rear position of any aircraft and was the most vulnerable area to be attacked and shot down from. "You bet I will."

The room took a collective, silent sigh of relief. Knots of officers broke up immediately, and everyone found their assigned seats. Karen fled. Chris saw tears in her eyes. Damn Brodie, she thought angrily.

Turning to leave, Chris almost collided with Dan at the door. He gave her a strange look and watched as she walked toward the community locker room to stow her gear.

Dan ambled down the aisle, noticing the absence of noise. He felt a tenseness in the room. What had happened? Everyone was strangely quiet. His gaze slid over to Brodie and his clique on the other side of the room. Brodie looked like he was ready to kill someone. Pursing his lips, Dan went to the lectern and paged through the text. This was not the place to find out what had happened. Chris had murder written in her violet eyes. Taking a deep breath before beginning his lecture, Dan knew without a doubt the first verbal salvo had been lobbed. Now it was his job to find out who was involved and dress them down in private and stop it before it got out of hand.

"CHRIS," DAN CALLED as the pilots began to disperse for the day, "I want to see you in my office."

Chris nodded. "Okay. Give me five minutes. I need a cup of coffee."

"Five minutes," he agreed. He saw Brodie's head snap up when he had ordered Chris to his office. And Rondo looked almost as guilty, too. It bothered him that the whole class was still subdued by the end of the afternoon. Whatever had occurred was serious because it had adversely affected everyone. And in this school, confidence, positive outlook and an upbeat attitude was a must for each pilot. It was a grueling forty-six-week course that demanded the class work together as a unit in order to survive. Closing the notebook in one heavy motion, Dan picked it up, walking with slow deliberation to his office.

"Okay, what's up?" he wanted to know as Chris entered his office and sat down in the only available chair. Dan sensed Chris's tightly throttled anger. These days, he could see right through her, sensing her true feelings. Had it only been three weeks since meeting her? He roused himself, gently shutting off those warming thoughts and centering on untangling the present difficulty. He looked up at Chris. "Well?"

Chris sat there, relating the entire event. She glanced up at Dan.

"I'm not going to take this from anyone, Dan. And Karen shouldn't have to take it, either. She's not even vying for test-pilot status, and he's picking on her. The Brodies of the world are nothing but—"

"Brodie is a macho jock. He was a hotshot lieutenant who made a reputation in F-4s during the closing days of the war."

"There's no war now," she answered coldly. "If he tries it again, I'll shoot him down."

Dan's mouth quirked upward. "I'd say you already singed his wing tips."

"The only thing his kind respects is meeting force with force."

Sitting up, Dan placed both elbows on his desk. "Look, I need you to understand where Brodie and his bunch are coming from. We won't allow this kind of abuse to happen again, but there was bound to be some friction sooner or later. Brodie will never accept a woman as a test pilot. I don't care how well you do. It won't change his mind. He's buried in the belief of outdated traditions that says women are second-class citizens and have no business behind the stick of a fighter or the yoke of a bomber."

"I'm not trying to change his mind," Chris said. "I just don't want Karen or me harassed by him."

"When I get done with him, he won't," he promised grimly. "But for the sake of the psychology, I'm asking you two women to understand his behavior and realize you don't need to defend yourself against that kind of childishness. After a while if you don't react, he'll stop. But—" he held Chris's gaze "—if you keep challenging him every time he pulls one of his cheap shots, he'll know he's getting to you. Ignore him and he'll fade away."

Chris choked on an expletive. "That'll be the day!" she retorted, and turning on her heel, walked out of the office.

DAN GLANCED AT HIS WATCH. It was almost 2100. Had three hours passed since talking with Chris? Pushing a group of papers away from him that still needed to be corrected, he leaned back, rubbing his face. Captain Brodie would be stopping by at any moment now. Frowning, he pushed a lock of hair off his brow and sat back up in the chair.

More than anything, he wanted to be with Chris right now. Since that night he had impulsively kissed her on the ramp, he had controlled his desire to push her too fast, too soon. He contented himself by flying with Chris almost every evening and on the weekends. A smile flickered in his eyes. She was slowly responding to him, just like a stubborn fighter plane in a dive. Glancing at the paperwork she had done for this morning's flight, Dan noticed how neat it looked. There wasn't an ink smudge anywhere. All the relevant numbers and figures were carefully recorded, making the report look professional in every sense of the word.

He didn't want to work anymore and put the pen down. Flying twice a day was beginning to take its toll on him. If the commandant found out, he would cancel the extra sessions immediately. Grimacing, Dan shook his head as if in denial that it would happen. In just three short weeks Chris had proven beyond a doubt that she had the sensitivity to be a damn good test pilot. Would she be as sensitive to lovemaking? He knew the answer to that, feeling his desire for her heightened once again. God, how he wanted *all* of her.

Ruefully Dan smiled to himself. *You are special, Captain Chris Mallory,* he told her silently. *No man in his right mind would want to just take you to bed and be done with it.* There was something incredibly exciting about Chris. *Patience,* he told himself. *Patience and give her a lot of care, and she'll come around.*

CHRIS WEARILY RUBBED HER FACE, glancing at her watch. It was almost ten-thirty and she was exhausted from the intensity of her studying. Her textbooks and manuals lay in a semicircle around where she sat on the carpeted floor. Leaning back against the couch, she yawned. The day had been incredibly stressful. A soft knock at the door pulled her from the reverie. Frowning, she wondered if it was Karen. Usually she came over every night for a quick visit.

Clad in only a pair of well-worn jeans and a loose-weave purple sweater, Chris opened the door. Her eyes widened. It was Dan McCord. Her lips parted as she looked up at his lined features. He looked as tired as she felt. Dan offered her a semblance of a smile.

"I know it's late—"

"That's all right, come in," Chris invited, trying to

quell her hammering heart. Ever since he had kissed her that night on the ramp, Dan had stayed out of her life except in an official capacity. Chris was incredibly happy to see him again.

Dan took off his blue flight cap and walked into the room. He was carrying a briefcase bulging with reports to be graded. Chris quietly shut the door, meeting his warming gaze. "Like some tea?"

He folded the cap and stuffed it into the left thigh pocket of his flight suit. "Just getting to see you again is enough," he answered.

Chris managed to return a smile. "You haven't changed at all, have you?"

"No. Did you want me to?"

She was glad to see him teasing her again. The past two weeks of flying had been all business with very little personal interchange. But she understood why. Dan was trying to get her qualified in the F-4 as fast as she could assimilate its flying characteristics. She motioned toward the couch. "A tiger never changes its stripes. Sit down before you fall down. I'm going to make us some orange-spice tea and lace it with a bit of brandy."

Dan ambled to the couch and gratefully sat. "Sounds great." He watched as Chris moved across the room to the small kitchen. She looked like a contented married woman. He surprised himself with that analogy. Maybe he was too tired. Or maybe it was the clash he'd had with Brodie an hour earlier. Dan wasn't sure. He leaned back, closing his eyes, musing. Being with Chris in her comfortable quarters gave him a sense of overwhelming peace. He had longed to see her socially, but the heavy demands placed upon them both had effectively squelched that. He rolled his head to the right, opening his eyes, studying her in the lulling silence.

There was a lack of tension around Chris as she worked in the kitchen. In her bare feet she looked positively beautiful, with a girlish quality to her. Her black hair flowed freely, brushing her proud shoulders. Normally her beautiful violet eyes were shadowed with weariness. Now they were clear, flecked with gold, which seemed to indicate she was happy. Had coming to see her tonight been responsible for that change? Dan didn't know. A smile quirked one corner of his mouth as he rose and ambled into the kitchen. He would like to think he was responsible for part of this change.

"Smells good," he commented, moving over to where Chris stood. He leaned over her, inhaling the freshly brewed tea.

Chris felt his shoulder lightly brush against hers for a moment. She smiled, removing the tea bags from the pot. "Let's go sit in the living room. I need a break, too," she confided.

Dan made himself comfortable on the couch. Chris sat on the floor near her textbooks, her arm resting against the sofa. She looked like a graceful cat curled up, her long legs drawn up beneath her body.

"You think I'm going to attack you if you sit up here with me?" Dan teased.

"Yes." Chris smiled and took a sip of the tea.

"You're probably right," he responded, grinning.

Chris liked his honesty. "I was just kidding. I'm a floor person by nature." She became more serious. "You look beat."

"It's common the first month of school," he explained, balancing the mug on his right knee. "You're holding up well under the circumstances," he noted with satisfaction.

"I don't know, Dan. After that run-in with Brodie today...."

"You hit him right between the running lights," he said, trying not to smile.

Her violet eyes darkened. "He's an eighteen-year-

old kid instead of a mature man in his early thir-
ties!''

"Brodie never grew up in some ways, Chris."

She tilted her head, studying him in the softened
light. "You sound as if you've known him for a
while."

"He was in my F-4 squadron a number of years
ago."

"And did he go around telling people to watch
their six?" she asked, anger lowering her voice.

Dan studied her for a moment. "He said that to
you?"

"Yes, in front of the whole class."

"He must have said it in jest."

To Dan, that particular phrase carried plenty of
weight and feeling behind it. It was reserved for a
confrontation that would set up a demarcation line
never to be crossed by the other person.

Chris grimaced. "If we were living in the Middle
Ages, it would have been akin to Brodie throwing
his gauntlet and challenging me to a duel."

After talking at length with Brodie, Dan had been
convinced that the pilot was going to continue trying to get to Chris. This extra bit of information confirmed his original impression. Dan held the mug in
both hands, looking down at her upturned face.
Right now all he wanted to do was take Chris into
his arms, to hold and kiss her. His body tightened
with desire. How could she look so vulnerable and
trusting now, and so professional and unreadable at
the school? Would her background as an orphan
have forced her to take on this chameleonlike quality? Dan pushed aside his personal feelings for a
moment. "Look," he began heavily, leaning forward, "I've dressed Brodie down for his actions, and
he's given his word it won't happen again."

Chris gave him a stare of disbelief. "You actually
believe him?"

"More importantly, will you?" he asked tensely.

She gave him a silent look, narrowing her violet eyes. Then she bowed her head for a moment. "Is that why you came over here? To get my reaction to his promise?"

"Yes." That was part truth, part lie. He had been feeling lonely after the harrowing day's events and needed her nearness. But she couldn't know that. Not yet. Dan didn't want to be impatient, however. He could see that because he had backed off and given Chris room to accept him, she was responding more openly and trustingly. The look she gave him made his heartbeat quicken. So she *did* care about him after all. That piece of knowledge made Dan breathe an inner sigh of relief. He softened his stance slightly. "You know me. I'll use any excuse to come over and spend a few minutes off duty with you."

Chris was torn between Brodie's threat and Dan's sincerity. "Business before pleasure, though."

"In this case, yes," Dan responded. "How do you feel about Brodie?"

"That I'd better watch my six."

"You don't trust his promise?"

"Would you?"

Dan pursed his lips, staring down into the contents of the mug he held. "Look, I need one of the two of you to behave responsibly in this situation."

Chris was on her feet in seconds. "Then why does it have to be me? I didn't start this thing! Brodie has a twisted attitude about all women, not just me."

Dan felt his stomach tighten. Calmly he looked up into her distraught features, compassion flooding his heart. "We're in a messy situation," he began carefully. "I could have Brodie kicked out now because of his attitude, and it would certainly ruin his career. He'd run screaming to every damn newspaper and magazine in this country. It would harm the opportunity for other women who want and deserve test-pilot status.''

Chris's face paled. She clenched her fists at her sides. ''You know exactly how to get to me, don't you?'' she whispered tautly.

Dan put the mug on the coffee table and got to his feet. Exhaustion showed deep in his eyes. ''We're all in this together, Chris. I don't like it. You don't like it. Nobody does. It's simply the battle of the sexes over one more career position.'' He rubbed his eyes. ''And it's not your fault you were picked to be the first woman. The first few women going through TPS as test-pilot nominees are going to draw the most fire. After a while, the furor will die down, and you won't have men like Brodie overreacting to a woman being in class.'' He spread his hands in a gesture of peace. ''If it will make you feel any better, Brodie doesn't get along with a lot of other people, including myself.'' He searched her pained features. Shadows were visible beneath her large eyes, her translucent skin drawn tightly across her high cheeks, the corners of her mouth pulled in with unspoken pain.

''Raven, you're an exceptional pilot. And right now, you're number five in class standings. If you were a man, the Brodies of the world wouldn't care. But you're a woman and his kind are going to react. He's going to keep sniping at you. He'll train his sights on you from now on because you openly challenged him in class.''

She gave a shrug and sat back down on the floor. ''I've always fought for the underdog. I guess I can do it for myself in this situation.''

''I'm beginning to understand where your sense of loyalty comes from. You protect your friends and slay your enemies,'' Dan said, sitting down once again on the couch.

''Figuratively, not literally!''

Dan smiled at her. "You know, I named you well. Ravens are a clannish lot that protect their own kind with a fierce kind of courage. We have plenty of them here at Edwards. I've even seen ravens attack hawks or eagles if they get too close to their young ones."

Chris sighed. "Just like I attacked Brodie in front of everyone."

"He had it coming. I'm just sorry I wasn't there to intercept and put a lid on it once and for all."

She gave him a tender look, a soft smile appearing on her lips. "Don't tell me there's a little bit of the knight on his white charger in you."

A careless grin came to Dan's mouth as he regarded her in the growing warmth being woven between them. His heart stirred, his body craved her. "If Brodie heard that, he'd tell you I was Don Quixote, not a Sir Galahad."

"Oh? Why?"

"Goes back to my days in Nam."

"Want to tell me about it?"

Dan hesitated. He had rarely spoken about his two tours over the skies of Nam and Hanoi. It brought up too many painful memories. "Brodie was assigned to my squadron during my second tour. We flew the F-4s. I had a bit of a reputation among the marines up in the demilitarized-zone for hedgehopping. Brodie became my wingman."

"Did he like you going down that low?"

Dan shook his head. "No."

"Why did you?"

His eyes grew dark as more of those days in his life were dredged to the surface. "I guess I'll always hear the radio crackling with the voices of pinned-down marines on the ground screaming for help again. Chris, I—" He hesitated, giving an embarrassed shrug. "This is going to sound silly."

She leaned forward, her face calm, eyes penetrating. "No, it won't. At least not to me," she coaxed. "You risked plenty by going down on the deck, Dan. Why?" *What made him run,* Chris wondered. Dan always appeared buoyant and devil-may-care. But anyone who would take the cantankerous Phantom down to the treetop level where it could be hit by ground fire and missiles was either very foolish or very confident of his skills. And she didn't see Dan as being a fool about anything.

Dan stood up, and walked to the end of the room, his features composed and thoughtful. "I guess I'm like you, Chris. I don't like seeing the underdog get beaten down. If I can do something about it, I will." He shrugged. "It got so that certain marine companies would call in air support and ask for me by name. They knew if they went into a tight spot, I'd be there to help them."

A memory stirred in the back of Chris's mind. What had Jim said one time? Her fiancé had spent two tours in Vietnam with F-4s. She gave Dan a keen look. "What was your name?"

"Cowboy. The marines dubbed me with it because I'd ride the F-4 down during any kind of situation or weather condition. Brodie hated going low level."

Chris's mouth went dry and her heart pounded at the base of her throat. Cowboy...Cowboy...Jim had known an F-4 pilot by that name! Her eyes widened. Was the world that small? Had Dan known Jim? The next thought paralyzed her: what if Dan knew about the crash? She swallowed hard, unable to think coherently for a moment. Jim had talked fondly of a pilot by the name of Cowboy, having nothing but admiration and praise for his flying ability. She looked guardedly up at Dan. She couldn't forget the conversations she and Jim had shared. How many times had he laughingly told her about Cowboy? Her world felt as if it were collapsing around her. Above everything, no one must know of the crash! Not her colleagues at TPS. And especially not Dan.

If word got around about the crash claiming Jim's life, her reputation at TPS would be destroyed. Chris frowned, getting to her feet. And what would Dan think? How close had Jim been to Dan before he had died? Had Jim ever told him of his engagement to her? A voice told her it was unlikely. Still, the way Jim had talked of Cowboy, Chris felt it was almost a brotherly relationship that had existed between the two pilots.

"The guys on the ground were worth that risk, though," Chris murmured.

Dan pursed his lips. "I thought so. Brodie didn't, but that was inconsequential to me." Reluctantly Dan glanced down at his watch. "As much as I've enjoyed coming over and talking with you, I'd better get going."

Where had the time gone? Chris looked at her watch to confirm it. A sense of disappointment washed over her. Their personal time together was rare, and she hungrily looked forward to those small, placid moments when they could meet on equal ground and discover new facets about each other.

"Tomorrow is going to be a tough day," he reminded her.

"Test day," Chris agreed, walking to the door and opening it. Tomorrow she would be given the final flight test in the F-4 that would qualify her to take up another student engineer, navigator or fellow pilot. But the test held less fear for her than the fact that Dan might have known Jim. If Jim had told him.... Chris stopped thinking as Dan drew close. Regardless of her spinning, tumultuous thoughts, she responded to his lean maleness. Raising her chin, Chris met his warm blue gaze, and felt his tender caress as he smoothed a stray tendril from her cheek.

"You know," he murmured, his voice becoming husky, "it's too bad you can't wear your hair down all the time. You look pretty this way."

Chris momentarily closed her eyes, her heart racing. She could still see his strong, chiseled mouth in her mind's eye. Memory of the branding kiss he had placed on her lips sent an ache of need throughout her. "Thank you," Chris whispered, meaning it. His eyes had darkened to a thundercloud intensity, sending a warming shiver down her spine. All he had to do was reach out, and.... Her breath caught when she read the intent in his eyes.

One part of her cried out for Dan's touch once again. Another shrank in fear from him. She had just lost someone she had loved. It can't happen again, a voice screamed. She never again wanted to feel the kind of pain that still persisted over the loss of Jim. "I think we should say good-night, Dan," she said firmly, her voice more businesslike than she intended.

If he was disappointed, he did not show it. Offering her a smile, Dan nodded. "I'll see you in the morning, Raven. Good night."

5

IT WAS 0600 when Chris arrived in her flight gear at TPS. She saw Dan's Corvette parked in the rear lot. The sky was still dark with stars although a gray hint of dawn nudged the silhouetted mountains in the background. Her fingers tightened in the pockets of her flight jacket as she quickly took the steps two at a time up to the door. Dan was busy with paperwork when Chris stepped into his cramped office. He looked up, giving her a slight smile.

"Grab a cup of coffee and then go check the weather. I'm going to be tied up with this stuff for another half hour."

"Sounds good," she murmured, meaning it. The coffee was like a shot of adrenaline to her exhausted mind. Sleep had been impossible, and Chris wanted to be perfect on the test flight today. Dan was a fair, but tough instructor. She called up operations and got in touch with the meteorologist, jotting down the wind direction, knots, the temperature and dew point. All these factors would have a great deal to do with the rotation or takeoff point of the jet that she would pilot this morning. Gathering up the flight-plan information, Chris met Dan as he was coming out of his office. He glanced up at her.

"All set?"

"Ready, ready now," she replied, dropping into B-52-bomber slang. It brought the expected smile to Dan's face.

"Okay, let's get Double Ugly checked out and then you can take me for a ride."

A new feeling penetrated her exhaustion. She recognized it as a shot of badly needed adrenaline. *Today was the day!* Resolution coupled with desire to do her very best on the test catapulted through her. Not only did Chris want to make the highest scores possible, but equally important, she wanted to make Dan proud of her. He was giving up a great deal for her sake. More than once she had heard some of the other instructors teasing Dan about the flight overtime he was logging for her benefit. Chris felt her heart expand in silent gratitude for his sacrifice. Dan personified the image of the ideal officer and gentleman.

She picked up her flight bag at the locker and doggedly walked out to the flight line where Dan was waiting. Hopping into the waiting van, they were driven out to the ramp in the grayness of the burgeoning dawn that outlined the black shapes of the awesome F-4 Phantoms.

As always, it was business only in the cockpit. Conversations were kept to a minimum, covering only the technical exchanges that were needed to complete the preflight list. Suddenly her fatigue vanished, and Chris placed all her concentration on the present. The shiver of the throbbing twin engines of the jet filled her with confidence. Working the rudders, she gave the crew chief a thumbs-up and inched the throttles foward, pointing the black-nosed fighter toward the taxi way. In an hour and a half she would know whether or not she had the right stuff to continue flying the fighters....

IT WAS ALMOST 0900 when Chris landed the Phantom. After she completed the final landing, Dan ordered her to bring the bird in from the grueling hour-and-a-half test. Chris pushed up the dark visor that covered the upper half of her face. When she unsnapped one side of her oxygen mask, it brushed the left side of her cheek. She grimaced, feeling the familiar trickle of sweat from between her breasts and from beneath her armpits. It had been one hell of a test.

"Switch to private," Dan ordered, breaking into her thought.

Chris reached down and switched the dial to PVT. "Go ahead," she said, holding the mask that held the communications device up to her mouth.

"You looked pretty tired when you came in this morning."

She managed a low laugh. "Is that a statement or question?"

Dan's laughter floated back into her ears. She relaxed, loving the huskiness of his voice. "A statement. What did you do? Stay up all night studying the F-4 manual?"

"Couldn't sleep so I decided to read through it one last time," she admitted cautiously.

"It showed. I'm giving you a ninety-four percent on your overall grade. Congratulations."

The shock of his statement almost disrupted her concentration as she taxied the F-4 toward the ramp.

"What's the matter?" Dan drawled. "Did I finally surprise you?"

She blinked and then choked on a laugh. "Sort of! A ninety-four?"

"You earned it," he said. "And just to celebrate all the hard work you've been putting in, I'm taking you out for dinner tonight. No argument."

Chris didn't know what to do first: cry, laugh or yell with happiness. She had passed with flying colors! A new sense of pride overwhelmed her momentarily. It had been a long hard road back since that crash—she had fought her own fears every time she had sat in the cockpit of a jet. By passing the test for the F-4, she had reconfirmed so much about herself that Chris lapsed into silence, too emotional to trust her voice.

"Hey, when I said 'no argument' I didn't mean for you to completely ignore my invitation."

Chris willed back her tears and popped the canopy hatch, allowing fresh air into the cockpit. As she slowly brought the F-4 into parking position with the help of the ground crew, she said, "I'm in shock."

"Over the test score or my invitation to dinner?"

Chris managed a smile, unbuckling the complicated harness and placing the safety pins back into the ejection seat. "Both, frankly. I'm going to unhook. See you down on the ramp."

Several other students and instructors were on the ramp, preparing to fly. Among them was Brodie who was climbing into the F-4 next to them. Chris ignored the glare Brodie leveled in her direction. She pulled the camouflaged helmet off her head, carefully tucking it back into the flight bag and released her chignon. Her ebony hair swung across her shoulders, framing her face once again. Dan sauntered around the wing and joined her. An irrepressible grin lurked at the corners of his mouth. Without the helmet, his hair was mussed, giving him a boyish look. Chris couldn't help but return his smile. Suddenly her exhaustion disappeared. All the nights of sporadic sleep coupled with the replay of the crash now seemed far away.

Dan shortened his stride in order to walk at Chris's side. A glint of pride shone in his blue eyes as he looked down at her. "I'll pick you up tonight at eight, Raven. Oh, and one more thing. Put your dancing shoes on. We've got some heavy celebrating to do."

She grinned. "Roger, roger, read you loud and clear."

IT HAD BEEN ONE LONG, EXCITING DAY. Written tests on calculus and aerodynamics were given that after-

noon. They had to be graded, but Chris knew from
long experience that her answers were correct. Begging off from joining Karen and Mark at the O'Club,
Chris went directly to her room at the BOQ. She
stripped off the flight suit, wrinkling her nose at the
odor her nervousness had created during the demanding flight test. After taking a hot, invigorating
shower, the tiredness that she had held at bay overwhelmed her. Slipping into her pale-pink robe,
Chris lay down on the couch, intent upon a quick
nap to refresh herself.

Her nightmare began insidiously, interwoven with
the exhausted sleep she desperately needed. First,
there was the G-buildup as the T-38 jet aircraft suddenly nosed downward at a frightening angle, crush-
ing her against the ejection seat. She felt as if a huge
hand were pushing in on her chest. Chris moaned,
calling to Jim.

"Jim, what's wrong?"

"I don't know."

The pressure of the dive increased as the sleek,
needlelike T-38 dived toward the earth thirty-nine
thousand feet below them. The Gs were so awesome
that Chris was smashed against the seat, barely able
to move her hands from their position on her thighs.
Her heart was racing. She heard Jim's harsh breathing coming through the earphones.

"Damn—Chris, grab the stick and hit the left rudder hard. I can't unlock the right rudder."

Her heart pounded as the T-38 hurtled into the
spin, its long nose pointed at the dry Texas desert,
now thirty-thousand feet below them. Was it hydraulic failure? It took every vestige of strength to
get her hand to the stick. Her fingers wrapped
strongly about it. She shoved her booted left foot
forward, putting all her weight on the rudder beneath it. Nothing moved! The scream of the jet continued. Her head was pressed against the seat, and

she was unable to move it one inch either way. The altimeter showing their altitude was unwinding like a broken spring.

"We've got to punch out!" she cried. "It's locked! It's locked!"

"No!" Jim gasped. "It's not hydraulic. Something's jammed under the rudder. Damn! Pull harder!"

Fear twisted through her. Her eyeballs felt as if they were getting pushed through the back of her skull. The T-38 spun in an almost vertical dive toward the parched brown earth. Chris could feel the right rudder give slightly. But not enough. Not enough! "It's stuck!" she gasped. "Punch out!" Sweat bathed her body, and a scream tore from her lips as the altimeter showed only fifteen thousand feet left between them and the ground. As always in the recurring nightmare, everything from this point on became a slow-motion blur. She was on the edge of blacking out, Jim's frantic breathing rasped over the headphones. In wild desperation he tried to work the right rudder free.

Chris moaned, crying out. Suddenly she was thrown violently awake by the ejection sequence. Another man's voice broke through the chaos of wind howling at her, pounding her body, tearing the visor off her helmet. Chris became aware of arms around her, holding her, rocking her. A sob tore loose from deep within her. The scent of Dan's body, his warmth and lean strength sponged slowly through her fragmented, cartwheeling brain. Chris felt the texture of corduroy against her wet cheek, heard the steadying beat of his heart against the turmoil of hers. "Oh, God," she whimpered, burying her head more deeply against his cradling shoulder. "Oh, God...."

Dan held her tightly, one hand against her blue-black hair, the other around her trembling sweat-soaked body. "Ssh," he soothed softly against her ear, "it's all right. You're here now and you're safe, Raven." His eyes mirrored the anguish he heard. Dan had arrived at exactly eight and knocked on the door. There had been no answer at first. And then he heard Chris cry out. He called her name. She had not answered. Grimly, he had put his hand around the doorknob, twisting it open. Luckily it was unlocked, and he stepped into her apartment. She was lying there on the couch, face contorted in sleep, sobbing.

Her words were almost unintelligible as he sat down on the couch, taking her into his arms. He was no stranger to nightmares himself and recognized that Chris was reliving some tragic flying sequence. Words such as "punch out" and "it's locked" were torn from her lips as she wrestled to escape the clutches of the event clothed in the mantle of sleep.

Dan held her, stroking her ebony hair, whispering words of comfort. Her body was damp and trembling. He closed his eyes, pressing his head against her fragrant hair. How many times had he awakened in a sweat after his days in Vietnam. Far too many. It was no different for Chris. What trauma from her past had caused this kind of reaction? His mind raced with questions as he rocked her gently, listening to the last vestiges of the horror fleeing from her. Had she been involved in a crash? If she had, there was no one at TPS who knew about it. And if she had, how long ago? He ran his fingers down her long curved back, delighting in the firmness of her muscles. Experience told him the crash couldn't have been more than a year ago because of her violent reaction.

Slowly Chris's breathing began to return to normal. He felt her breasts pressed against his chest, aware of the wild beat of her heart. Dan embraced her more tightly for a moment, dizzied by her ability to trust him. She was like a small child that had been frightened by a storm, clinging to him in muted silence. She stirred other awakening desires to life within him, but Dan made no move to capitalize upon the moment. She needed help and someone to hold her.

"It's all right, Raven," he told her in a hushed voice. "You're here, in the present now. The nightmare's over. You're here, with me, in your room at the BOQ." How many times had he wakened in his barracks room thinking he was still reliving the horror of SAM missiles streaking toward his F-4, intent on obliterating him from the skies? And how long had it taken him to talk himself out of that state even though he had been pulled awake by his own screams? His own sobs? He had wanted to roll over and bury himself in the arms of a woman and find solace against those stalking ghosts of the past. Grimly Dan blinked back tears as he gazed down at Chris.

No one had ever held him in the throes of those horrible nights. At least he could do that for Chris. Dan understood better than most what the warmth of a steadying body could do to bring someone back into the present. He gently brushed the wetness from her cheek, his face filled with concern. Chris was still trembling, her lips parted, contorted by powerful updrafts of emotions he could sense were violently alive within her. "It's okay, honey," he murmured, leaning down, placing a kiss on her temple. "Work through the fear. Don't hang on to it. Just let it go...."

Chris squeezed her eyes shut, burying her face in the folds of his coat. "Oh, Dan..." she cried hoarsely.

"I know, I know," he crooned. But he didn't know. Dan was stymied. If a crash was this traumatic, the pilots were put on waivers and given medical or psychological help to pull them through it so they could fly again. Chris had to have conquered it, or they wouldn't have allowed her to come to TPS. Especially because of the pressures she would be under in order to learn to fly fighter planes. The medical people would not have certified her fit for flight duty if she hadn't gotten herself together after the accident. It had to be something else. But what? He pursed his lips, gazing down at her pale drawn features. His heart felt torn from his chest. God, she looked so damn broken. So vulnerable. A soft groan escaped Dan, and he simply held her within the safety of his arms for a long, long time.

Dan eventually shifted his position. He rested against the couch with Chris safely ensconced in his arms. The watch on his wrist read 9:00. Chris's heart had quit beating like a frightened bird, her breathing was less chaotic, telling him she was now past the worst of it. He brushed her flushed cheek with his fingers one last time, aware of the smoothness of the skin. His body contracted with need of her—all of her. The natural fragrance of her skin, the smell of apricot that lingered in her black hair were all powerful aphrodisiacs to his heightened senses. Dan controlled his desire to kiss those full, parted lips. But the desire that coursed through him was more than just physical desire for Chris. He wanted to love Chris, protect her. He needed her.... Love? He tested the word carefully in his mind and heart. A tranquil sigh came from deep within Dan as he nuzzled his face against the silk of her hair.

His heart soared with that knowledge. He took his time to assimilate the gamut of feelings that she effortlessly brought forth in him. He had known many women in his thirty-five years. But never one like Chris. There was a magic that flowed between them. A new tenderness flooded Dan's chest, and the warmth he experienced in that moment of

knowing took his breath away. He placed a small
kiss on her cheek, and felt her respond, the tentative,
hesitant sliding of her arm around his neck, the resting of her brow against his jaw.

Dan tried to sort out all the emotional impressions
he was picking up from Chris. There was an excru-
ciating level of anguish and loss surrounding her.
Somehow, he wanted to fill the void. Following his
instincts, he cupped her jaw, bringing her face close
to his own. He studied her thick lashes wet with
tears, the flawless peach color of her fragrant skin
and finally her waiting, full lips. Leaning down, he
caressed them tentatively. They tasted of salt, of life.
Dan felt her lips tremble beneath his own, and he
pressed more surely, lost in the warming texture of
her flesh. A small cry tore from her as she weakly
struggled to push away.

"Don't," he whispered. He had felt her immediate
response when he had first brushed her lips. Pressing more firmly, Dan moved his mouth across hers
in small, teasing motions. Chris's breath quickened,
telling him that he was affecting her just as much as
he was dizzied by their tentative exploration of each
other. Gradually her resistance disappeared. He inhaled her scent, barely able to control his raging desires now begging to be released. Her lips parted
against his like an opening flower to sunlight, allowing him to explore her. He groaned as he tasted
the sweet depths of her mouth, and coaxed her into
mutual exploration, his tongue teasing, tantalizing.
Chris almost melted against him, her fingers curling
into the hair at the nape of his neck, her breathing
ragged.

Dan tasted her thoroughly, his own body hardening with a desire so overwhelming that he felt
himself tremble for want of her. But something cautioned him to go no further. Dan had lived all his life
by his instincts, and reluctantly, he obeyed. He

wasn't thinking: only sensing, feeling, glorying in the fact that her mouth was warm and responsive against his. Her body was supple, her soft feminine curves fitting perfectly to him.

Chris slowly pulled away, her eyes dark with passion as she studied Dan. He had soothed her anguish with just a kiss. It was a kiss meant to heal her ragged, scared emotional state—given unselfishly and without the carnal reasons that normally went with a kiss. She regarded Dan gravely, realizing that he could have taken advantage of the situation. But he hadn't. She was unable to sort through the violent emotions that had been unleashed by the virulent nightmare. Chris gave him a searching look, reaching up, touching her well-kissed lips.

"I'll be okay..." she whispered, her voice barely audible. Dan released her, allowing her to sit up. The robe had become loosened, revealing the creamy texture of her skin and the shadowed cleft between her concealed breasts. Oddly, she felt no embarrassment as she rose to her feet, rearranging the folds and tightening the sash once more. The silence pervading the room was comforting. The quiet of healing, she thought suddenly.

"Maybe a shower will help you." He got to his feet, slipping his arm around her slender waist. "Go on," he coaxed. "I'll make us some tea."

Dan took off his corduroy sport coat, hanging it over one of the chairs. He unbuttoned the shirt, rolling the sleeves up on his forearms. By the time Chris emerged fifteen minutes later, the tea was prepared. Dan offered her a reassuring glance as she padded quietly into the kitchen. Her hair hung in damp strands, framing her face and shoulders, a rosy glow to her skin attesting to the fact it had been a very hot shower.

"Come on in the living room," he invited. "We'll sit on the couch."

Chris followed him without protest. She wore a lavender terry-cloth robe instead of the pink one. Dan put the tray on the coffee table and then sat down next to her.

"Your tea has a hefty dose of brandy in it," he warned, handing it to her.

Her fingers trembled as she took the mug. Dan continued to hold the mug, watching her. Chris felt as if a devastating emotional war had taken place inside her. It had left her shaken on all levels, even physically. Taking a good grip on the mug, she glanced at him. "I've got it now."

She leaned back, tucking her legs up beneath her, cradling the mug in both hands. The warmth of the tea combined with the brandy made her feel more in touch with reality. Dan held his own mug between his hands. After a few more sips she tried out her strained voice. "Thanks, Dan...for being here...."

He regarded her solemnly. "I wouldn't have it any other way, Raven."

She pushed a wet strand away from her temple. "You always seem to catch me when I'm down and out."

"I'm not sorry. Are you?"

Chris pursed her lips, remembering the fiery imprint of his mouth upon her. "No..." she admitted hesitantly, "I never expected the nightmare to happen. I just lay down for a short nap." She saw his eyes narrow, and her stomach knotted. He was going to ask....

"You're having a pretty strong reaction to something, Chris. Maybe it would help if you talked to someone about it."

She stared down at the tea for a long time. "I can't...."

"You mean you won't," he corrected without censure.

Chris felt broken; as if she was scattered into so

many emotional pieces. She looked directly into Dan's kind eyes. "Please," she begged, "I feel so fragile right now, Dan. I hurt inside...."

He reached over, his fingers sliding around her arm and capturing her free hand. "Okay," he murmured, "I understand. Some other time, then."

The mixture of tea and brandy quelled her screaming nerves but made her feel drowsy. Placing the mug on the coffee table, Chris leaned back.

"You look as if you need to be held," Dan said. "Come here." He reached out, expecting Chris to balk. To his surprise, she acquiesced without one word of protest. She fitted against him perfectly, her head resting in the hollow of his shoulder, her hands against his chest. "That's better," he murmured. Instinctively she nuzzled against him, feeling his arm momentarily tighten around her shoulders.

His breath was warm and moist against her face. "Talk to me, Dan, about anything," she murmured.

He recognized the symptoms Chris was displaying. After a particularly brutal nightmare he often tried to shift his mind to anything else other than it. "What do you want to hear?" he asked.

Chris blinked tiredly. "About you. Where you grew up. What you did as a little boy."

He took a deep breath, loving the trust building between them. "I'm a country boy from Texas," he said in a soft voice. "I was an only child, born in Fort Worth. My father was an oil wildcatter who found more producing wells than dry holes. He was usually away from home hunting down his next lease or well. I spent most of my childhood with my uncle who owned a cattle ranch in the Panhandle."

"And were you as precocious then as now?" Chris asked, closing her eyes. She craved the warmth in his voice, the vibration a soothing balm to her recently distraught emotional state. Being held by Dan chased away the dread.

He responded softly, "Let's put it this way: I was the kid who would drop a horny toad in your cowboy boot." His eyes crinkled with silent laughter over those fond memories. "Of course, I spent plenty of time doing penance for those jokes by helping the ranch crews replace fences."

"You were lucky to have a family."

"In a way," he mused, a frown forming on his brow. "Although being born with a so-called silver spoon in your mouth isn't always to be envied."

She wanted to listen, but the fingers of sleep dragged her into oblivion. And without meaning to, Chris fell asleep in Dan's arms. He had felt her body relax against him, but he continued to talk in a subdued tone. Dan made no move to leave her for almost an hour afterward. He wanted to make sure that those nightmares would not start stalking Chris again. It was almost ten-thirty before he gently picked Chris up and carried her to the bedroom. Leaving her robe on, he placed her on the bed and tucked her in. Dan turned on the small lamp that sat on the nightstand. Bending over, he gently caressed her cheek.

"No more nightmares, Raven," he whispered. Straightening up, he stood watching her sleep. Gone were the lines of tension from around her mouth. Black hair framed her face, the shadowed lighting accentuating Chris's clean features and full lips. Lips that he wanted to kiss again. *Soon*, he promised her. *I know you care for me, Raven.* Dan gazed at her longingly, unable to deny the burgeoning feelings of joy that threatened to overwhelm him. A slight smile played on his lips as he turned and left as quietly as he had come.

CHRIS DROWSILY AWOKE. The February sun filtered through the lace curtains, casting muted shadows on the opposite wall. What time was it? She rolled over on her side, forcing her eyes to focus. Ten o'clock! Adrenaline shot through her, and Chris jerked the covers off. She had a flight at 10:30 this morning! Confusion momentarily made her halt. What was she doing in her robe? Her eyes widened and she halted at the doorway, the entire memory of the night before avalanching upon her. Chris groaned, running quickly to the kitchen to ring Operations. She saw a note on the kitchen table and picked it up.

Raven,
   Take the day off. That's an order. I've canceled your morning flight. You've been through enough in a month's time. Call me when you wake up and I'll take you to breakfast.

                                          Dan

Chris took a deep breath, her violet eyes mirroring the sudden warmth she felt coursing through her body. It felt as if a hundred tons of weight had just slipped free of her shoulders. Today, for the first time, she could have a cup of coffee and read the paper without racing through her morning routine. A small smile played up on her lips as she picked up the phone and dialed the number Dan had placed at the bottom of the note.

"Hello?"

Chris loved the sound of Dan's voice. "Hi."

"Did anybody ever tell you how sexy you sound when you first wake up?"

"Here we go again!"

"Of course. Anything to get you to laugh a little."

She sobered. "I have been crying a lot, haven't I?"

"Hey now, let's not go into a tailspin over your tears." His voice was alive with good humor.

"I don't understand why Karen didn't stop by this morning," she added, fighting off the sleepiness. "Or did you fix that, too?"

"I called Karen and gave her strict instructions that you were to be left alone. I told her you had a late night."

Chris groaned. "Wonderful! Now I'll never hear the end of her teasing me about it." Karen would love nothing better than to rib her about Dan's coming to visit her.

"I don't think she will," Dan hedged. "Had coffee yet?"

"N—no, I just charged out of bed when I saw what time it was. Thank God you left a note, or I would have made it to Ops in record time."

"Then invite me over for a cup. You don't sound as if you're ready to meet the world yet."

"Well—"

"Listen, I tucked you into bed last night, so I know what you look like when you're exhausted. Besides, I think you're gorgeous au naturel."

She felt the heat of a blush. *My God, had something else happened last night?*

"No, nothing happened last night," he said, as if reading her mind. "Unfortunately."

"Give me a break." She laughed. Dan had seen her at her worst, so why should she be worried? "Come on over."

"Be right there."

Chris hummed softly, pouring herself a cup of the freshly brewed coffee. The aroma filled the kitchen and she inhaled it, enjoying the fragrance. Earlier she had run a brush through her ebony hair and now felt comfortable enough to meet Dan in her robe and bare feet.

A knock at the door announced Dan's arrival. Chris opened it, meeting him with a smile.

He looked so handsome in his snug-fitting jeans

and a dark-gold sweater that brought out the gold highlights in his brown hair. He shared a welcoming smile with her and closed the door behind him.

"You look great," he murmured, meaning it.

Chris took the compliment, motioned him to the kitchen and handed him a cup of coffee. "Thanks to you."

He raised the cup to his mouth, taking a tentative sip. "And I intend to collect, my raven-haired lady," he promised.

She met his azure gaze, caught up in the euphoria of simply being with Dan. "Oh?"

"Yes, ma'am. I've decided that you need a day off from all your studies and flying."

"Is that your professional opinion, major, or are your motives questionable?"

Dan grinned. *God, she looked incredibly beautiful this morning.* There was a translucence to her skin, her dark-violet eyes shining with life. A smile was finally touching those lips that were meant to be worshiped for a lifetime. Dan roused himself from his torrid thoughts, and gave her a look of pure innocence. "Strictly professional, you understand."

Her laughter was lilting, infectious. "You know, your nickname serves you well. You *are* like a cowboy. Always roping somebody into a situation."

"And hog-tying them when necessary if they don't do as I suggest," he warned darkly.

Chris picked up the gauntlet he had thrown in her direction. "And if I don't agree with your professional opinion?"

He shrugged his broad shoulders, enjoying the repartee. "Then I'll just have to throw you over my shoulder and carry you off."

"Now who's a chauvinist of the first order?"

He grinned wickedly. "Lady, when it comes to getting your attention, I'll even be a chauvinist if I have to."

Shaking her head, Chris murmured, "You won't have to. I'm ready for a break. What did you have in mind?"

He balanced the cup between his hands, studying her warmly. "How about a trip to the ocean? We're two hours from the beaches near L.A. I checked with meteorology, and they say it's going to be a bit chilly but sunny. Are you game?"

Her violet eyes sparkled. "With you at the helm, you'd better believe it."

Dan hooted with glee. "Finally! The lady trusts me enough to make a decision for her. This *is* a special day."

Chris got to her feet. "What am I getting myself into?" she asked just as dramatically.

He gave her a warning glance. "Being a test-pilot student, you ought to be excited about exploring the unknown."

She gave him a backward glance over her shoulder, hesitating at the bedroom door. "Right now, I think I'd feel safer testing a jet than trusting your intentions."

"Only one way to find out, isn't there, Raven?" he posed softly.

Her lips curved into a full smile. "I'm game."

"That's my lady. Hurry up. We'll grab breakfast on the road."

For their outing, Chris chose a pair of dark-brown slacks, a crisp white shirt, and a pale-pink sweater. Was this all a dream, she wondered. Dan had rescued her from the drowning depths of a nightmare and lifted her into the cloudless blue of utter happiness. As they traveled the freeway toward busy Los Angeles, she felt drowsy in the warm confines of his Corvette. Breakfast had been a wonderful break in Riverside, the conversation light. Her heart sang with sheer joy. How long had it been since she felt like this? Had Jim ever made her feel quite this happy? Chris closed her eyes, resting her head against the seat, trying to find her answer. Jim had been a more intense, quiet individual. They had shared a meeting of minds. She wanted to share both mind and emotions with Dan. That thought jolted her and Chris opened her eyes.

There was no longer any denial of the physical attraction she felt for Dan. He was ruggedly handsome, and possessed an undeniable charm. Out of the corner of her eye, she watched Dan drive. His profile was clean, his eyes ever alert, his entire demeanor that of a man who was in complete charge of his life in every way. And was he also in charge of hers? She avoided confronting the answer. Today all Chris wanted to do was relax, forget the past and the pressures that had dogged her quest for test-pilot status.

She dozed lightly until Dan woke her. Chris roused herself, rubbing her neck where a small kink had developed. "I'm sorry," she murmured, sitting up. "I didn't mean to go to sleep on you."

He simply smiled, opening the door. "Don't worry, I'm not going to think you fell asleep because I was boring company."

"Hardly. It's the strain of the past month catching up with me," she admitted.

He winked. "Come on, Raven, let's go for a walk. Some fresh salt air will do you good."

It seemed natural to feel his hand gripping hers. The beach was dotted with people walking their dogs, joggers and a few families. The sky was a bright blue, and white gulls with black-tipped wings sailed effortlessly on the invisible up and down drafts, skimming the calm ocean for unsuspecting prey. Chris fell into step with Dan, relishing his closeness. The wind was brisk, lifting strands of her dark hair across her face momentarily.

Dan looked down. "Cold?" Before she could

answer, he released her hand and slipped his arm around her waist.

Chris made no protest, content to languish against his strong body, head resting on his shoulder. The crashing waves frothed and foamed, spilling out upon the dark sand at their feet. Above and to their right stood eroded sandstone cliffs. It looked as if a giant hand with sharp fingernails had raked their face, creating deep, scarring indentations. Driftwood ranging from pine to rare myrtle wood from the Northern California coast lay graying in the strong rays of the sun, thrown to shore by the latest storm. Chris stared at one piece of driftwood bobbing in the surf, finding a parallel.

"Do you ever feel like that," she asked, pointing to the gnarled wood struggling against the relentless tide.

Dan slowed his walk and they halted, watching it. "Drifting?" he prompted, reading between the lines of her statement.

"Yes, sometimes I do. That sounds pitiful, doesn't it?"

"No. It's not pity. Matter of fact, Raven, people like us ought to be less hard on ourselves," he murmured, resting his chin against her hair.

"What do you mean?"

"We're pushed by our past. Me to escape the shadow of my less than exemplary parents. You were alone so much of your life that you set your own goals instead of comparing yourself against others' accomplishments." He frowned, searching for the right words. "When you have no comparison, you sometimes overexcel."

"My life hasn't been very moderate," she returned dryly. "As a matter of fact, it has been one of extremes."

Dan turned her around, resting his arms lightly on her shoulders, looking deeply into her violet eyes.

"You are an extremist, like me," he agreed. "But by being one, you've accomplished more than most people. So you see, it's not all negative. But I think right now you need to learn more moderation. Allow yourself to let down and relax. That's something I've already learned. Be yourself, Raven."

Chris gave him a curious smile, basking in the warmth of his gaze. "I am myself."

Dan's eyes crinkled with silent laughter. "A fascinating, mysterious, provocative sensual woman. That's you."

She gave an embarrassed laugh. "Oh, stop it! You and Mark Hoffman! I don't know which of you can out-compliment the other."

"As long as the compliments are sincere, what do you care?" he mocked gently. "Just accept them with grace. Beautiful women should always consent to homage being paid to them, Raven." He leaned down, placing a light kiss on her nose.

"And judging from your past, you've had ample opportunity to sample a world full of beautiful women," she noted wryly.

"Guilty on all accounts," he admitted. "That's why you should take my compliments with even more validity. I know what I'm talking about."

Chris grinned ruefully, pulling out of his warm embrace. It was easy to fall against him and bury herself in his arms once again. So easy.... "You're so full of it," she retorted, beginning to walk slowly, hands thrust deeply into the pockets of her slacks.

"Sometimes I get the feeling you think I give women exactly what they want to hear."

Chris glanced up at him. "That's true. Ever since you told me about your past I can't help but think that you were raised and polished to be the consummate social animal."

He frowned. "I was raised on a ranch, Raven. I'll admit I played around for the first twenty-three

years of my life like any bachelor would. But the war
sobered me up real fast. Up until then I sort of
moved through life but didn't really get too seriously involved."

"Including no serious involvement with wom-
en?"

Dan hesitated, pursing his mouth. "Yes, including
women."

"I wondered why you weren't married."

"I never found a woman who could complement
all my diverse facets."

She gave him a wry look, trying to curb a smile.

Farther down the beach, she found a particularly
beautiful brown-and-white-spotted shell. Crouch-
ing down, Chris picked it up. Dan joined her.

"Look at this," he pointed. "The ridges are all the
same until they start flaring out at the end of the
shell."

The ridges were deep and identical as Chris ran
her sensitive fingertips across them. They began to
lose their shape and depth until finally, the last few
melted into a flat surface of the shell. "Nothing in
nature is an accident," she mused. "I wonder what
this means?" she asked, glancing over at him.

Dan shrugged, taking the shell and methodically
studying it. "Maybe there's a lesson in there for all
mankind," he remarked softly. His blue eyes darkened and held hers. "That we may be born into a
very fixed, rigid set of circumstances. If we persevere
and become our own person, we shed those old
ways and habits." He pointed to the smoothed area
of the shell. "In the end we can take on other facets
of ourself and grow, if given the chance."

"I think that's possible," she said, rising and
pocketing the shell.

The sun was moving to the west, the light dancing
off the quiet ocean, making them both squint. "I
know it's possible," Dan said with fervor. He slipped

his arm across her shoulder, drawing her near, needing to feel Chris against him as they started to walk once again.

"Are you talking philosophically?" Chris challenged, falling in step with him. How easy it was to become a natural part of Dan, she thought distractedly.

"No, factually."

"Explain."

He smiled grimly. "I'm an ideal example of what I just said. I walked away from the world my parents lived in and made a life of my own."

Chris heard the emotion behind Dan's words, as if some deep pain still existed within him.

"My father had my life planned out for me from the day I was born. I would take over the oil interests he had built. I would become an extension of him."

"Why didn't that appeal to you, Dan?"

"Drilling for oil wells never excited me."

"But flying did?"

He grinned, sharing his smile with Chris. "It grabbed me by the throat and has never let go."

She could identify with that. "So what happened when you told your parents you were going into the Air Force?"

Dan pursed his lips, his eyes growing distant for a moment. "Let's just say all hell broke loose."

Chris looked at him guardedly. She could feel the intensity of Dan's commitment to his freedom. He had broken the shackles of his past and stepped free. They continued to walk in silence another mile before she finally spoke. "I've got a ways to go yet."

"Oh?" He pulled her to a stop, placing his arms around her shoulders.

She chewed on her lower lip, unable to meet the warmth she knew rested in his blue eyes. Chris took a deep breath and said, "I've still got a chip on my shoulder."

His laughter was sensual, low and nonthreatening. "Raven, do you want to know what I think?" he whispered near her ear. He placed his hand beneath her chin, forcing her to meet his eyes.

"Yes." Her heart began a slow pound of awareness. He was so male, so intoxicatingly close, and so appealing to her heightened senses.

"You're so intent on the distance that you've traveled in life that you try to measure what's ahead, rather than appreciate what you've accomplished." A gentle smile touched the corners of his mouth as he scanned her upturned features. "You react strongly from your growing-up days." His voice dropped. "You need to shed that hardness, Raven. You no longer need it." He stroked her velvety cheek with the back of his hand. "All you have to do is see what you've accomplished and allow that vulnerable woman who lives in there to come out."

A burgeoning warmth centered in her heart, and Chris felt the heat of tears forming in her eyes. Dan caressed her cheek, tilting her head, brushing her lips in a slow, worshipful kiss. She trembled outwardly and moved into his waiting embrace, a supple willow against the hard oak of his body. A jagged bolt of heat tore through her as he pressed more demandingly against her yielding lips.

"Open your mouth," he whispered thickly, "I want to taste you. All of you...."

A shudder vibrated through his body, and Chris felt it move through her own like a delicious caress. His fingers stroked the nape of her neck, entangling in her ebony hair, sending thrilling messages to her overwhelmed senses. His mouth moved teasingly across her lips, his tongue tracing, probing and stroking all of her. He tasted male; he was hungry, and in control. There was an overwhelming tenderness to his onslaught as he drank deeply of her. Dizziness washed like an ocean wave through her, and she felt as if her entire body was exploding with pulse-pounding heat as he savored her, kissing each corner of her mouth with sureness before he drew inches away from her parted, glistening lips.

Languorously, she forced open her eyes. Dazed by the liquid fire now racing through her, she stared wonderingly up into his eyes, now pure cobalt with desire. A gnawing ache spread throughout her lower body, and her fingers tightened around his neck as she pressed herself closer. The intense longing in his eyes freed her of her own fear of giving herself willingly to him, on all levels and in all ways. Dan slid his fingers up her delicate jawline, framing her face between his hands. His head descended, and he placed a soft wet kiss against her waiting lips.

"This is the woman I had seen all along," he husked. "So warm, so vulnerable and trusting...."

Her thick ebony lashes fell against her flushed cheeks as she returned his achingly tender kiss. The licking flames of desire were melting every barrier. She wanted him—all of him. His maleness. His gentleness. His understanding of her that made her rapturous with joy.

"God," he groaned, lifting his head. "I want you, Raven. All of you."

Chris looked up at him wonderingly, needing his physical support in order to keep standing. She saw the corners of his sensual mouth draw upward into a wry smile.

"Of course, I would have to pick a beach with people on it."

A slow smile of understanding pulled at her thoroughly kissed lips. "Of all people, I'd never have thought that a test pilot would have such bad timing, McCord."

A glint of mirth danced in his eyes as he ran his hands down the length of her delicately curved back. "If that gets back to base, my reputation will be

ruined as a test pilot," he agreed. The turbulent blue
of his eyes grew lighter with amusement. "But what
I lack in timing, I'll more than make up with other
skills," he promised her huskily.

Chris leaned up on her toes, placing a kiss on his
smiling mouth. "No complaint there, believe me."

"Really?" He grinned down.

"McCord, I can't even stand on my own right
now."

He gave her a pleased look. "You look absolutely
ravishing, my raven-haired beauty. And believe me,
if we were on a deserted beach, you wouldn't be
standing. You'd be in my arms, and I would be making love to you right there."

Chris trembled, resting her head against his shoulder, closing her eyes. "I know," she confided in a
wispy voice. "And I wish there weren't any people
around, too."

Dan smiled tenderly, holding her for a long, long
time, simply feeling the woman of her against the
man of him. Pressing a series of small kisses along
her hairline and temple, he whispered, "We'll do
this again, Raven. We both need this. We need each
other. I need you...."

6

THE CLASSROOM HAD EMPTIED at lunchtime, leaving Chris to grapple with some last-minute studying before the next test. Resting her head against her hand, she drank in the technical information on aerodynamic theory. A headache was lapping at her temples and she sat back, raising her shoulders, trying to get rid of the accumulated tension. *Where had the first four months gone?* Dan had been right: the pressures at the school were accelerating to the point where everyone was experiencing mental burnout.

Putting down the pencil for a moment, she rubbed her aching eyes. Memories of their day at the beach two weeks ago soothed her present worries and concerns. It had been the last time they had been together in a nonprofessional situation. With Dan and her pulling extra flight duty to get her qualified in the two other aircraft, the remaining time was filled with study and fretful sleep. *Well,* she thought, *I have been trying to put my past behind me.* Karen had noticed it, just last night remarking, "You're—softer," she had said. Her blue eyes danced with mischief. "Can't be because of Dan McCord, could it?" she hinted broadly, grinning.

"Could be."

"Well, whatever it is, I like it. You're not so brittle with the guys. They feel it, too. It's a great change, and everyone is reaping the benefits from it."

"I know. I don't go around ripping everyone's head off anymore," Chris acknowledged.

"No, you never did that. You were just aloof,"

Karen explained. "Now you get along with everyone except Brodie."

One eyebrow moved upward, and Chris stared
across the table at her friend. "Tell me, who *does* get
along with Brodie?"

"No one. You'd think after all this time he'd cool
his heels and begin to accept you."

"Over his dead body," Chris muttered blackly.

"Better his than yours, honey."

Chris reluctantly pulled her mind back to the
present, but it didn't stay there long. As always, her
heart dwelled with Dan McCord. She rested her
head against her hands, closing her eyes for a moment. So far they had been able to keep their budding relationship a secret. At school Dan treated her
no differently than any other student. And although
Karen and Mark knew about their on-again, off-
again relationship, they said nothing to anyone. Occasionally Brodie would drop an innuendo that she
was carrying out her education with the instructors
in the bedroom. It had angered her until she had
finally parried his venomous attacks with a cool response.

"Hey, didn't somebody tell you it's lunchtime?"
Dan asked, sauntering into the room.

Chris looked up and met his smiling eyes. A blanket of warmth flooded her body as she scanned his
handsome features. "Has anybody ever told you
you're a sight for sore eyes?" she said, returning the
smile.

Dan raised his brow in mock horror. "I don't believe it! A compliment! Finally, after four months...."
He halted near her desk.

"Stow it, major. I'm busy studying for your
lousy aerodynamics-theory test this afternoon,"
she growled, trying to get serious.

Dan turned and looked toward the door to make
sure no one was passing by. He then slipped his

hand beneath her arm, pulling her to her feet. "My goodness, it sounds like you're picking up a lot of navy language from your friends in the class. Looks like I'll have to brainwash you back to Air Force lingo. Stow it, indeed." He gave her a dark look filled with humor. "Grab your flight cap. I'm taking you out to eat. And before you open those beautiful, inviting lips to say no, that's an order, captain."

Chris stood there, enjoying his fingers upon her arm. Her imagination took flight for an instant, and she again wondered what it would be like to make love with Dan. "Okay, hot-rock jet jockey, let's saddle up. I'm starved," she returned, settling the cap on her black hair, which swung in a page boy around her shoulders.

Once in the car, he drove off the base, heading toward Lancaster. Chris looked at her watch. "We've only got an hour and a half," she protested worriedly.

"So, I'll drive fast. Ever see a Corvette fly without wings?"

"The silver wings on your uniform will never make up the difference."

Dan grinned good-naturedly, reaching over and covering her hand. "How have you been, Raven? I've had one hell of a time trying to work in some time and space alone with you."

She warmed to his touch, returning the pressure of his fingers against her own. "That's your fault, not mine. If you'd quit piling on the homework so I wouldn't have to study until midnight, I might get to see you occasionally."

"Not to mention our nightly flights."

"Or weekend sorties," she agreed.

Dan squeezed her hand firmly. "But you're doing fine, Raven. Everyone is proud of you, believe me."

She pursed her lips. "Except Brodie and his clique."

"Brodie's opinions don't count. Mine and the other instructors do," he reminded her.

She groaned. "Thank God for small favors!"

"Hey, can we get serious for a minute?"

Her violet eyes twinkled. "Sure." And then she looked at her flight watch, setting it for exactly sixty seconds. "Ready, ready now!"

"Wench," he accused. "How about dinner tonight? I'm dying of loneliness."

"That's not bad. It only took you ten seconds flat. You're a fast mover." She glanced up at him. "You've got another forty-five seconds. Want to add to that invitation, major?"

Dan gave her a wicked look. "What I have in mind is less talking and more action."

She blushed beautifully. Chris wanted to share some of her personal discoveries with him and relished the idea of a dinner alone. "You don't scare me. I'll accept your dinner invitation."

"You're a brave woman, Raven."

She laughed. "Either that or very trusting."

"And the trust becomes you." He raised her hand to his lips. "You keep changing and showing your softer side, and I won't be held accountable for my actions," he murmured, kissing her hand.

After the grueling two-hour mathematics test, all the TPS students stretched or got coffee. Dan had left the room during the fifteen-minute break, and Chris forced herself not to watch him leave.

"How did you do?" Chris asked her classmate, Frank Conway.

"Flying is fine, but this damn math is a bitch!"

"You did okay," she reassured him.

Frank slowly got to his feet. "You like some coffee?"

"Love some," Chris responded tiredly. "Put a shot of whiskey in mine," she kidded.

Frank grimaced. "How about in an hour over at

the O'Club? Major McCord will probably only hold us for another forty-five minutes since it's Friday."

"Thanks, but no." Chris looked at him. "You guys do it for me."

"Chris, you *never* go out and celebrate! All you do is go to the barracks and hit the books."

Chris rose and stretched, placing her hands against her hips, leaning slowly one way and then the other. "Just my nature," she explained, smiling.

"Well, I'll get our coffee," he said as he sauntered away. The room was partially empty, with Brodie and four of his sidekicks lingering behind. Chris ignored them, walking around the room to loosen her tight muscles. Another six pilots were discussing the test in lowered voices.

Brodie eyed Chris across the aisle. "Hey, Mallory," he called, his voice carrying enough so that everybody could hear.

Chris lifted her chin, turning and meeting Brodie's glittering gaze. "Yes?"

He grinned, easing his whipcord body onto the desk top, a wolfish smile on his narrow features. "I stumbled upon a pretty interesting piece of information about you."

"Oh?" She immediately went on guard, realizing Brodie was going to start harassing her. He always chose a time when the instructor was absent. Another half-dozen students filed back into the classroom armed with fresh cups of coffee. Chris tensed. Why was Brodie openly challenging her this time?

"Yeah." His gaze drifted around the room. Now he had everyone's undivided attention. "I don't know about anyone else here," he began loudly, "but if I were an engineer or navigator in this class, I sure as hell wouldn't be flying with you, Mallory."

Chris froze, her lips thinning as she glared over at the pilot. "What's your game, captain?"

Brodie laughed. "No game, Mallory. You eject when it gets down to the nitty-gritty." His voice lowered to a deadly snarl. "The way I hear it, you left your buddy to die in a T-38 in Texas. The least little thing goes wrong and you're ready to call it quits instead of staying to help the air commander with the situation. Just think of it, guys. Would you like to be with Mallory when she puts a T-38 into a spin? Only thing was, her AC stayed with the plane trying to control it and died doing it." Brodie gave her a chilling smile. "You chicken out when the chips are down. That's not what I'd like to see in a test pilot."

A roar engulfed Chris, and she fought against the sudden deluge of emotion that Brodie had torn loose within her. A hundred questions caromed through her mind. How had he found out? Who had told him? That was privileged information! And every pilot in the room was staring at her, expressions suddenly closed, guarded and measuring. Her throat constricted as she stared disbelievingly over at the smiling Brodie.

"Well?" he prodded. "You're white as a sheet, Mallory. It must be the truth."

Frank Conway had entered with coffee in hand just in time to hear the accusation. "Probably a third of these pilots have punched out at one time or another," he defended swiftly.

Chris managed to leash her emotions. "It's all right," she told Conway. She turned on Brodie, her violet eyes black with anger. "I did punch out, Brodie. And I don't know who gave you that information, but you've screwed it up."

Brodie rose, very sure of himself. "Wrong, Mallory. You're the one who's screwed up. You left the pilot alone in a bird that was heading for the ground. You left him to die—"

"That's enough!" McCord snarled, stepping into

the room. His voice cut like a knife through the turgid, confused atmosphere. Dan walked between Chris and Brodie, glaring at both of them. His thundercloud blue eyes were narrowed upon Brodie. "Captain, sit down. Nobody throws unsubstantiated accusations around in my classroom. Is that understood? I won't have anyone throwing stupid attacks like that in this school." Dan stepped within inches of Brodie. "Is that clear, captain?"

Brodie glared back. "Yes, sir, major."

Chris felt her knees weaken, but she forced herself to walk to the chair before she collapsed. Dan ordered everyone to sit down, and launched immediately into another hour on aerodynamic theory. Her heart was pounding relentlessly, her body bathed in a cold sweat as Brodie's words sank deeper and deeper.

Chris had lost the entire hour. She remembered nothing of Dan's lecture, but was aware of only renewed pain, embarrassment and agony.

McCord walked up to Brodie after class had been dismissed. As badly as he wanted to, Dan could not console Chris. It had taken every bit of his concentration to continue to lecture that hour. He had seen the paleness of her features, her violet eyes wounded holes of pain, and watched her retreat within her shell. His anger was barely controlled as he stopped at Brodie's desk. "I want to see you right now, captain."

GRIMLY DAN THREW THE LECTURE NOTEBOOK on his desk and waited until Brodie had shut the door to his office. Then he turned menacingly on the pilot. "Just what the hell are you spreading now?"

"Nothing that isn't the truth, major."

"I told you once before, Brodie, we won't tolerate attacks on anyone here. Male or female." He pointed his finger at Brodie. "You've really overstepped your bounds this time, mister."

"Think so, major? Then just what the hell is the truth about Mallory and that T-38 incident?"

Dan gauged him in the shattering silence that built between them. Normally when Brodie was caught in the act, he became conciliatory. This time he was belligerent. Dan's instincts warned him that Brodie wasn't lying. His mind spun. None of the other instructors had been informed about Chris being in an accident and having to punch out. A new fear began eating at Dan. "I want the whole story, Brodie. Now," he ground out.

"It's short and sweet, major. She and Captain Jim Rosen were up getting proficiency flight hours in a T-38 when it went into a dive."

"Uncontrolled?" Dan asked sharply.

Brodie shrugged. "I don't know."

"You don't know? You just sat out there an hour ago and accused Captain Mallory of not being able to fly! You'd better get your story straight. And in a hell of a hurry!"

"I don't know all the details!" Brodie snarled back. "She punched out and left the AC. Word has it that she should have stayed. Some think that if Mallory had stayed with the bird they both could have pulled it out in time."

Dan's breathing was harsh. "I want facts, captain. Not goddamn stories!"

The captain paled. "Check with Reese Air Force Base in Texas. You'll get all the info you want, major. I'm surprised none of your people knew about this," he threw back boldly.

The tension thrummed palpably in the small office between them. Both men were tense, squaring off. Dan forcefully unclenched his fists as he grabbed his flight cap and walked around the desk. He was several inches taller than Brodie and stopped, glaring down at him. "You'd better hope for your sake that you're right, Captain Brodie," he breathed softly, his voice lined in steel. "Because if you aren't,

I'm having you disqualified from TPS. There is no place at this school for a pilot who operates on half-truths. We rely on facts here, mister. And yours had damn well better be correct."

Brodie stood a step away, his eyes widening momentarily. "It's a pretty sad state of affairs when a student has to find out about another student's lousy flying ability. I ain't going up with anyone who's a chicken in the clutch, major. Man or woman," he breathed hotly. "And I'm not worried about being on waivers, either. I'll stick to my story and what I said. All you need to do is confirm it."

Dan punched Brodie in the chest with his finger. "Captain, until you hear back from me, you keep your mouth shut concerning this incident," he ordered. Dan left the office, heading toward the commandant's quarters. The halls of TPS were deserted. It was late Friday afternoon, and everyone was taking well-earned breaks and letting off some steam from the grueling work.

Dan walked into Peggy Dube's secretarial office. "Peg, where's Colonel Martin?"

Peggy lifted her head, detecting anger in Dan's carefully modulated voice. "He's gone up to SAC Headquarters at Offutt Air Force Base in Nebraska. He's going to see if he can't wangle a B-52 bomber out of them for the class later on. Why?"

Dan quickly ran his fingers through his dark hair. "Something just occurred in my class, and I need to verify some data through the files."

"He's already locked the files," she apologized. "Maybe I can help?"

Dan sucked air in between his clenched teeth. "It's regarding Captain Mallory. I need to know if she was involved in a T-38 crash at Reese. I don't know when. I need to verify the information."

Peggy's green eyes widened slightly, her brows dipping. "Oh, dear," she murmured.

He shot her a keen look. "You know about it?" Of

course, what secretary didn't know her boss's business?

Peggy nervously shuffled some papers together before meeting his demanding gaze. "I only know that it occurred, Dan."

Scowling he asked, "Do you know if she was cleared of the incident?" Reason told him she had to be, or else no one would have allowed her to come to TPS. Dan couldn't figure out why the instructors weren't told of it.

"I don't know. Look, come back Monday morning. I'll leave a note on the colonel's desk, and you can discuss it with him further, Dan."

"That's not good enough, Peg. I've got one officer who knows bits and pieces of this incident and is beginning to spread the story around the whole damn base. It needs to be stopped now before it goes any further."

She gave him a helpless look. "All I know, Dan, is that the colonel kept the information to himself. He felt the fewer that knew, the better. That way there was less chance of it getting out to the press and putting more pressure on Captain Mallory."

He clenched the flight cap in his hand. "Unless I can find out the truth about this, Captain Brodie is going to do some real damage. Right now I've ordered him to maintain silence until I could do some investigating of his allegations."

Peg shook her head, giving him a shrug. "No one can get into the colonel's files until Monday, Dan. I'm sorry."

Dan turned, capping his desire to explode at anyone who got in his way. "Well," he muttered, "I guess I'll go to Captain Mallory, then."

"I'm sorry," Peggy said as he left.

"Yeah," he breathed softly, "so am I." He strode quickly down the polished hallway, throwing open the back door and taking the concrete stairs two at a time. His heart was beating heavily with fear—fear for Chris. Brodie was on to something. As he drove toward the BOQ he began putting the jigsaw puzzle together. Chris had never lost her skill, confidence or courage to fly jets. If she had been in a crash, it wasn't showing up in her flying performance. His mind snapped back to the time when he knew a pilot by the name of Jim Rosen. In the last few years he had lost touch with Jim except to run into him at the O'Club whenever he flew to Reese on business. Dan frowned. Reese was where Jim had been flying as an instructor pilot. Chris had also been an instructor at the base. Dan tiredly rubbed his face. And how had Brodie gotten this information? Brodie had sworn to find some dirt on Chris. The colonel wasn't even allowing his own instructors to know about the incident. Why? Exhaling forcefully, Dan parked the Corvette, getting out. It was up to him to put a halt to the rumors surrounding the woman he loved.

7

TAKING OFF HIS FLIGHT CAP, Dan walked to the end of the hallway on the first floor of the BOQ, where Chris had her quarters. His knock was firm against the door. He swallowed hard, realizing that Chris was probably in severe emotional turmoil by now. His heart wrenched. He wanted to protect her and felt helpless because he wasn't sure how to do it. Knocking again, he called out her name. "Chris, it's Dan. Open up." His voice carried down the hall. Another thirty seconds fled by with agonizing slowness before the door was unlocked. Putting his hand on the knob, Dan twisted it and opened the door, coming face to face with Chris.

Chris stared at him. "Come on in," she said tonelessly, stepping aside. She had changed from her flight suit into the pink silk robe. Droplets of water still clung to her black hair, evidence that she had taken a recent shower. Her stomach knotted as she saw the anger in Dan's narrowed eyes. Chris walked nervously toward the couch, her arms crossed against her chest. Tensing, she heard the door close quietly behind him. The silence was brutal, and Chris squeezed her eyes shut. She wouldn't cry! Now everyone would know about the crash. The heartache was too personal.

She felt Dan's hand upon her shoulder, turning her around. His touch was firm, yet gentle with insistence as she tried to resist.

"I don't want to do this," he said hoarsely, "but I need to know the truth, Raven. I want you to tell me what happened."

She lifted her violet eyes upward, tears swimming in their depths. A sob threatened to choke off her voice. "It's too late!" she whispered painfully.

Dan gripped her shoulders. "It's not! Look, I tried to find out about this crash through Brodie. All he has is half a story leaked out by someone at Reese. I tried to find out through the commandant, but he's gone for the weekend." Dan gave her a small shake. "I didn't want to have to drag it out of you, Chris. No one, not even the other instructors, knew anything about a T-38 crash at Reese. Brodie is going to spread this rumor around if I don't find out what really happened," he said, frustration choking his words. "And I can't get that information without your help. Did it happen?"

Chris began to tremble, dislodging herself from his hands. She turned her back to him, staring at the curtained window. Tears trickled down her cheeks. "Yes, it happened," she admitted, raw with pain.

Dan walked up to her and drew her back against his body. His anger at Brodie forced him to ask, "Were you cleared after the investigation?" The words were out and could never be taken back.

Chris turned, her features ravaged with pain. "That's all you care about, isn't it?"

He grew tense. "The commandant wouldn't let you come to TPS if the crash had been your fault, Chris. So it's a very small part of why I'm here," he explained levelly, tryng to maintain a conciliatory tone to the conflict escalating between them. "I need the truth in order to keep Brodie quiet."

She was hurting inside so much that her anger toward Brodie was aimed at Dan instead. Her lips trembled, tears flowing down her face unchecked now. "All you care about is your lousy school image!"

His lips thinned. "Dammit, Chris, quit overreacting. I don't like this any more than you do."

She lowered her lashes, everything blurring. "The

commandant must have been worried that the crash would affect the school's image."

Dan growled an epithet, reaching out and placing his hands on her tense shoulders. "Get that chip off your shoulder and hear what I'm asking of you," he ordered tautly.

Chris glared up at him. Dan was excruciatingly close. His breath was hot and moist against her face. The anger in his blue eyes was laced with thunderstorm black. His fingers tightened against the flesh of her upper arms. "I hear you asking whether or not I'm cleared of that crash!"

"No! Do I have to tear this out of you piece by piece? Is that what you want? I can put some of it together. I knew Jim Rosen. He was a fine pilot. And I also know you. Your flying skills are excellent, Chris. If there was a crash, then there had to be something mechanically wrong with the aircraft." Dan lowered his voice, realizing he was nearly shouting. His tone became roughened with emotion. "I know what your nightmare was about now. You were crying 'punch out' and 'it's stuck.' And I also figure that the crash happened no more than a year ago because you're still too emotional about it."

With a strangled cry, Chris fled from his captive hands. She ran to the other side of the room, whirling on him, her face contorted with naked anguish. "I should have stayed!" she screamed. "I should have stayed and helped Jim!"

Dan froze, stunned by the ferocity of her cry. What he was seeing and hearing was more than just a reaction to a plane crash. He groped, blinking back an unexpected reaction: tears. Holding out his hand in a calming gesture, Dan walked slowly toward Chris. She had put her hands across her mouth, shoulders drawn upward, shaking. *Oh, God, her eyes.* Her eyes were brittle with hurt. His throat constricted as he halted a few feet from her, his hand still outstretched.

"Raven," he called softly. "I'm sorry. I shouldn't have shouted at you. Come here...." His stomach twisted as he saw her eyes widen with despair. She was trembling visibly. All he wanted to do was hold her and take away all the pain he had just forced her to confront. Damn Brodie. Damn the whole double-standard system. He realized that he had just broken her emotionally. Acid stung his mouth. "Come..." he begged hoarsely.

As she hesitated, Dan closed the distance between them. He groaned her name, taking her into his arms, pressing her tightly against his body. A sob wrenched loose from her and Dan could only hold her, a feeling of helplessness crawling through his heart and soul. Stroking her unbound hair, he whispered, "I'm sorry, honey. So damn sorry. Let go of that pain. Don't hang on to it...."

Chris wept brokenly. After a while she became oddly silent, huddled against him, numb, after her emotional outpouring. There was a measure of safety in Dan's arms as she forced herself to talk in a raw, almost inaudible voice. "Jim was AC on the flight. We both were logging proficiency hours in the T-38." She winced, reliving that day again in her mind. "It was in the late afternoon, and we were flying at thirty-nine thousand feet. It was just straight flight, no acrobatics or anything. We had just leveled out and were flying toward Lackland Air Force Base when the plane suddenly went into a spin. The right rudder was stuck." Chris shuddered, hearing the scream of the wind, the wail of the jet engines and Jim's calm voice describing the problem. "He asked me to help him," she mechanically went on, as if she were a robot describing the incident. "No matter what we did, the T-38 wouldn't respond. At twelve thousand feet, Jim ordered me to punch out. I said no. We had worked the rudder a little, and I could feel it freeing up slightly and so could he." She sobbed, hiding her face against Dan's body. "I punched out at seven thousand because Jim screamed at me to go. I thought he was right behind me...and he rode the bird into the ground...."

Dan took in a shaky breath. "My God, you punched out at seven thousand?" he asked incredulously. He could feel the warmth of her body against him. She should be dead. Ejecting at that altitude in a spin usually killed the pilot. Dan pulled her away from him, searching her pale features.

Chris barely nodded. "You don't understand. Jim—" she looked up at him "—was my fiancé. We were to be married last December. I should have stayed with him." She pressed her hand against her mouth. "I should have stayed. Maybe I could have made up the difference—"

Dan gripped her harshly. "No!" he breathed, giving her a shake. "Dammit, don't you realize that you're lucky to be alive? Jim made the mistake by trying to pull that bird out at too low an altitude. He should have punched out like you did." He searched her face, disbelief in his voice. "You must have been injured in that ejection." He couldn't believe it. She was whole and functioning after a close call like that. Further, the fact that she had loved Jim Rosen must have impaired her emotionally. Dan was awed by her strength and will to survive such a crippling incident. And it only made her that much more special in his eyes. Truly, Chris Mallory was an exceptional woman beyond any he had ever known.

Her shoulders drooped with dejection. She muffled a bitter sound, pulling from his grip, walking aimlessly around the room. "I had back compression and ankle problems for a while. No big deal. Every pilot who punches out gets it."

Dan turned, watching her guardedly. "They put you in the hospital?"

"Yes." She halted, staring down at the coffee table. "I wasn't in very good condition for a while."

"More importantly," Dan murmured, walking to her side, "is how you were dealing with Jim's loss."

Chris barely looked over at Dan, feeling as if someone had taken a knife and gutted her emotionally. "They kept me at the hospital for observation. I was tested by the base psychiatrist, interviewed by my commander and helped by the chaplain." She managed a weak smile. "The chaplain pulled me through the worst of Jim's death."

Dan nodded, the silence gathering in the room. "How long ago did this happen?"

"Ten months."

"And what did the investigation show?"

She sighed brokenly. "That one of the mechanics who worked on that T-38 had left a wrench behind. The wrench slid and jammed under the right rudder, causing us to go into an uncontrolled spin." She shrugged. "Pitiful, isn't it? A man's life is wasted because a mechanic got sloppy on the job and didn't count his tools when he was finished servicing the T-38."

Dan understood her bitterness. "You could have died, too."

"All the Board of Inquiry saw was the loss of one pilot and the loss of a two-million-dollar plane. I was cleared after the investigation. I got a reprimand for not bailing out earlier when I disregarded Jim's orders."

"And then you went back to flying status?"

She nodded. "Yes, three weeks later my commander checked me out in a T-38, and I was off to teach recruits to fly again."

"But you're still blaming yourself, Raven."

Chris jerked her head up, glaring at Dan. "That's my business!"

"No," he countered swiftly, "you're wrong. It's my business."

Her eyes widened. "Do you think I won't do as I'm ordered?"

"I'm more concerned that you'll ride a bird down trying to save it when you ought to be punching out."

"You needn't worry about that, major."

Dan eyed her speculatively. His gut instinct said not to believe her. He had heard the anguish in her voice earlier about punching out and leaving Jim behind. And he recalled the force of her nightmare that had held Chris in its grip. What would happen if she and another student put a bird into a spin and they couldn't pull it out? Would she ride it down because of this past trauma, trying to atone for a supposed mistake on her part?

He searched her wan features, and his heart contracted with compassion. She was emotionally wrung out, broken by the confrontation. "I'm going to put a lid on this, Chris," he began, putting the flight cap back on his head. "I'm going over to talk to Brodie now. I want to find out how he got hold of this information."

Chris grimaced. "That wouldn't be too hard. Any crash becomes common knowledge at a base. If Brodie has a buddy at Reese, it was bound to come out."

"Well," Dan said grimly, "Brodie knows bits and pieces of what actually occurred." He walked up to her, cupping her chin, forcing her to look up at him. "When I get done with Captain Brodie, I'm coming back over here. I think we both need to get away from here for a while."

"And go where?" she asked, bitterness tinging her voice. Was there any place far enough away from this caldron of anguish?

"Just away," he returned quietly, catching her violet gaze. "I feel like driving until we're too tired to stay awake. We'll get a couple of rooms and sleep until we decide to wake up. No schedules to meet. No demands."

Chris felt her heart exploding with emotions she had never before experienced. The touch of his fingers against her cheek possessed a healing balm. "All right," she murmured brokenly.

Dan released her, taking a steadying breath. He cared for Chris and was frightened of what the unstable future might hold for both of them. Brodie wouldn't be detoured. He knew in his gut that the vindictive captain would spread his own version of Chris's supposed incompetence. What would it do to her? How would it impact on her flying? Would it destroy her proud spirit and wash her out of the school? All of those possibilities were very real. And because he believed in Chris, he had to move quickly to try and shore up her broken defenses so that she could continue at TPS and graduate as she deserved. "I'll be back," he promised, opening the door.

As an hour passed, lethargy stole upon Chris. She had slowly changed from her robe to a pair of comfortable jeans, a sweater of pale lavender to match her eyes and a light jacket of white trimmed in dark-blue piping. Her ebony hair fell in soft planes around her face. Only the application of makeup took away her pallor. Putting the delicate pearl earrings in her earlobes, Chris added a touch of light perfume to her pulse points—anything to halt her spiraling depression. When Dan returned he was also in jeans, a plaid shirt and a dark-brown leather jacket. He gave her a reassuring smile as he held out his hand to her. "Come on, Raven."

She picked up her overnight bag and, without a word, slid into the Corvette. The sun was dipping below the western horizon, its long rays outlining the sagebrush and Joshua trees across the desert valley. Just being close to Dan helped assuage some of the raw pain she was experiencing. His hand rarely left hers as they drove out the gate of Edwards, heading toward Lancaster in the distance. Little by little, Chris felt herself stabilizing. Dan had made no effort to force her into conversation. The silence acted as a healing cocoon to her charged emotional state.

Darkness fell rapidly, and Chris continued to grope her way through the trauma. The lights of the Corvette stabbed into the blackness of the asphalt highway. Oddly, it brought a parallel to her mind about Dan and herself: he was like light in the darkness of her soul. He, more than any other man in her life, had unselfishly given her strength, encouragement and belief in herself. A new kind of warmth invaded her and she turned her head, looking at him as he drove.

"You're a special man, Dan McCord," she whispered.

He glanced at her, a tentative smile barely pulling at the corners of his mouth. "Think so? I forced you into reliving that incident." He grimaced. "That's like some jerk asking me to talk about my days in Vietnam. It's a pretty ugly episode, and I wouldn't want to drag it up again."

Chris responded to the bitterness in his voice. "You had no choice," she countered softly. "It wasn't your fault."

He lifted her hand, kissing it. "That's another one of your fine assets, Raven. You always forgive the other person." His eyes were dark and searching as he looked over at her. "But more important, I want you to be able to forgive yourself. You were right in punching out. Jim was wrong. I've been in enough spins to know when to eject. And so had he. Let it go, Chris. It won't bring him back."

She winced at his gently spoken words. "You're right."

"Whether you want it or not," he said firmly, "I'm going to be here to help you."

Her lips curved into a tender smile. "I wouldn't want it any other way."

His eyebrow rose. "Sure?" he queried.

"Very sure."

Dan sighed inwardly with relief. She was over the loss of Jim Rosen, the man she had loved. That admittance alone lifted the heaviness he had carried in his heart since finding out Chris had been engaged. He spotted a restaurant up ahead and pulled off the interstate. Parking, he turned, putting his arm to rest behind Chris's shoulders. Shadows and light played across his strong, concerned face as he carefully observed her. "Look," he said softly, "I feel like driving forever with you, Raven. I think we both need this time away from the base." He leaned forward, caressing her silken hair, his fingers coming to rest beneath her chin. "You need this time." His voice grew husky. "And I need the time with you."

Chris trembled. The invitation was there, gently being offered to her on her own terms. Her lips parted and she closed her eyes, leaning against his cradling hand. "Yes," she whispered fervently. "I wanted to be with you, Dan...." Gratefully, she felt him pull her forward. The instant his mouth brushed her waiting lips, she melted against him. A small cry was torn from her throat as his kiss deepened with tenderness.

As he drew away, his eyes smoldered with barely contained passion. He caressed her cheek. "Come on," he said huskily. "We both could use a breather and some food."

Chris didn't dare trust her legs. She waited until Dan walked around, offering his hand to help her out of the car. It was so natural, leaning against him, his arm going around her waist, protecting her. He kissed her hair. "You're an incredible creature," he whispered against her ear. "I never realized how much courage you possess, Raven."

She responded to his gently spoken admission by simply laying her head on his shoulder. Dinner was a quiet, intimate affair. The black leather booths were in the shape of crescents, effectively blotting out any nearby diners. She wasn't hungry, but Dan forced her to eat a small salad. A smile came to her lips as the waitress brought the beef Stroganoff for Dan. He ladled some of it out in the small plate and put it in front of her.

"Eat," he ordered.

She picked up the fork, holding his gaze. "When I first met you, I never thought you had so much sensitivity."

He tilted his head, studying her. "Just thought I was some hot-rock jet jockey on the make like all the rest?"

"But you aren't," she returned, meaning it. Chris searched his relaxed features. There was a depth of peace in him that she longed to reach out and possess. There was no peace within her. There never had been. Dan gave her that serene feeling that no matter what storm she had yet to weather, she could do it if he was at her side. That thought shocked her into a new discovery about how she felt toward him. She had never relied heavily on anyone during her life. Up until now all those vague feelings of happiness had simmered deep within her every time she thought of Dan. He hadn't forced or cajoled her to move any faster than was emotionally possible. Now, looking deep in his eyes, Chris felt the depth of his commitment to her. It left her shaken.

"We're all complicated human beings," he said in answer. "And I think test pilots are more so than most. Our Jekyll-Hyde personalities, if you will. What I'm like as an instructor pilot, I'm not necessarily like in my personal life."

"I want to know the personal side of you," she heard herself say. Chris blinked, shocked at herself. Suddenly she didn't care if it was the right or wrong thing to admit. That was how she felt about Dan.

Dan gauged her in the gathering silence. "If I have my way, you will, Raven." He reached over, capturing her hand momentarily. "And just as important, I want to explore and know the woman, Chris Mallory."

She compressed her lips. "That's dangerous, Dan...."

"I'm used to taking calculated risks with touchy aircraft. I'll take my chances with you."

That was true. Dan had proven he was able to deal with her better than any man in her past. She picked disinterestedly at the Stroganoff until Dan finished eating. Paying the bill, he led her out into the starry night. Even in April the cold winds were cutting across the high desert. Dan drew her close, walking slowly toward the car. "While we were sitting in there, I got an idea," he said. "You know what I'd like to do?" he asked, kissing her temple.

She shook her head, looking up into his face. "What?"

"Head north on the interstate toward the sequoias that sit above Bakersfield. I'd like to share tomorrow up in the mountains with you, just hiking or sitting and watching the world go by."

Chris slowed to a halt, slipping her arms around his neck, pressing her body against him. Right now, more than at any point in her life, she realized the importance of living for the moment. She would not continue living in the past because that was dead and gone. "All right," she agreed huskily. "Let's do it."

His eyes widened briefly, surprise written in their depths. His arms tightened around her waist. "Going to throw caution to the wind?" he asked, a smile beginning to tug at his strong, mobile mouth.

"I think it's about time I did."

"Sure?"

Chris leaned up, brushing his mouth with her lips.

"Very sure," she whispered against them. "Take me away, Dan," she breathed. "All I want to do is be with you."

IT WAS NEAR ELEVEN AT NIGHT when they finally stopped. A motel situated near the base of the Sierra Nevada had looked inviting.

Dan came back to the Corvette, leaning down to speak to her. "They've got a single left," he said, watching the play of shadows across her exhausted features. "What do you want to do? We could keep going and—"

Chris wearily rubbed her eyes. "I'm too tired to go on, Dan."

Darkness lingered in his blue eyes. "Raven, I'm no saint. I won't promise to keep my hands off you if we sleep together," he admitted gruffly.

Chris looked up at him. "Then I'm in good company, because I'm far from sainthood myself."

Dan managed a deprecating smile. "As tired as we both are, we'll probably be asleep the instant we hit the pillow." He reached out, giving her shoulder a firm squeeze. "Hang on, and I'll sign us in."

The room was small but cozy, the rough paneling reminding her of a log cabin. The intimacy between them both remained strong and unbroken. Perhaps under ordinary circumstances Chris would have been nervous or worried. But she was fatigued to the point where her mind refused to work any more. Dan noticed her sluggish movements and took over, getting the shower started and then urging her into the bathroom.

"Go on," he coaxed, handing her the overnight bag. "I'm going out to lock the car and get a map from the motel manager. I'll be back in a few minutes."

Chris nodded. The warmth of the shower increased the exhaustion that stole into her mind and body. Slipping into the floor-length nightgown, she stepped from the bathroom fifteen minutes later. Dan was sitting on the chair, intently studying the map of the sequoia region when she padded into the room.

He lifted his head, his eyes intent upon her. Chris was immobilized by his hungry, disturbing look. She was drained, yet her entire body reacted instantly, the desire mirrored in Dan's gaze. Without a word Dan put the map aside and stood, coming over to her.

"You look positively beautiful," he breathed. The silk gown molded to each curve of her body, the plunging neckline revealing the shadowed valley between her breasts. Her hair was damp, the blue-black tresses framing her pale face, her eyes the richest hue of violet he had ever seen. He leaned over, kissing her lips like a brush touching canvas. "Get in bed before you fall over," he commanded huskily. "I'll be joining you in a little while."

Her heart pulsed heavily in her chest as his light kiss stirred her desire for him. Dan gave her a pat on the rear and Chris turned, catching the twinkle in his blue eyes. He made her happy by just being himself. Sliding in between the cool sheets, she wondered when a bed had ever felt so good as her eyes began to close. She had meant to turn off the light, but had forgotten. Seconds and minutes seemed like unrelenting hours as Dan showered. She was nervous, excited and aching to fulfill their collision-course destiny. Yet, despite everything, her black lashes dropped closed, and Chris slid into the abyss of sleep despite her intentions to stay awake.

She was pulled briefly from sleep when Dan joined her in bed. Chris groaned, rolling onto her back, forcing her eyes open. Her black lashes barely rested against her cheeks as she gazed up at Dan. There was a thoughtful, concerned look in his eyes as he studied her. She was wildly aware of the naked length of his body against her own; the thin cotton of his drawstring pajamas the only barrier between her and his lower body. Reaching over, he snapped off the light and then brought her close.

"I didn't mean to fall asleep—"

Dan pulled up the remaining cover to ward off the chill of the April night. "No apologies needed," he husked. "Go back to sleep, Raven. Neither of us is in any shape to share the moment."

Sleepily Chris snuggled into the crook of his arm, a new sense of comfort surrounding her. "If you're bucking for sainthood—"

Dan gave a low laugh, settling back, giving her a reassuring embrace. "Not sainthood, just common sense under the circumstances. Go to sleep," he ordered gruffly.

CHRIS NUZZLED LIKE A LOST LAMB, seeking the warming embrace of the arms that held her during sleep. Slowly she fought off her drowsy state. She was lying against Dan, her body fitted perfectly to him. Her head on the crook of his shoulder, Chris heard the drumlike beat of his steady heart in his broad chest. During the night, she had snuggled close, one arm and leg thrown across Dan's lean, muscular body. His skin was heated and fragrant, and she inhaled his scent. Small silken hair that spread like a carpet across his chest tickled her nose, making her wrinkle it to halt the itching. Moonlight streamed through the loose-weave drapes, lending the room a muted radiance.

She felt rested, having no idea how long she had slept. And when had Dan come to bed? Chris inhaled deeply, aware only of the peace that enveloped her. Looking up, she breathed in with awe. Dan's face was devoid of the usual tension. Lines no longer appeared at the corners of his eyes or around his

mouth. In fact, he looked years younger when he
was relaxed. And for a moment she felt distressed
because the school was just as hard, if not more demanding on the instructors than on the students. The
responsibility that rode upon Dan's broad shoulders
was not to be taken lightly.

Reaching up, Chris allowed her fingertips to brush
the bridge of his nose, which had a small bump on it.
Had he broken it as a young boy? She allowed her
imagination to recreate Dan's childhood. He had
worked on a ranch in Texas. Had he broken his nose
by falling off a calf, or off a horse that needed breaking or by getting into a scrap with another boy?
That thought made her smile tenderly as she continued to trace the planes of his face. Her fingertips returned to his strong, pliant mouth. She loved it
when Dan smiled or teased her mercilessly, always
drawn to the need to kiss him there.

Obeying the command of her needs for Dan, Chris
leaned up, tentatively brushing her lips against his
mouth. His skin was warm to the touch, inviting.
Suddenly Chris felt him shift, gently lifting her and
placing her protectively beneath him. Her eyes widened as she stared up into his. There were remnants
of sleep in the azure blueness coupled with the
warmth of his desire and tenderness. Her heart ex-
panded and she reached up, sliding her arms around
his neck, drawing him down upon her.

His mouth was strong, coaxing, stealing the breath
from her trembling body. His hands freely roamed
the length of her yielding body. A hunger consumed
her and she arched against him, whispering an en-
dearment against his mouth. Dan groaned her name
over and over again, uttering a litany of reverence as
he kissed her deeply, possessively. An almost uncontrolled fire swept through her as his fingers slid
the straps of the nightgown off her shoulders. His
hands moved down her shoulders, brushing the

curving fullness of her breasts, tasting her until she thought she would go mad with desire. Deftly, he released her from the confines of the silken gown and divested himself of his clothes.

Her breath came in short, shallow sobs as he finally tore his mouth from her soft, swollen lips, trailing a series of branding kisses down the length of her neck to her breasts. She tensed as she felt the warming moistness of his breath lingering above her. Her fingers dug deeply into his back and she moaned his name.

His mouth settled over the hardened nipple, teasing it, provoking a fiery caldron of raging, unchecked desire to tear loose within her. A small cry rose in her throat and she arched upward, wanting, needing all of him. Each time he teased the firm, upright nipples, it was as if an electrical surge jolted down her body to center on her aching need. A pulsating sensation began, blacking her mind, increasing her hungry need to be one with Dan. She barely felt him shift position as she wordlessly begged him to enter her to forge the union that had to take place.

"Now," she murmured throatily against his ear, "please, Dan, now. I need you...." An explosion rocked her as he thrust deeply into her body. A cry of joy fled from her lips, and their hearts and breaths melted into a rhythmic oneness. Sensation dissolved into light as they joined in their fiery union. Then a spiraling explosion rocked her, leaving her breathless and satisfied in its wake.

Gradually, ever so gradually, they both floated back to earth in each other's arms. Chris nuzzled Dan, aware of the dampness of his skin against her own. She inhaled deeply, loving the natural masculine scent of him. Their hearts pounded in unison, and she arched against him as he ran his hand down the long curve of her back, coming to rest on her hip. Dan kissed her eyes, nose and then her mouth. His eyes were wide with spent passion and wonder as he gazed down at her. Their noses and mouths almost touched, the moisture of their breath intermingling on the pillow they lay upon. Chris closed her eyes, savoring his nearness, his love. She realized that she was in love with Dan McCord. Searching his guileless blue eyes, Chris marveled at his depth of kindness and tenderness. Had she ever known any man who possessed such wonderful sensitivity? *No.* "You're so special," she murmured throatily, reaching out and running her fingers through his tousled hair.

Dan returned the smile, kissing the tip of her nose. "No way, Raven. You're the special one."

"Two special people, then," she whispered, leaning forward to rest her lips against his strong, loving mouth.

He ran his tongue across her lips, watching her eyes widen as the fires of passion returned to their incredible violet depths. "You have the most beautiful mouth, too," he said, tasting the salt from them. "So responsive and loving...." He molded his mouth against her lips, delighting in her responding fervor. She was just as courageous in returning love as she was at flying. There was no fear in opening her heart to him, and it left him breathless with wonder. Despite the harshness of her life up to this point, her ability to trust and love him without restraint was a miracle. And for Dan, she was a wonderful new miracle in his life. All that, and more.

He moved up on one elbow, lingering above her, a glimmer of wonderment mirrored in his eyes. Her black hair was in disarray, making her look as if she were a wild, spirited animal. It did nothing but accentuate the sensuousness he had been aware of since the day he had met Chris. "You are all woman," he told her quietly, pulling up the covers and then gathering her back into his arms.

"Coming from you, that means a lot," Chris

whispered. She placed her leg across his long muscular thigh, delighting in the hardness of his body. Chris closed her eyes, completely satiated. Another miracle had occurred: her heart no longer felt shredded and torn. She reached across Dan's chest, seeking, finding his hand and covering it with her own. "You're a healer," she whispered, her voice becoming inaudible as she fell into the returning folds of sleep.

Dan lay awake for a long time afterward, holding the woman he fiercely loved within his arms. Her breathing became softened and shallow, signaling that she had found a corner of peace in her sleep. Dan gently stroked her black hair, loving its silken texture as he absently moved strands of it between his thumb and forefinger. Chris had stunned him with her ability to love him so fully, so selflessly. As much pleasure as he had given to her, she had returned to him. He was amazed that the woman he held and the professional pilot were two entirely different people. When flying, Chris's voice was devoid of any emotion, her mind on the business at hand, her intelligence and ability to fly the plane first and foremost. And there in bed, she had removed those barriers and allowed him complete access to her heart and soul. She was warm, willful, pleasing and desirous, all at once. Her voice shook with emotion, her body was a sensitive, calibrated instrument highly attuned to each of his grazing, meaningful touches. Her eyes danced with joy, shining with passion for him alone. Dan drew her near him, placing a kiss on her temple. "I love you, Raven," he whispered into the night. "You've stolen my heart, and I don't want a day to pass without loving you, honey."

8

THE SECOND TIME CHRIS AWOKE, the melodic song of
birds roused her from sleep. Drowsily opening her
eyes, she realized Dan was sitting on the edge of the
bed watching her, a slight smile touching the corners of his mouth. She was trapped between his
body and his right arm, which rested near her waist.

"Has anyone ever told you how beautiful you are
when you sleep?" he asked, tracing the curve of her
cheek with his fingers.

Chris sighed languorously, pressing against his
hand. "No," she murmured. Dan was dressed in a
pair of jeans and long-sleeved plaid shirt, his hair
wet and gleaming from a recent shower. There was a
flame of undeniable happiness that she saw in his
eyes as she gazed up at him. Reaching out, she slid
her hand up his arm, delighting in the firmness of
his muscles. "How long have you been awake?"

He leaned down, tasting her lips, caressing them
longingly. "I woke about an hour ago," he murmured, kissing her more demandingly. He had discovered another facet to Chris as she slept like some
lost kitten on the large expanse of the bed. The stress
that always shadowed her features had disappeared,
leaving her mouth full and relaxed. Normally she
thinned her lips while concentrating, or when she
felt threatened. Dan gently moved his thumb across
her unlined brow, just beginning to realize how
much tension she was carrying during her waking
hours. Dan gazed deeply into her eyes. They were
free of pain this morning, thank God. Their ame-

thyst depths clear. Her skin smelled of sun-warmed apricots. "Raven, you're going to entice me into coming back to bed."

Chris smiled sleepily, her heart warming as she rolled over to hug him. "I'm glad sainthood didn't win out."

He grinned, running his fingers through her beautiful black hair. "Never. I'm afraid I have feet made of clay where you're concerned. You're in good shape, Raven." There wasn't an inch of fat on her long, graceful body. Her shoulder and upper-back region were strong, for sometimes, hauling a fighter around was sheer physical labor. The G-forces would build up to such a degree in a dive or spin that it was the upper-body strength that wrestled the stick back in order to bring the bird out of the dive.

She was like a cat, aroused by his fleeting touch. Sitting up, Chris slipped her arms around Dan's shoulders, drawing him against her, kissing him. No one had ever loved her so thoroughly and with such sensitivity. The warming bond that ebbed and flowed between them was there, as always. It was almost as if it were a living electrical charge throbbing between them, making her ultraresponsive to his slightest change. The admittance scared her badly. She had just lost one man she loved to a plane.

"Hey," he chided, lifting her chin. "I see trouble lurking in your eyes."

She gave a low laugh, shrugging off her morbid thoughts. "Don't mind me. What's on the agenda today?"

Dan cradled her in his arms, relishing her closeness as she rested her head on his shoulder. He leaned down, pressing a kiss on her nose. "I scouted around a little earlier. There's a rustic restaurant about a half mile away. The road is clear of snow up to the sequoia groves, although there's a good foot or two of it on the ground."

Chris gave him a surprised look. "Snow?"

"This is only April and they get some sudden, heavy snowfalls up in Sierra Nevada." He grinned. "Just because we live in the desert and in California doesn't mean the state doesn't get its share of snow."

She sighed, content to be in his arms. "Snow..." she murmured. "Do you realize how long it's been since I've seen some?"

"No. How long?"

"At least seven years." Her features gave way to her underlying excitement and in that moment, she looked like a little girl to Dan. "I can hardly wait!"

He gave her a tight embrace and then released her. "Great. After breakfast we'll go up and find a spot to make angel's wings and have a snowball fight." His blue eyes narrowed. "Of course, I'll win the snowball fight."

Chris slipped out of bed, taking up the challenge. Her body tingled hotly at the hungry intense look he gave her. She felt no embarrassment. "Don't be so sure, hotshot jet jockey."

"I've had a lot more practice aiming rockets and missiles than you," he murmured, appreciating her beauty. With or without clothes, she had a glorious body, and he capped the desire to pull her back on the bed. "You don't stand a chance, Raven."

She turned, giving him a confident look. "Think so, huh? I'm pretty good when it comes to hitting targets myself."

Dan laughed fully, standing. "Honey, you won't get any argument from me on that."

Chris smiled and wordlessly slipped into the bathroom, eager to start the day with Dan at her side.

They lingered over the enjoyable breakfast. Chris was finishing her second cup of coffee when she asked, "What are angel's wings?"

Dan's eyebrows rose upward. "You don't know?" Disbelief was etched in his eyes. "Every kid knows—" He hesitated, forgetting that she was an orphan without family, brothers or sisters. He lost some of his teasing tone, not wanting to hurt her. "You flop on your back in the snow and move your arms in an arc from the side of your body up to your head and back. Then you get up and all you see is an imprint of a human with wings. We call them 'angels in the snow.'"

"Sounds pretty," she confided, "but wet."

Dan grinned. "Depends upon the consistency of the snow up there. We'll find out soon enough," he said, pointing out the window. Above them, beneath a sunny, blue sky, the Sierra Nevada range rose, a cape of snow on its upper elevations.

"Well, Chris, let's saddle up and take off. I for one want to get back into the wilderness."

She agreed, getting to her feet. Although the temperature was in the lower sixties, Chris realized that as they drove up to the seven-thousand-foot elevation, the temperature would drop dramatically. Dan caught her hand, drawing her next to him as they walked out to where his sports car was parked. How could she feel so happy? Chris didn't try to sort out the possible answers. She only knew she craved Dan's presence and support.

It took an hour up a narrow, winding road to reach Giant Lodge, one of the areas where the towering sequoia grew. Chris was like a child, gawking at the world's largest trees. They parked near one set of cabins and got out. Chris leaned back, staring up in awe at one group of three sequoias that stood near the main lodge opposite them. "Look, Dan!" she whispered. "They're beautiful!"

He came around, drawing her near, pleased with her joy over being up in the mountains. "I call those the Three Sisters. It's interesting that the seeds for these magnificent trees come from a pine cone no larger than a silver dollar."

Chris glanced at him. "Come on!"

"No, I'm serious. I'm not pulling your leg, Raven." He laughed. "You warm enough in that jacket?"

She nodded. "Warm, happy and feeling like a child!"

Dan returned her ecstatic smile. "Good, it's about time you let that kid inside of you come out. Let's take the upper trail across the street. It looks pretty beaten down by other people using it."

Chris held Dan's hand, following his confident lead. Very soon they had left the large grouping of cabins and the main lodge behind them, the awesome silence of the sequoias engulfing them. The temperature was in the midforties and the snow was turning slushy beneath their feet. But Chris didn't care, making the most of their spontaneous outing. Dan halted, putting his arm around her shoulder. "Look." He pointed to the right. "There," he whispered near her ear, "do you see it?"

Chris quickly spotted a squirrel sitting on a fallen log. "I see him! A red squirrel."

Dan looked down at her. "Very good. For a city girl, you're not doing too badly."

"You're such a show-off, McCord. Just because you were raised on a ranch doesn't give you license to know everything about the country!"

"No?"

"No."

He leaned down, removing the snow until the ground came into view. "Here," he said, placing a very small pine cone into her palm. "This is a sequoia cone. The squirrels gather them up for food during the winters up here. Kind of hard to believe that something this small could create something so great as these trees, isn't it?"

Chris nodded, turning the cone over in her hands. "But don't all great things come from small beginnings?" she asked, musing.

He brought her around, holding her against him. "You're like that cone, you know," he said softly, placing a kiss on her hair. "You came from a small, unknown background, and you've made a place in history for yourself."

She blushed at the inference. "I don't see myself that way, Dan."

"No?"

"No. I didn't get into the Air Force Academy or become a pilot just because I was a woman. And I'm certainly not struggling to get test-pilot status for that reason, either."

He sighed, a smile edging his mouth. "Some trees just don't know they're giant until they're fully grown and look down to see how far the ground is beneath them." He became more serious. "Your talents for flying are incredible, Chris. No, now don't deny it. Just stand here and listen to me. I've been an instructor at TPS for two years, and I've seen plenty of test pilots graduate. And no one, no one has your hands. You have that incredible ability to sense what a bird will do before it actually departs control." He managed a quick smile as he paused momentarily. "You can never tell when the day will come when you'll need that extra touch, that 'something' you possess. Hell, the Air Force needs your talents. But more important, I need you...."

Chris managed an embarrassed laugh. "Okay, Aesop, cool the fables. I get the hint. I don't give myself enough credit for what I've accomplished."

Dan gave her an appraising look, guiding her up the path once again. "Very good. Hey, you know you're pretty smart, lady. I think I might keep you around for a while."

She gave him a jab in the ribs. "That's because I'm

the only one that can keep up with that steel-trap mind of yours," she said, laughing.

Dan hugged her fiercely. "That's true," he whispered. "You enthrall me, you make me want to explore every facet you own." He looked gravely into her wide eyes. "You fascinate me, Raven, like no woman ever has."

If she had not trained herself to hear the slightest change in sound vibration, she would have missed the tremble conveyed in his tone. As it was, Chris responded to that admission. "How have you escaped marriage, Dan McCord? That's what I'd like to know."

They resumed walking, moving up a small trail to the right that led them back toward a small stream. Dan shrugged. "Just never quite found the right lady," he admitted.

"But your attributes," she said, shaking her head, mystified. "You have *everything* any woman could want." She flashed him a grin. "The Air Force must have kept you at some pretty isolated bases where women couldn't get to you, then."

He laughed in return, savoring her closeness and companionship. "That's true enough. I spent the first six years at Northern Tier bases in North Dakota and Michigan flying Buffs. That's enough to make you a confirmed hermit."

"From what I understand, you could become almost celibate up there," she returned, smiling. It was true: at isolated B-52 bases placed in the northern U.S., the population was small or almost nonexistent. That kind of environment didn't encourage single pilots to be assigned there.

"Well, I was single and it was hell, believe me," he answered fervently.

"Somehow," Chris drawled, "I think you managed to survive."

His smile deepened. "I did."

"And you still never found a woman you wanted to marry?"

Dan shook his head, becoming more serious. "You know when you get out of the Academy and go into flight school, there are always women around that want to marry a career military officer. Let's face it, Raven, I'm set for the next twenty or thirty years of my life. A woman looking to marry for security reasons would see me as a pretty good catch."

Chris wrinkled her nose. "God, those are all the wrong reasons to get married!"

"Roger that. So I escaped the first wave of women who came after me and successfully graduated from flight school still single."

"And then?"

"Then my past caught up with me."

"Your father's money?"

"Yes. I had plenty of women who wanted to marry the rich son of...."

Chris felt sorry for him. "That must be terrible, Dan," she confided. "To wonder if a woman is with you because of yourself or your money."

He pressed her closer to him. "Yeah, and I nearly got married to a woman who almost fooled me."

"How did you know what her ulterior motives were?"

An impish smile crossed his handsome features. "The final test was when I told her that my father had disowned me and I didn't have a penny to my name except what I earned from my Air Force salary."

Chris stared at him. "You had to do that in order to find out where her motives really were?"

He stopped her, embracing her tightly, laughing. "You are so naive in some ways," he murmured against her hair. "Being streetwise, I would think you'd come up with some similar type of ploy to find out someone's true feelings and colors."

Harlequin Temptation™

Have you ever thought
you were in love
with one man...only
to feel attracted to another?

Exclusive Harlequin home subscriber benefits!

- CONVENIENCE of home delivery
- NO CHARGE for postage and handling
- FREE *Harlequin Romance Digest* ®
- FREE BONUS books
- NEW TITLES 2 months ahead of retail
- A MEMBER of the largest romance fiction book club in the world

GET **FIRST IMPRESSIONS** FREE AS YOUR INTRODUCTION TO *Harlequin Temptation* ™ PLUS A FREE TOTE BAG!

 ® No one touches the heart of a woman quite like Harlequin

YES, please send me FREE and **without obligation** my *Harlequin Temptation* romance novel, *First Impressions* and my FREE tote bag. If you do not hear from me after I have examined my FREE book, please send me 4 new *Harlequin Temptation* novels each month as soon as they come off the press. I understand that I will be billed only $1.75 per book (total $7.00). There are no shipping and handling or any other hidden charges. There is no minimum number of books that I have to purchase. In fact, I may cancel this arrangement at any time. The FREE tote bag and *First Impressions* are mine to keep as a free gift, even if I do not buy any additional books.

142 CIX MDF3

Name _____

Address _____ Apt. No. _____

City _____ State/Prov. _____ Zip/Postal Code _____

Signature (If under 18, parent or guardian must sign.)

This offer is limited to one order per household and not valid to present *Harlequin Temptation* subscribers. We reserve the right to exercise discretion in granting membership.

PRINTED IN U.S.A.

TBPT584

Get this romance novel and tote bag
FREE as your introduction to

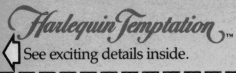

See exciting details inside.

Chris felt the heat of a blush rushing upward to her face, unable to meet his warming blue gaze. "I'm streetwise only in the sense I survived, Dan. I never had the kind of problems you had with women. Most of the guys were too threatened by that chip I used to carry around on my shoulder." She felt his grip on her become firmer.

"There's a vast difference between a boy and a man, Raven," he began gently. He forced her chin up so he could stare into her lovely violet eyes. "A boy would definitely be threatened by a woman of your intelligence, confidence and leadership qualities." He caressed her cheek lovingly.

"And a man?" she asked, her voice barely above a whisper, her heart pounding.

A knowing smile played around his mouth. "A man would be completely captivated by you, Raven. A man who's confident in his masculinity wouldn't be frightened by you. Rather," he continued, leaning down and brushing her parted lips tenderly, "he would drink you into him like some fine rare wine." He tasted her lips. "You do taste like sweet wine," he murmured against her. "You're rich, filled with the wonder of life, honey. So much of you is woman, child and a wonderful combination of magic mixed with mystery." His azure eyes deepened in color as they swept across her. "Your womanliness is like a spell to me, Raven. I'm fascinated with how you think, what you feel and the way you express yourself when we love each other." He cupped her face between his hands. "You've cast a spell over me, my magical lady. And somehow, we're going to see more of each other regardless of our heavy responsibilities." He brushed her lips, feeling her returning ardor, the skipping of her heart as she pressed herself against his body. "I've just found you, and I'm damned if I'm going to allow you to escape."

She melted into his arms, reveling in his strength

of conviction. "Oh, Dan," she murmured, burying her head on his shoulder, "do you always say the right thing?"

He laughed, whirling her around several times before setting her back on the ground. His eyes sparkled with unabashed joy as he touched her chin. "I don't know. Do I?"

Chris joined his laughter. "You know you do! You're such an arrogant jet jock, McCord." She broke free, running several feet and halted, sweeping up a handful of snow. "Take this!" she taunted, hurling the snowball at him. The snow splattered against his chest. His eyes widened in surprise and then they narrowed with hunterlike intensity.

"Why, you little—" he growled, springing after her.

Chris shrieked, trying to escape. Bu she was no match for Dan's sureness in snow. Running down the small incline, Chris suddenly realized that the path dipped to the left and across a small stream. She heard his footfalls coming up fast and laughed, slipping in the slushy snow. In a blinding instant he had tackled her from behind and then Chris screamed, throwing up her arms to protect her head as the ground raced up to meet them.

She couldn't stop laughing as Dan padded her fall, pulling her on top of him at the last moment. They landed heavily in the snow together, their laughter melting into the quiet of the forest around them. Chris struggled free, grabbing handfuls of snow and throwing them into Dan's face.

"No you don't!" he growled, and threw her on the ground beneath him, pinning her mercilessly. Their breath came out in white, wispy jets, their laughter nonstop as they stared at each other. Dan tightened his grip on her arms. "I ought to stuff snow down your blouse."

She giggled helplessly. "You look funny!" She had

managed to place snow down inside his jacket and shirt. Dan grinned good-naturedly. "You're going to pay for this, Raven," he threatened, leaning closer. His breath was moist and warm against her flushed cheeks.

"Whatever the stakes, it was worth it," she gasped, trying to struggle free. She choked on her laughter, trying to talk. "I'd say I did pretty well for somebody who wasn't raised around snow."

Dan nodded, mesmerized by her uninhibited joy. Suddenly she was a child. A child who had never been able to be one before in her life. He reveled in the fact that she was sharing this side with him. "Yes, you did too well. And now, you're going to pay."

Chris closed her eyes, leaning up to meet his descending mouth. She moaned as the pressure of his kiss tore at her senses, calling a fiery caldron of desire to life within her once again. She felt him release her hands, his arms sliding around her body, bringing her against him. Her heart pounded from the high, thin air and from the masterful touch of his mouth upon her own. Finally he released her, only their hard, rough breathing mixing with the silence around them. Dan idly picked up bits of snow from her hair, a tender smile lingering on his mouth as he gazed down at her. "Come on," he urged, "we can't leave here today without making snow angels."

Chris took his hand and he pulled her to her feet. It was as if the rest of her life had ceased to exist except for this moment in time with Dan. The love blossoming fully in her heart would not be stilled. She longed to reach out and whisper those words to him. A part of her still was not ready for that commitment and she balked. They had time to grow to know each other better over the next few months. And wasn't something good worth cultivating and working toward? She stole a look over at Dan, lov-

ing his ruddy features, dancing blue eyes and effort-
less smile that always seemed so much a part of him.
He had made her laugh. He had shown her a way to
free her emotions. Grasping his hand, Chris threw
herself into his arms, giving him a long embrace.

"What's this for?" he asked, returning the embrace.

"Because," she whispered, her voice trembling.
"Just because, Dan McCord."

9

CHRIS WEARILY DROPPED the armload of books on the kitchen table. Her brain felt as if someone had taken a bottle brush to it and wiped it clean. The testing was becoming much more demanding, extracting every ounce of her knowledge about aerodynamics until she thought her mind was going to blow a fuse. Every morning was spent flying in a series of demanding tests. She had just completed the spin and recovery tests in the A-37 Dragonfly. The stress of Gs was monumental. If it hadn't been for wearing the G-suit, from the waist down to her ankles, she could have blacked out. The bridge of her nose ached where the oxygen mask had been situated. During particularly heavy G-loads, the mask was pulled downward by the force of gravity, bruising the bone and flesh. Going through the motions of making herself a cup of coffee, Chris enjoyed the quiet of the Friday afternoon. It was late May. The temperature of the Mojave desert was beginning to reach the high nineties during the day, and the lake beds were drying beneath the sun's blinding rays.

She sat down in the living room, released her hair from the chignon and unlaced her flight boots, nudging them off her feet. Tiredly she leaned back, closing her eyes. A soft knock at the door roused her.

"It's unlocked," she called.

Her eyes widened as Dan slipped inside. Instantly, a pulse leaped at the base of her slender throat.

"Figured I'd catch you over here," he said. He shut the door and shared a smile with her.

"There's fresh coffee," she murmured, gazing up into his strong, loving face. "I'm too tired to move."

He sauntered over, sitting next to her. "I'm coffeed out." He ran his hand down her thigh. "I have a surprise for you."

Chris groaned. "Not another damn test!"

"No," he said, smiling, "another chance to get away. You realize this is Memorial Day weekend and we get four days off school?"

She warmed to his touch. Their time together had been limited at best. "I look at it as downtime," she offered. "Why? What's the surprise?"

His blue eyes grew warm. "Well, all you need to do is pack a small overnight bag, get into your flight gear and we'll take off."

She groaned again. "Oh, come on, Dan! I've flown so much this last month I ought to be sprouting permanent wings here at my shoulders."

He laughed, taking Chris into his arms, cradling her against his body. Inhaling the apricot scent of her hair, Dan rested his head against hers. "I've got a T-38 being fueled right now, and we're going to take off for Carswell Air Force Base."

She stole a look up at him. "But that's in Fort Worth, Texas."

He pursed his lips, mesmerized by her deep violet eyes, reveling in the expression in their depths. "Yes, ma'am. I want to take you home and let you see where I grew up."

Chris felt her heart contract in fear. An old insecurity surfaced, and she fought against that feeling. His family was rich, affluent, and from the right side of the tracks. She had been dirt poor, struggling for every penny she ever earned. Stop it, she told herself. She knew it was ridiculous to have those feelings, but her emotions were still adolescent about that tender, raw episode of her life. She felt Dan's arms tighten around her.

"Well?" he prompted.

"I—yes," she whispered, gazing up at him. "I'd love to see your home."

Dan leaned over, brushing her lips tenderly. Her mouth was always warm, responsive, sending a fiery torch of desire throbbing through his body for her alone. Reluctantly he pulled away from her enticing lips. "I love your courage," he said simply, meaning it. "I know you probably feel uncomfortable about meeting my parents. But the real reason I wanted you to come, Chris, is to meet my Uncle Howard. He practically raised me. I've talked to Vanessa, my mother, and she's reluctantly agreed to pick us up at Carswell. Once we spend the obligatory night at their home, we'll fly out to my uncle's ranch, which lies north of Fort Worth." His eyes lightened, his voice taking on an edge of underlying excitement. "We'll spend two days at the ranch. I'll take you riding and show you all my old haunts."

She slid her arm around his neck, nuzzling close to him. "You make it sound like we'll have to endure one night for two wonderful days at your uncle's ranch."

"Perhaps," Dan said evasively. "Then you'll go?"

Her violet eyes became warm. "More than anything, Dan, I'd love to meet the people who mean so much to you. No matter what you say, you're still lucky to have a family." She stopped, her voice betraying the feelings behind her words.

"Well," he murmured against her ear, "my uncle and his wife, Melvina, are going to love you. They're excited about meeting you." He smiled, kissing her cheek. "So come on, my raven-haired beauty. Let's go get suited up, and we'll take off to the sky where everything is always all right."

In no time they were airborne, the white skin of the needle-nosed Talon T-38 dancing with the brilliance of sunlight off it's delta-shaped wings. Chris was content to sit in the second cockpit behind Dan and be the navigator for the flight. They climbed rapidly to thirty-nine thousand feet, and Dan pointed the bird in a southwesterly direction. Chris gazed around, pushing up her dark visor momentarily to drink in the deep blue of the sky that surrounded them.

"I love it up here," she confided in a hushed voice.

She saw Dan nod his helmeted head. "Next to making love with you, this is the second greatest pleasure on earth," he returned.

Chris smiled, although the oxygen mask strapped tightly to her face hid the fact. "Roger that," she teased, remembering the few times that they had shared together since the trip to the sequoia region. She reached up, pushing the dark visor down to protect her eyes from the harsh sunlight. All pilots wore a helmet equipped with a visor to screen the sun's rays. Her entire face was then protected in case she ever had to eject. Chris tried to push the ugly memory aside, unwillingly recalling the last time she had had to punch out. The force of the wind had slammed against her tightly strapped-in body, ripping the visor off her helmet and subjecting her eyes to over six hundred knots of wind blast during the initial seconds. She had sustained lacerations from the plastic visor snapping and flying back into her face. *I was lucky*, she thought. *I could have lost my eyesight.* It wasn't uncommon to have that all-important, protective visor ripped away during ejection. She sighed trying to shake the memory away.

"Uncle Howard is going to fall in love with you," Dan said, breaking into her morbid thoughts.

She rallied. "It's either feast or famine, isn't it?"

"Don't kid yourself, Raven. There's more than a couple of guys in that class that have their eye on you."

"Jealous?"

"You'd better believe it," he confirmed.

Chris smiled, knowing that he was teasing her. Rondo had approached her on more than one occasion to ask her to go over to the O'Club for drinks and dinner. She had gracefully declined the invitation. Julio Mendez idolized the ground she walked on. Despite the damage she had thought Brodie might wreak, Chris had been pleasantly surprised by the attitude of most of the pilots. They had been professional, refusing to accept Brodie's gossip. A few of them had approached and queried her about the accident. Leaving out the personal part, Chris had told them the story. They seemed satisfied, trading stories with her of their own accounts of being forced to punch out. And always, there was Dan's silent support. He had already qualified her in three different types of combat aircraft and helped her summon forth the ability to doggedly meet the severe demands of the school. Everyone needed someone going through TPS, she admitted. The husbands had their wives to support them. And with all the test-pilot-student families living on Sharon Street, it became a tight-knit, supportive community while the men labored under the demands of the harsh rigors.

Even Karen and Mark Hoffman. She smiled, pleased at their budding relationship. As much as Karen unmercifully teased her about Dan, Chris knew her best friend was in love with Hoffman. They were fortunate, though. They didn't have to hide their feelings.

"You ever ride a horse?" Dan wanted to know.

"A couple of times."

"Good. Ever been around a working ranch?"

"No. Will I have to work?"

Dan laughed. "Not unless you want to. I'm going to ride some fence, feel a good horse under me and share that time with you. You'll probably be on a horse more than on the ground," he promised.

"Just as long as I don't come back bowlegged, McCord. And I don't want a hot horse. Just find me something that will plod along at a nice, quiet gait."

"What's this? My Raven who can outfly me in an F-4 Phantom wants a *quiet* horse."

She grinned. "I can't outfly you in Double Ugly."

"Oh, yes you can," he said seriously. "You have a great touch with that fighter. Few pilots have taken to the F-4 like you have, Chris. They either love or hate it. We need good people who can handle that touchy bird."

She warmed to his praise. That was another wonderful quality about Dan: he was quick to give sincere compliments. He had done more to boost her ego and confidence than anyone else in her life. "I'm looking forward to doing more complicated testing with the Phantom when we get back."

"You'll do fine," he returned. "Well," he said, "in another hour we'll be at Carswell."

"I can hardly wait, Dan."

"Just remember, Vanessa will probably appear upset. Don't take it personally."

Chris frowned. She noticed Dan didn't call her "mother," and that puzzled her greatly. Everyone should be thankful they had parents. If she had had parents, she would have called them mom and dad, not by their first names. "Okay, I'll remember," she answered softly.

It was near eight in the evening when they landed the T-38 at Carswell. After they climbed down the ladders and exchanged a few pleasantries with the ground crew, Dan led her to Operations. The wind was hot, the sun setting low on the western horizon, giving the sky a blood-red cast. She noticed Dan's step seemed lighter. His smile devastated her as he checked his stride for her sake.

"You look absolutely beautiful," he murmured.

"Quit looking like a wolf ready to pounce."

Dan raised an eyebrow. "Is it that obvious?"

She suppressed a smile, trying to remain serious. "You'd better believe it."

"I'm having a hell of a time keeping my hands off you."

She glanced up at him, her violet eyes dancing with happiness. "I am too," she admitted, meeting his dazzling smile.

All too soon they were in Ops, traversing the highly polished tiled halls. Chris received several startled looks from those who manned the flight and meteorology desks. Out of some twenty-three-thousand Air Force pilots, only one hundred seventy-five were women. She was always an oddity and novelty wherever she went. But after seven years, she tended to disregard the amazed stares of the passersby.

"There's Vanessa," Dan suddenly warned.

Chris lifted her chin from her reverie, looking toward the front doors of the Ops building. A tall regal woman with gray hair stopped pacing after consulting her gold watch. Her hair was coiffed in the latest fashion, and a designer dress of pale beige was tastefully draped on her slender body. Vanessa moved like a queen, Chris thought, immediately impressed with the woman's entire aura of control.

"Daniel! I thought you'd never arrive," she chided in exchange for a greeting.

Chris curbed a smile. She never thought of Dan as "Daniel."

"Actually, Vanessa," he said, coming to a halt and putting his arm around Chris's waist, "we had a good tail wind and we're fifteen minutes early. I'd like you to meet Captain Chris Mallory. Chris, this is my mother, Vanessa McCord."

Chris smiled warmly, extending her hand. "Mrs. McCord, it's a pleasure to meet you."

Vanessa eyed her coolly. "My, you are a tall one, aren't you?" she murmured, taking Chris's hand

and shaking it weakly. Vanessa glanced over at her son. "Well, come along dear. I've got to get back to supervise the setting up of the party in your honor tonight."

Dan groaned. "Vanessa, I told you, I didn't want a party."

She gave an eloquent shrug of her shoulders, waiting for Dan to open the door. "Daniel, it's the least I could do for you. I know how bored you get around home, and I thought a party would bring out some of the lovely women who are just waiting for you to drop by." Vanessa gave Chris an apologetic look. "Sorry, Captain Mallory, we didn't know you were coming. Daniel is terrible about telling us all the details. He just drops in without warning and then leaves us a few days later." Vanessa walked primly down the steps toward the awaiting black limousine.

Chris felt Dan tense beside her as they caught up with Vanessa. "I told you Chris was coming," he growled, giving his mother a black look.

With a wave of her elegant, carefully lacquered fingernails, Vanessa glided like a swan into the limo. "All these details! Really, Daniel. You can't expect me to remember everything, dear. Come, come. We must hurry, or I'll miss Dee Dee's transatlantic phone call." She consulted her watch again. "She's to call in forty minutes."

Chris got in, glad to be sitting next to Dan. She tried not to allow the sense of awe to become apparent on her features as she gazed around the richly appointed car. The limo looked almost two car lengths long and came with a lavishly stocked bar. Dan gripped Chris's hand, holding it in his lap. "We'll make it in plenty of time," he growled, staring across the aisle at his mother.

Chris withdrew into her shell, fully aware of the

tension that eddied and swirled between Dan and his mother. If it weren't for Dan's reassuring grip, she would have broken out into a sweat. Vanessa was truly beautiful. If she was in her midfifties, it wasn't obvious. Her dark-gray hair did nothing but enhance her aristocratic bearing. Chris glanced discreetly at the number of emeralds, diamonds and rubies that adorned Vanessa's slender, artistic fingers. Swallowing nervously, Chris tried to appear calm despite her rolling stomach.

Vanessa looked sharply at Chris, her dark-blue eyes penetrating. "So Daniel tells me you're a woman pilot," she drawled.

Chris managed a smile. "There's a few of us around, Mrs. McCord."

Vanessa managed a cutting smile, her eyes skimming over Chris, missing no detail. "Well, in my personal opinion, women don't belong in the military."

Dan's hand tightened. "You didn't think I belonged there, either," he replied coolly. "So it's a moot point, isn't it, Vanessa?"

Chris breathed a sigh of relief, grateful for Dan's protective presence. She sensed Vanessa's displeasure that she was with Dan. Why? Had she planned to parade several eligible females in front of Dan at the party to tempt him into marrying and perhaps getting out of the disgusting Air Force? Suddenly Chris understood what Dan had said all along. He belonged in the Air Force doing what he loved best—instructing and flying. She could not picture Dan at the head of any major corporation. His need of freedom and space was stamped all over him, as it was over her. Those thoughts warmed her heart, and Chris looked over at Dan, sharing a tender smile with him.

"Your father's health is deteriorating, Daniel. I

would think you would give some serious thought to leaving the Air Force and coming home to pick up your duties."

Dan scowled. "My home is the Air Force. Has Preston been having more heart pains than usual?"

Vanessa set her petulant lips. "The fool doesn't slow down. And the cardiologist has warned him so many times. Maybe *you* can talk some sense into him, Daniel. Unfortunately he won't be home tonight. He's in Europe completing another oil transaction."

Dan gave a twisted smile; one that did not reach his eyes. "When has he ever listened to me, Vanessa?"

She clucked her tongue. "Or me, for that matter!"

"I guess all McCords are hardheaded," Dan returned, sharing a warmer smile with Chris.

"Humph! You got a double dose of it, Daniel, if you ask me."

"Just because I don't see life your way, Vanessa, doesn't mean I'm wrong."

Chris breathed a sigh of relief once they arrived at the luxurious home outside of Fort Worth. The home reminded her of a Southern mansion with its six white fluted columns. The lawn and rose gardens surrounding it were stunning. Vanessa waited impatiently until the driver came around to open the door.

"Daniel, have the maid show Chris to her room. I'll see you two later." Vanessa halted, looking directly at Chris. "Captain Mallory, I presume you have something to wear tonight other than a dress military uniform?"

Chris allowed the stinging comment to pass. "I think so, Mrs. McCord."

Semisatisfied, Vanessa fled up the white marble steps like some exotic bird who was fully aware of her royal plumage. Dan lifted out their individual bags. "Come on," he murmured, grinning. "I'll show you around myself."

Chris followed Dan into the mansion. The maid was courteous, murmuring the proper greetings as they walked into the highly polished foyer of pale-pink marble. Dan grabbed Chris's hand, pulling her up the long flight of stairs.

He opened a door halfway down the hall and placed his bag on the beige carpet of the bedroom. Chris entered, looking around. It was a decidedly masculine room with antique mahogany furniture. The balcony doors had been opened, allowing the evening breeze to waft through, carrying the scent of oranges with it.

"This is fantastic," Chris whispered, her eyes widening with awe.

Dan shook his head. "Give me a nice little home with the woman I love and I'll be happy. Follow me—your room is next door."

Chris gave him a hesitant look. "Next door?"

Dan opened it. "Yeah. Any problem with that?" he asked, smiling.

Chris carefully stepped across the expanse. "From the leer in your eyes, jet jockey, I'd say there is."

"I don't have a problem with it," he said, ushering her into the next room."

"I don't, either. But your mother might."

Dan snorted softly, pulling her to a halt in the center of the feminine bedroom. "The crowd Vanessa runs with wouldn't bat an eyelash, believe me."

A sadness filled Chris as she gazed up at Dan. She moved into his arms, sighing as she pressed her body against him. "It sounds bizarre," she whispered, closing her eyes, relishing his nearness.

Dan placed a series of small kisses on her neck, jaw and finally, on her waiting lips. His mouth moved with sureness and tantalizing slowness across her lips, feeling her respond fully. Finally he pulled away, gazing down at her. "I never did hold with that kind of life-style," he murmured. "I was a black sheep from the day I was born into this family. I want to know that the woman I marry loves me and doesn't want to have a series of other bed partners. I want her to know that she is my whole life, not just an extension of myself like my parents are to each other." He frowned, caressing her cheek. "I guess I require loyalty from the woman I love."

Chris trembled within his arms. The warming silence grew between them, and she felt the heavy, steady beat of his heart against her breast. Reaching up, she touched his face, feeling the roughness of his skin. "I may not have had parents, Dan, but I grew up knowing I wanted the same thing." She shook her head, mystified. "And here I thought it would be so great just having parents. Maybe I wasn't so badly off as I thought."

Dan claimed her lips in a lingering, exploratory kiss. "The grass isn't always greener on the other side of the fence, Raven. Believe me."

Chris lay down for a short nap and was roused by the maid an hour later. It was dark, the music of crickets floating through the balcony doors.

"Captain Mallory, Mrs. McCord said to bring this up for you to wear. I'll just put it in the closet over here for you, ma'am."

Chris slowly swung her legs over the bed, groping to wake up. She had changed into a set of jeans and a tank top after taking a welcoming shower. The bed had looked inviting, and she had given in to the urge to sleep. Gathering her scattered thoughts, Chris gave the young Mexican maid a confused look.

"I didn't ask for a dress."

The maid curtsied shyly. "Mrs. McCord instructed me to bring this up, ma'am."

"Okay...thank you."

The girl dipped her head. "Yes, ma'am. If you need anything else, just ring this bell."

Chris stretched fitfully after the maid had left. She walked over to the closet, fingering the silver lamé dress that looked sinfully skimpy. A slow anger fanned to life within Chris as she stood there. Vanessa couldn't trust her to come down dressed well enough so as not to embarrass her in front of her rich friends. With a sigh, Chris turned away. Had Vanessa tried to run Dan's life in the same domineering manner? She thought so, truly beginning to understand why Dan had escaped the oppressive atmosphere of his mother's controlling hand.

It was nearly nine-thirty when Chris heard a knock at the inner door. She checked her hair one more time before skipping across the room in her nylon-clad feet. Dan stood there, his eyes lighting up in appreciation as his gaze swept over her. He gave a low whistle of appreciation, stepping into her room.

"Lady, you're going to cause a riot down there," he breathed softly. "God, you look beautiful."

She blushed fiercely, giving a nervous laugh. She wore a simple lavender dress to match the color of her violet eyes. The silky material fell in graceful lines over her body, emphasizing her small bust, slender waist and hips. The knee-length gown was held in place by small spaghetti straps that tied in a bow at the back of her neck. With her black hair down, falling softly across her shoulders, she felt incredibly feminine. Dainty earrings of amethyst emphasized her lustrous eyes. She made a nervous gesture, walking over to slip into the elegant high heels of pearl gray that matched her small purse. "I'm nervous enough without you looking at me like that!" she said, laughing.

Dan shook his head. "Raven, you're the most beautiful woman I've ever seen. I never realized—"

"Hey, you know we Air Force jet jockeys clean up pretty well," she teased, leaning upward to lightly kiss his mouth. Before Dan could trap her against him, she slipped away, laughter in her eyes. "You don't clean up too badly yourself."

Dan shrugged, looking devastating in the brown slacks and pale-pink long-sleeve shirt and light-brown corduroy sport coat. The tie at his throat was a dark-rust color, matching the color of his hair. "I suppose Vanessa brought you a dress to wear?" he asked, sliding his hand beneath her elbow and leading her out the door.

"How did you know?"

Dan grinned. "Because she sent the butler up with a tuxedo for me. I guess she feels we won't dress correctly for her guests."

Music and laughter floated up from below as they traversed the hall, stopping at the top of the stairs. Dan captured her firmly against him, giving her a reassuring kiss on the cheek. "Just remember," he murmured, "we'll be gone early tomorrow morning."

Chris grimaced. "Frankly, I'd rather be flying with Brodie right now than facing this."

Dan laughed as he guided them down the stairs. "You'll be doing that as soon as you get back, Raven. And don't worry, this isn't a firing squad. Just leave the maneuvering to me and be my 'co' on this flight."

She smiled secretly at his lingo. Co was another word for copilot. She placed her trust in Dan completely, allowing him to guide her through the groups of beautifully sleek guests. It was a night that Chris would not forget. She had never rubbed elbows with the rich or the jet set. And before it was all over, she understood Dan's desire to escape the cloying atmosphere of the hangers-on, fawners and doting, plastic people who orbited the McCord power structure.

Vanessa fluttered over, her eyes widening as she looked at Chris, disbelief written in her features. She cooed over both of them and congratulated Chris on her dress. Slipping her hand around Dan's free arm, she dragged them from one pedigreed, cluster of well-bred guests to another. On several occasions, Chris met beautifully appointed women who made subtle passes at Dan. And each time Dan remained a gentleman, introducing Chris at his side. Each of those women would stare at Chris and then murmur polite words to Dan and glide off, drink in hand. More than once, Dan took her out on the floor, dancing to escape Vanessa's matchmaking efforts.

They danced as one, the rhythm of the music invading their souls, stirring their hearts and rekindling their passion for each other. Dan held her close, molding her against his lean body, moving her effortlessly in time with the music. To him, it was just another provocative form of making love to her. He had known instinctively that, with her hands and feel for flying, Chris would be a good dancer. Dancing meant subliminally turning the music into form; changing the rhythm into a flow of expression by the human body. She followed him effortlessly, with complete trust in each of his guiding movements, a melding union taking place.

With Chris's head nestled against his chest, he inhaled her special female fragrance, feeling his body tighten with desire. She was so special in so many ways. One of a kind. A woman of rarity that would never be found again in his lifetime. Dan pressed a kiss to her brow. "Lady, I'm falling in love with you...." Before Dan realized it, he had uttered the words close to her ear. The need to admit it to her was overpowering and as Chris looked up to meet his eyes, his heart contracted with overflowing happiness. She had heard his softly spoken words; he could see it in her shining violet eyes.

Her lips parted in response, and Dan held her a little tighter. The music was ending, but neither realized it. They finally slowed to a halt, oblivious to everything surrounding them. Chris gazed up into Dan's darkened blue eyes, aware of some invisible joy that seemed to reach out and smother her with happiness. "And I love you..." she whispered in response, losing herself in his tender, returning gaze.

Dan captured her face between his hands, leaning down, sealing those promising words upon her full lips—lips that were warm and giving beneath his mouth. Raising his head, he stared intently into her eyes. "I need you, Raven," he whispered huskily, "forever."

Her heart pounded painfully in her breast as she responded to his highly charged emotional words. "Oh, Dan—" she whispered.

"Daniel!" Vanessa's voice cut through the aura that surrounded them. In moments, Vanessa had propelled them off the emptying dance floor, chatting airily about meaningless subjects that interested neither of them.

Near midnight, Dan escorted her upstairs. Vanessa had pouted beautifully when he firmly told his mother they were calling it a night. He stopped at the bedroom door, opening it for Chris. Placing his hands on her bare shoulders, he smiled down at her.

"You'd better get some sleep, Raven."

She nodded, excitement coursing through her body. She hungered for his nearness, needing to talk to him further of her feelings for him. It was as if Dan had read all this in her features because he leaned over, kissing her reassuringly.

"Not here," he murmured. "We'll have time at the ranch to do some more talking. Go on, beautiful lady pilot, before I lose all my control and follow you in there."

Chris nodded, stunned by the culmination of events. "All right. Good night, Dan...."

"Good night, Chris. I'll wake you up at six o'clock sharp tomorrow morning. Sweet dreams, honey."

THE MORNING WAS A WHIRLWIND of activity. To Chris's delight, Dan took a small single-engine Cessna from the hangar at the McCord Estate and flew the two of them fifty miles north to Howard McCord's huge cattle ranch. Emerging from the Cessna on an arid strip, Chris met the man whom Dan loved like a father. Howard McCord came forward, a burly man of six-three and two hundred pounds. He gripped Chris's hand in a shake that bruised her fingers.

"So you're the pretty young filly Dan's been tellin' us about. Proud to know you, Chris. Just call me Howard and forget standing on formality around here. This is family." He grinned fully, his parched, leatherlike skin crinkling like old paper. He released his grip and then strode around the small plane, gripping Dan by the shoulders and giving him a huge bear hug.

"Dan! You son of a gun. Damned if you don't look the best I've ever seen you, son." He gripped Dan's shoulders, holding him at arm's length, his dark eyes narrowing. "That filly of yours must be doing you some good, eh?" he asked, grinning fully.

Dan slapped Howard on the back. "She makes me pretty happy, dad."

The rancher smiled as he put his arm around each of them and escorted them to the Jeep in the distance. "We'll get you young 'uns settled back at the homestead. Melvina's dying to meet you, Chris," he whispered in a conspiratorial tone. "My missus thinks the world of this boy of ours, and she's straining her corset to see who Dan finally settled on."

Chris shot Dan a distraught look. Dan grinned

happily, giving her a wink. "Why do I have the feeling I'm getting railroaded?" she asked, trying to halt a smile of her own. Howard helped her into the back seat of the Jeep.

"Naw, Dan don't railroad anybody, Chris," he corrected, starting the Jeep up. "Vanessa and Preston do, but this boy escaped their clutches in time. He always says 'please' first before he shoves somebody into a mud puddle. Ain't that right, son?" He chuckled.

Chris couldn't halt her grin. "I have a feeling I've lost both the battle and the war with you two around."

Howard's big Texas laugh boomed across the dry sagebrushed land. "You'll find out something real quick, pretty filly. The McCord's *always* get their way." He drove off at high speed, the Jeep bouncing and jerking along, kicking up a high cloud of yellow dust in its wake.

The ranch house, nestled among cottonwood trees, was a sprawling affair fashioned out of adobe brick, set off with a red Spanish tiled roof. Chris felt free there and marveled at the difference in life-styles between Dan's parents and his uncle. There, she felt relaxed; as if she could be herself, and no one could tell her any different. There it didn't matter what she wore. What counted, as Dan had said earlier, was the genuineness of the people.

Melvina McCord stood awaiting their arrival at the front-porch door, her chunky fists embedded deeply into her fleshy hips. Chris smiled brightly as the woman of some sixty years of age broke into a wide, welcoming grin.

"Ain't she purty!" Melvina crowed, throwing her arms open to envelop Chris. "Dan, you outdid yourself!" she cried, hugging her until Chris thought she would lose her breath. "Why, child, you are even prettier than what Dan said. Let me take a good look at you." She put Chris at arm's length, her watery blue eyes dancing with pleasure. She cast a dirty look at Dan who stood there grinning. "She's too skinny, Dan!" Melvina returned her attention to Chris, eyeing her shrewdly. "Child, what you need is some good home cooking to put some meat on those bones of yours."

Chris managed a warm smile. "Really, I'm fine, Mrs. McCord—"

"You call me Aunt Melvina or auntie. None of this formality. That's for the birds. And you noticed *they* ain't bowing and say'n how'd you do to each other."

Laughing, Chris obeyed. "You got a deal, Aunt Melvina."

"That's better," she said gruffly, moving over to Dan. "Now you, you young upstart of a pup, come here."

Chris felt tears coming to her eyes as Melvina embraced Dan for a long, long time. She cast a glance over to Howard, whose face had suddenly softened.

"Why ain't you been home lately?" Melvina asked, brushing a tear from her plump, ruddy cheek. Her frizzy black-and-gray hair was all over the place, but it seemed to fit Melvina's spunky image.

Dan wiped tears from his own eyes, keeping his arm around his aunt. "Got tied up with another class coming in, mom." He cast a meaningful glance over at Chris. "Besides, I met a pretty wonderful lady, and she's taken up all my spare time."

Chris smiled warmly over at Aunt Melvina. "I've probably seen him about as much as you have," she replied in good-natured defense.

Melvina chuckled, patting Dan lovingly on the shoulder. "He was always known to tell a few white lies to cover his tracks. Both of you, come on in. I got hot coffee brewin' and fresh-baked cinnamon rolls. We'll just get your luggage moved in and settle down for a chat."

After a huge breakfast of sausage, eggs, home-made bread and the rolls, Chris felt like she was ready to burst at the seams. The atmosphere of the cozy ranch was warm, relaxing and happy. Melvina sat ensconced between them on the old tattered couch that was covered with a hand-knit afghan of various shades of green and blue. She patted Chris's knee.

"You know Dan is like a son to us? When Terry, our own son, died in a tractor accident at age seven, Dan was a godsend." Melvina's eyes got damp again as she cast a look over at Dan. "And he was such a good boy. I suppose you met Vanessa and her nest of cronies?"

Chris swallowed hard, surprised at Melvina's sudden change in voice. "Why—uh, yes, I did meet her," she said, hesitantly.

"You should have seen Dan when they dumped him on our front porch. Vanessa was young, foolish and didn't want nothin' to do with raising a child. Dan was only seven then. She was crying that the world was waiting for her and she couldn't stay home to play mother." Melvina snorted vehemently. "Best thing she did was give us Dan! Some people were never created to be parents, and Vanessa and Preston are two of them."

10

NEAR TEN IN THE MORNING Dan persuaded Melvina to free them for a ride. Capturing Chris's hand, he walked toward the huge horse barn that sat north of the ranch house. Everywhere Chris looked there were large corraled paddocks with either cattle or horses in them. She smiled winsomely up at Dan as he led her into the shade of the horse barn. "I love your aunt and uncle. I can see why you think so much of them."

"Howard and Melvina are my real family, Chris," he answered, sliding open the first door of the box stall on the right. "They're kind of taken with you, too," he said, leading out a small gray mare.

"The feeling's mutual. This might sound like wistful thinking, but they almost fit what I had wanted in imaginary parents." She cast him a shy look. "Sounds stupid, doesn't it? Even at my age I have a set of make-believe parents in my head."

Dan put the mare in the crossties, coming over and placing his arms around her. "It doesn't sound crazy at all, honey. I've tried to imagine what my world would be like without any family." A pained expression crossed his face. "I think I'd feel awfully empty inside and very much alone." He caressed her face with his hands. "That's why I've tried to make the effort to be here for you. You deserve it. You're a special lady."

Chris leaned up, kissing him soundly, glorying in the pressure of his mouth on her lips. She relished the hardness of his body on the softness of hers, his

hands sliding down the expanse of her back, coming
to rest on her hips. He drew her daringly against
him, making her aware of his arousal. "Mmm, you
are too tempting, Dan McCord," she whispered
against his mouth. "Let me go before I melt into
your arms."

He uttered a low growl, planting a hungry kiss on
her full, wet lips. "You won't be safe here," he
whispered seductively. "Even though there are two
guest bedrooms here at the ranch, I'm not sleeping
in the other room tonight."

Chris gave him an intent look. "Will your aunt
and uncle understand?"

"Yes. I don't come home with young ladies very
often. So they know you're somebody special to me.
They may look old-fashioned and are in some ways,
but they taught me to make my own decisions and
abide by them."

Chris gazed up at him. "Even in this short time I
can see their influence on how you make decisions
and the way you think."

Dan released her, going to the tack room and re-
trieving a saddle, blanket and bridle for the mare.
"They helped me become what I am," he admitted,
throwing the blanket on the horse.

Chris leaned up against the stall, watching him.
He looked so at home there. If she hadn't known he
was an Air Force officer, she would have thought he
was a Texas rancher. That particular occupation did
suit him, she thought. "Didn't you ever go back
home to Vanessa after she left you here?" she asked.

Dan cinched up the saddle. "I'd visit my parents a
couple of weeks every summer. The rest of the time I
lived here."

"Have you ever thought of taking up ranching,
Dan?"

He released the horse from the crossties, putting
the bridle over the mare's head. "Sometimes." And

then he gave her a wicked grin. "When things get murky in the rank and file of the Air Force, I often think I should have been a cowboy instead. But after the politics clear up, I always find my desire to sit in the cockpit of a jet fighter stronger than to throw my leg over a horse."

She smiled thoughtfully. "Maybe later when they ground you to flying a desk instead of a plane you'll get out."

Dan handed her the reins, going down to the next box stall and leading out a large black gelding. "That's crossed my mind," he admitted. "I don't think I want to be a desk jockey the last five or ten years of my career. But that's going to be a tough decision."

Within minutes, the gelding, known as Blackjack, was saddled and they were trotting out toward lush green pastures dotted with white Charlois cattle. The sun beat down hotly; the temperature was already in the high eighties. The sky was a light blue; the same color as Dan's laughing eyes as he watched her try to post in the Western saddle. Finally giving in, Chris pulled her gray mare to a walk. She marveled at Dan's natural grace in the saddle, but then reminded herself he had almost been born to one, having ridden from age seven until he was eighteen years old.

Several cowboys raised their hand in greeting as they passed them. Most of them were older men who slouched comfortably in their saddles, their weather-beaten features rough-hewn from a combination of sun, wind and rain. Dan rode at her side for almost an hour, telling Chris the layout of the huge working ranch. They neared a small stream and a grove of cottonwoods, dismounting and giving their charges a well-earned drink of water.

Dan hobbled both horses. Removing their bridles and putting them over the saddle horn allowed the horses to munch on the grass. Then Dan led Chris over to a stout cottonwood, pulling her down so that she rested in his lap. He touched her nose with his finger.

"You're getting sunburned, Raven. I should have thought to pick up some hats before we left."

"Somehow, I don't see myself in anything but a camouflaged helmet, visor and oxygen mask."

"No cowboy hat?" he inquired, his blue eyes dancing with merriment.

Chris shook her head. "The way my legs feel right now all I want is my bird and the straps of my ejection seat harness biting into my shoulders," she said, laughing.

"I have to remember you're a city girl at heart," he murmured, kissing her cheek.

"And you're a country boy at heart."

"Think that makes us opposites, huh?"

She closed her eyes, relishing his maleness. "We don't have many differences, really."

Dan nodded. "That's true," he conceded. The silence lulled them into the quiet of noontime. A noisy crow cawed raucously in the distance. The lowing of cattle increased the sense of peace in her. Chris was content to lie in Dan's arms and let her mind wander into bliss.

"Happy?" Dan murmured.

"Mmm, completely. You?"

"Never happier," he admitted huskily. He ran his fingers down her rib cage, caressing her hip. "You make me happy, Raven. Matter of fact, you touch many people with your warmth."

She nuzzled against his neck. "Some of the guys at the school think I'm a sourpuss of sorts and others—"

"Think you're one hell of a woman," he finished, sitting her up and forcing her to look directly into his intense azure eyes. "You don't hear the talk that goes on over at the O'Club afterward."

She smirked. "That's because I never go over there for a drink after classes."

"No one thinks you're a snob for not doing that. Most of the students think you're studying your fool head off."

Grinning, she said, "I am!"

Dan ran his fingers up her jawline, lightly brushing the nape of her neck. "Last night," he whispered huskily, looking levelly into her eyes, "I said something to you, Chris. Something that I've been wanting to say for quite a while."

She sobered immediately, aware of the tremor in his voice. "I know...."

His grip tightened on her shoulder, his face mirroring the intensity of his emotions toward her. "I love you, my sweet Raven. Like I've never loved another woman before." His eyes softened as he gazed at her. "Since the first day I met you on that aircraft ramp, you reached inside me. You made me feel things that I've never experienced. You're a dream come true for me."

She lowered her lashes, her heart pounding wildly in her breast. "I never believed in dreams, Dan." She swallowed hard, meeting his tender gaze. "Not until you walked into my life." She gave a helpless shrug, tears suddenly filling her eyes. "I'll have to admit, I tried to ignore you. I—after Jim's death, I just felt too hurt to open up again. But there you were—you made me laugh, you held me during some of the worst moments of my life and you accepted me as I was. You didn't want to change me or mold me into something else."

Dan caressed her cheek, cupping her chin. "Honey, I wouldn't change anything in you except about how you feel about yourself," he promised thickly. "If only you could see what you've accomplished."

Her lips parted in response as she heard the words fall like a loving hand upon her heart. "You've helped me realize some of it, darling," she murmured. "And really, I love being with you. Not just in a jet, but anywhere."

He grinned. "Even in a cowboy hat?"

Chris laughed softly. "Yes, even in a cowboy hat."

Dan pulled a small box from his left shirt pocket. "This is for you, Raven. Open it," he urged quietly, placing it in her hand.

Her heart stilled as she stared down at the small red velvet case. Her fingers trembled as she began to open it.

"Because we're both in the Air Force and we can't wear engagement or wedding rings during flight, I wanted to give you something that you could wear regardless," he said, watching her expression closely.

The latch was sprung and Chris lifted the lid. A small gasp escaped from her lips. Inside, with a gold clasp and chain, was a carefully crafted violet gem in the shape of a heart. Dan picked it up, fastening it around her neck.

"It's amethyst," he explained, watching how the precious gem settled at the hollow of her lovely throat. "The color of your eyes, Raven." He slowly looked up at her. "Eyes that I could lose myself in forever. I see every emotion in there, did you know that?"

She was speechless, overwhelmed with Dan's generosity and his outpouring of love. Touching the stone carefully, she choked back a sob. "I—no one has ever given me anything so lovely, Dan...."

He pulled her into his arms, embracing her fiercely. "I'm going to shower you with gifts," he promised fervently. "God knows, you deserve some happiness after the hell you've gone through."

"But I don't need things," she protested softly, unable to stem the tide of tears. Chris buried her head in his chest. "I just need you, Dan...."

He rocked her, smiling tenderly. "I know," he whispered thickly, "that's why I love you so much. You value people, not material possessions, not money. And more than that, I love your unquenchable spirit, do you know that?" Placing his mouth against her trembling lips, he shared the salt of her tears. It was a kiss sealing eternity. Dan put as much of his soul into that breathtaking molding of his lips against hers as possible. He heard her moan, feeling the hardening of her taut breasts against the wall of his chest as he deepened the exploration of his tongue into her sweet depths. Slowly he withdrew, his eyes burning fiercely with cobalt desire as he looked down at her. "I love you," he whispered rawly, "and I'm asking you to be my wife. I can't conceive of life without you, honey. I never knew what living was until I met you."

Her violet eyes sparkled with the wash of tears, her cheeks wet and flushed. "There is no life without you, Dan," she murmured throatily. "I can only answer yes. I love you so much that it hurts," she said, touching the area where her heart lay.

Dan groaned, pressing Chris against him, holding her so tightly that he was afraid he might crush her. "You're mine," he breathed fiercely. "Always mine and I'll love you forever...."

CHRIS CLIMBED INTO THE FRONT COCKPIT SEAT of the F-4. Once settled in, she took her helmet, which was sitting behind the windshield frame, and gently pushed it on her head. She tried to ignore the fact that Captain Brodie was climbing in the rear seat. Where had the past weekend gone? She hadn't wanted to come back to TPS after spending time at the McCord ranch. Howard and Melvina had been good tonic for both Dan and herself. At last she had a family, people who loved her openly and with a lavish show of affection. Melvina was a toucher;

someone who knew the value of making hand contact with Chris. And Howard doted upon her as if she were the daughter they had never had.

Chris's eyes shadowed briefly, remembering Melvina telling her of their second child, a daughter, who had died at birth. Even now, although it had occurred thirty years ago, Chris could hear the loss in Melvina's suddenly husky voice. And Chris had reached over out of genuine compassion, trying to console Melvina. That one touch had brought all of them together. The sense of family from that moment on had drawn Chris into their hearts, and they had bestowed love in return to her lonely heart.

Automatically her gloved fingers went to her throat where the amethyst necklace rested beneath her flight suit. It was a symbol of Dan's undying love for her. And how many times had she touched that beautiful gem, awed by its fiery facets glimmering with hues ranging from pale lavender to almost a crimson color? Was it true? Did her eyes truly reveal all her changeable moods as Dan had said?

Her body was still vibrantly warm from their lovemaking the night before. But now, the harshness of reality, of her other world, was demanding all her attention and skills. It was 0900, and many of the students and instructors were already up and flying. Chris looked to her left, watching as Dan and Rondo clambered aboard the F-4 next to them on the ramp. She raised her hand as Dan glanced in her direction. Her heart lifted as he returned the greeting.

"If you're through with the social amenities, captain, how about getting this show on the road?" Brodie asked, a growl in his voice.

Chris controlled her emotions, accepting her responsibility as aircraft commander on this test flight. She pulled the oxygen mask, which held a microphone, to her face. "I'll tell you when we're ready," she returned coolly. She knew Brodie would challenge the very limits of her power because she had been given the AC position by no one less than Colonel Martin himself. In a way, Chris was thankful that Dan had not done it, since Brodie would have screamed prejudice. She went through the final preflight checks on all instruments, sticking her hand high above her head, making a circular motion with her index finger to the ground crew below. It meant, start the engines.

She was all business now. Deadly, serious business. She and Brodie would be flying supersonic climb tests and high-angle-of-attack tests with the Phantom today. Brodie would be monitoring the speed, acceleration, climb rate and other factors as they flew above the Mojave for the next hour and a half. The straps of the harness bit deeply into Chris's shoulders as she pulled downward on them one final time. A slight smile pulled at her mouth as she flipped down the dark visor to cut the intense glare of the sun. The trembling power of a jet beneath her body felt good.

Chris gave a thumbs-up to the crew chief, slowly inching the throttles of the F-4 forward, the bird heeling to port at her command. Pointing the bulbous black nose of the Phantom toward the taxiway, they moved to the hammerhead area where Chris shoved down on the rudder and brakes system. Three airmen stood waiting, chocks dangling in their hands. Automatically Chris and Brodie put their hands in sight of the airmen, resting them on the cockpit frame. Instantly the team went into action. Their job was to check for any oil spills or hydraulic leaks beneath the surface of the bird. By the pilots having both hands visible, one of them could not mistakenly roll the bird forward and possibly injure one of the ground crew. The external check made, the airmen gave Chris the final signal. She ordered the canopies down and locked. The second F-4 containing Dan and Rondo was following them slowly off the ramp.

Brodie sullenly sat in the rear seat, his eyes narrowed in anger. He had spent most of his weekend at the O'Club, drinking and talking about Mallory to anyone who would listen. Few did, and it only made him hate her more. Ever since he had looked at the schedule last Thursday and seen the team assignment, he had swum in a dark sea of bitterness. Just watching Mallory move confidently through every phase of preflight this morning did nothing but increase his ire.

A plan lurked in his mind. A slight, thin smile pulled at his mouth. He would deliberately, on the third high-angle-of-attack test, "accidentally" pull the stick back, taking control without Mallory knowing in advance. By doing that, he knew the bird would depart from its flight path and become a twenty-two-ton projectile screaming out of control at an over twenty-five-degree angle of attack. Then Brodie would watch her try to recover control of the bird, knowing full well she wouldn't be able to handle the unexpected situation. He looked up, squinting at the sky above him. At the right time, he would take the stick and make the recovery, having successfully embarrassed Mallory, making her look like the incompetent fool that she was. Without telling Mallory, he switched their normal cabin intercom to "ground" so that everyone in the air and in the control tower could hear. It was a "hot mike" situation and rarely done while students were testing. Nevertheless, Brodie knew it would seal Mallory's fate once and for all by shaming her in front of everyone on the base.

Dan watched as Chris's F-4 took off. The jet hurtled down the runway, both afterburners lit and glowing in the early-morning air. He could feel the tremors from the thunderous display as he sat in his jet waiting his turn for takeoff. Something nagged at him, but he shrugged off the intuitive feeling. He was worrying because Brodie was with Chris. He didn't like the captain's sullen attitude that morning, aware of the angry black glare in Brodie's eyes as he watched Chris.

Dan's gut tightened and once again he dismissed the premonition as nothing more than his overprotective attitude toward Chris. "Okay, Rondo, let's stand on it," he ordered as he heard clearance given by the tower. Sitting in the rear seat, Dan gave control of the Phantom over to the other pilot. This would be Rondo's last check flight before he would be ready to fly with other student pilots, navigators or engineers aboard an aircraft. Dan felt some solace knowing that he and Rondo would be flying chase for Chris. It was the chase team's job to stay no farther than a mile away from the spin-test jet. If the jet did not recover from its maneuver by eighteen thousand feet, it would be Rondo's responsibility to alert the pilot of the spin jet. At that point, if they hadn't recovered by fifteen thousand, Dan would order them to pop the canopies and eject.

Dan strapped the small placard on his left thigh, noting the type of spins Chris would be doing with the aircraft. It would be Rondo's job to make large circles around the spin jet, watching for other aircraft traffic in the area. After every spin, the chase plane would join the other jet at twenty-four thousand feet. Rondo would fly within two hundred feet, checking all external surfaces, looking for telltale leaks of pink hydraulic fluid. If too much fluid showed on the spin jet, the rest of the tests would be scrubbed and they would be ordered back to base. Without proper levels of the life-giving hydraulic fluid, the bird would be unflyable. At least Dan would be in constant radio contact with them and could eavesdrop on the conversations between them to dispel the dark hunch hovering over him.

Chris listened closely to Brodie's voice while aiming the bird upward into the dazzlingly blue sky above them for the first series of supersonic climb tests. He called off knots, angle of attack and the temperature on the powerful, throbbing engines. The Phantom felt good, beautifully responsive to her slightest hand and foot pressure against the stick and rudder. Joy replaced her initial dread of working with Brodie as they spent almost an hour working as a close-knit team on the test problems. After each run Dan or Rondo would check the F-4 and then pronounce them "clean and dry" for the next one.

"All right," Brodie said, "we're to hit Mach two at thirty-nine thousand and hold, leveling the bird off at forty-five."

"Roger," she replied. At forty-five thousand the air was quite thin and the Phantom would be less responsive. The engines would voraciously eat up the oxygen needed in order to keep forward speed. She glanced at the altimeter indicating their present altitude: fifteen thousand. A smile crossed her face: she loved the incredible power that the Phantom could deliver. It would be only a matter of seconds before they would reach the top of their test altitude and she would have to level off. Still, it was a thrill to her each and every time.

"Ready when you are," she responded.

"Roger. Ten seconds and counting..." Brodie returned.

Chris listened carefully, her heart accelerating with each count. Her fingers closed more firmly over the throttles, getting ready to notch them above normal flight into the afterburner range. They were going to tempt the gods once more, roaring into their

mythical heaven. Would the god of thunder, light-
ning and the sky be angered? She frowned at the
analogy, ready to challenge those invisible spirits
that created the ever-changing weather patterns
around them.

"Now!" Brodie commanded.

The Phantom roared, hurling itself at an almost
vertical angle. Chris was pressed back into the seat,
the G-forces building up within seconds as the engines accelerated. Brodie called out the knots. She hit
Mach two exactly on time and at the proper altitude.
The Phantom shivered and Chris watched the angle
closely, feeling they were a hairbreadth away from
losing control. The Phantom screamed on, the sky becoming a midnight blue as they left the heavy shackles of earth behind them. She leveled off at forty-five
thousand, gently easing the throttles back. Her body
was pulled forward into the harness, her eyes feeling
as though someone was pushing them outward from
her skull. The straps bit more deeply into her shoulders as she slowed the Phantom to subsonic flight.

Chris felt the angle of attack build as she main-
tained level flight. Her fingers sensitively monitored
the pressure against the throttles as "alpha" or angle
of attack approached nineteen degrees. The aircraft
trembled as it passed Mach one, on the verge of losing its straight flight. Chris nudged the stick forward
a bare quarter of an inch, bringing the nose down,
feeling the Phantom become more stable.

Suddenly Chris felt the stick jerk backward. She
opened her mouth to shout something but it was too
late! The Phantom's nose swung abruptly to the
port, the entire front end of the plane pitching upward. Within a matter of split seconds, the bird careened, slicing hard to port, rolling upside down as
it broke into a screaming spin.

"Come on," Brodie cried, "get this bird under
control!"

Anger roared through Chris as she fought to bring the Phantom back beneath her hand. The G-forces built up rapidly, pinning her heavily against the seat. It felt as if the flesh from her face was being pulled downward. She was frozen in position, her one hand gripping the stick, her other hand over the throttles. The G-suit inflated, tightly squeezing her whole lower body. The bird plunged into a yawing rolling dive. "You bastard! What are you doing?" Chris shouted. A thousand thoughts raced into her mind. A hundred possibilities, the ways to correct the spinning bird and Brodie's despicable trick ran through her steel-trap brain. Test pilots were taught to think no matter what the circumstance. And at that instant, Chris was reacting out of hours of training and reflexive action. She shoved the throttles forward, igniting the afterburners, and rammed the stick forward. They were at twenty-five thousand, and the earth was rushing up to meet them. The jet fell on its back and corkscrewed like a falling leaf. The power of the engines slowly forced the screaming Phantom to grudgingly come out of the spin. She kept the angle of attack low so that the plane would respond.

"Cobra Two to Cobra One," Dan called, his voice taut. "What happened? Is there a problem?"

The Phantom was responding to her hand. Chris was going to answer Dan's call when Brodie jerked the stick back again. She sucked in a breath of air, unable to believe what he was doing. Did he want to kill them both? The bird departed a second time. It was worse at lower altitude and airspeed, and the plane became even more slothful. The altimeter unwound like a broken spring. Blood rushed to her head, the pressure on her eyes tremendous as an invisible hand of the G-forces pulled downward against her entire body. Blackness began to rim her vision for a moment as she fought to control the Phantom.

"Come on!" Brodie yelled, a sudden catch in his voice. In his anger to make Chris look incompetent, he had forgotten how low they were flying after the first recovery. It was too late to regret his action. His eyes bulged as he watched the Phantom screaming downward toward ten thousand feet. "Pull it out! Pull it out!" he cried.

"Cobra Two to Cobra One!" Dan called. "Coming up on nineteen thousand. What's wrong?"

They were too low! Chris ground her teeth, gripping the throttles. She would have to light the afterburners again and pray that she would break the spin and pull out before it was too late.

"Eighteen thousand!" Brodie cried.

"Read me the altimeter settings!" she snapped hoarsely, hearing Dan's voice once again in her helmet. The bird strained, bucking against her steady hand. *No, no*, Chris silently shouted to the plane, *come back, come back!* She wasn't going to lose another plane! Not another!

"Fifteen! Goddamn, we're not going to make it!" Brodie screamed through the intercom. "Punch out! It won't come out of the dive soon enough. Punch!"

"No!" Chris ordered tightly, "we're staying!"

The brown-and-green speckled earth loomed through the cockpit windows at Chris. Sweat drenched her body, her arm aching as she hit right stick and hard right rudder. The bird shivered with the torque of wind tearing at its exotic metal skin, the thundering engines threatening to tear them apart.

"Twelve! You're crazy. You're dead if you don't punch out!"

Chris ground her teeth, forcing a gulp of air into her body to try to ease the pressure of G-forces that were smashing against her. "I've got it!" she croaked, feeling the bird grudgingly respond.

Brodie jerked the T-handle, making sure only his

seat and not Mallory's would be blown. "You're crazy! Ten thousand! Ten thousand! Punch out!"

Before she could order him to stay, Brodie had popped both canopies. Chris felt a huge, invisible fist of air hit her bodily, momentarily blacking her out. A cry was ripped from her lips. She vaguely heard the explosion of the back ejection seat. Wind tore relentlessly at her, buffeting her wildly as she stubbornly remained at the controls, willing the bird to come back beneath her steadying hands. The Phantom came out of the spin, going into a dive. Her only thought was to save the plane. Shoving the throttle forward, afterburners on, the wind velocity increased across the open cockpit, threatening to rupture her internally from the concussion of wind blast created by the speed. Her hand tightened around the stick and she wrenched back, her muscles feeling as if someone was tearing her apart.

The brown of earth filled her fading line of vision. Chris valiantly fought off the telling blackness as the blood was pulled from her brain. She was losing it! *Come on, come on,* she silently begged, her voice screaming in her ears. It was a mad rush between her and the ground. Six thousand...five...four...three...she could see each mesquite bush, each Joshua tree....

Ground observers who had heard the frantic conversation at the tower watched as the gray Phantom tumbled from high altitude. Twice they heard the roar of afterburners being lit. And twice, they held their breath as the fighter careened earthward, the pilot pulling the nose up, trying to recover from the dive. The F-4 skimmed across the sunbaked earth, screaming like a banshee. Men scrambled for fire trucks as the call came in from Cobra Two that a bird was in trouble. Air-traffic controllers stood tensely in their tower, helplessly watching the drama unfold before their eyes as the Phantom slowly gained altitude.

Chris called to the fighter, the G-forces pounding her body. The bird was responding! It was coming out of the dive, leveling out. Just as she got it into controlled flight, moving the howling jet across the desert floor, an invisible column of air caught the plane, throwing the bird up. Worse, the concussion and blast of air tore viciously at Chris, ripping the visor away from her eyes. From sheer instinct, Chris pulled the throttles back to decrease the wind resistance, keeping the jet's nose on a gentle climb out of the valley. The plastic visor snapped, cutting her flesh, leaving her eyes unprotected and exposed to over six hundred knots of wind.

"Mayday!" Chris called, her voice sounding light years away to her. The wind roar was deafening as she again hit the button. "Cobra One... Mayday!"

"Cobra One, this is Tower," said a disembodied voice through her helmet. "What is your status?"

Chris fought down panic, barely able to see the instruments. She pulled the throttles back slowly, fearful of stalling the fighter. "Tower," she gasped, "This is Captain Mallory... canopies blown... I can't see... visor's gone... rear seat ejected...."

"Cobra One, roger. Is the bird flyable?"

Where was she? Real panic began to eat at Chris as she raised her gloved hand with great difficulty to wipe away the blood streaming into her eyes. For a brief second she could see her position to the land below. She was at five thousand feet and holding the Phantom in fairly level flight.

"Yes... bird's fine. Can't see instruments clearly...."

"Cobra One—" the voice hesitated a second "—can you land it?"

Chris's lips tightened beneath the mask. "I'll need

help. Got to have someone talk me down. Can't
see—"

"Cobra Two to Tower—" Dan's voice floated over
her earphones "—we're three miles away and have
visually sighted Cobra One. We'll talk her down if
the damage isn't too bad."

Chris nearly cried out Dan's name. A sudden
surge of emotion nearly overwhelmed her. Blindly
Chris groped to clear her eyes, trying desperately to
read the altimeter and check the horizon indicator to
see if she was flying toward the ground or climbing
away from it. Wind buffeted her mercilessly. Her
head was pinned against the seat, and she was unable
to move it in either direction. Her mouth was sticky
with the metallic taste of blood that had somehow
leaked beneath the tightly fitting mask on her face.

"Cobra Two—oh, hell...Raven? Do you read me?
It's Dan."

Her eyes were tearing badly from the lashing of
wind across the open cockpit. Chris thumbed the intercom. "Dan...I'm in trouble. I can't see. Blood
keeps blurring my vision, and I can't open my eyes
because of the wind. Tell me if I'm level."

Dan forced his voice to remain neutral. "Your
wings are level. You're at five thousand." His heart
surged with emotion as he heard Chris's calmness.
She had more courage than he had ever expected
under the circumstances.

"Rondo, let's fly about a hundred feet off her starboard wing. You fly, I'll talk her in," he ordered
tightly.

"Roger. God, look at that," Rondo whispered,
pointing at the injured Phantom.

Dan's eyes narrowed, quickly evaluating the damage to the jet. After Brodie had ejected, there was
nothing but a gaping black hole where the seat
had once been. Both canopies were missing. His
heart hammered painfully in his chest as he assessed

Chris. They had heard the entire sequence between her and Brodie. Dan had ordered Rondo to turn immediately, flying to where her jet was in trouble. They had seen Brodie punch out, the chute opening and safely taking him earthward. Dan had watched in silent anguish as Chris had fought for control of the spirited Phantom and almost cried out, thinking she would crash. Now he shoved all those thoughts away, concentrating on the present.

"She's blind," Rondo said, his voice drained of emotion. "Even from here I can see blood on her face. God, how is she flying that bird?"

Dan swallowed hard. "With her heart," he answered grimly.

He hit the button on the stick, which would link him with her aircraft. He knew the whole base was probably listening by now, but he no longer cared. "Raven, your wings are level and you're holding your altitude." He glanced at the speed gauge. "You're at two hundred fifty knots. You can ease back the throttles gradually so there's less wind resistance on you. Do you copy?"

"Yes...."

He hesitated. Chris was blind. Only fifty percent of the pilots forced to fly blind were able to land the aircraft. The others died in a fiery crash trying.

"I think we'd better get the bird enough altitude so you can eject," he said.

"No!"

Dan's eyes narrowed, feeling the authority of Chris's voice.

"For your own safety," he argued.

"I'm not losing this bird, dammit! I can fly it. I know I can."

Dan put a clamp on his fear for her life. "You can't see!"

"I'm AC," she snapped back. "It's my final decision whether I leave or stay."

Dan felt an incredible surge of pride in his chest for Chris. The lady was made of the right stuff. She wasn't going to throw away a multimillion-dollar aircraft, but had opted instead to utilize her full range of skills to bring it safely in. The only question was: could she survive? Who could land a jet blind on feel alone and voice instruction? Some deep gut answer said: *Chris can.* Dan's mouth thinned with tension as he hit the intercom button.

"Okay, Raven, I'll go along with your decision. I'll talk you down."

Relief was apparent in her voice. "Just keep talking to me, Dan. I'll bring her in. Talk to me, Dan...."

He nodded, his narrowed, intense eyes never leaving her. "Don't worry, honey, you'll get sick of hearing my voice before this is all over."

Chris made a small, choked sound. Every time there was silence, panic ate at her. "Never. What can we do, Dan? Where can I sit this bird down?"

"We're fifteen miles out from the lake-bed landing area," Rondo interrupted.

"Raven, we're fifteen miles from Edwards. The only way I can get you down is to land with you."

"I know."

"You're flying at one hundred sixty knots now. Drop the nose slightly. Good girl. Looking good," he reassured her.

Dan switched to inter-cabin. "Rondo, raise Tower. Tell them we're coming in on the lake bed. I need wind-direction information."

"Roger."

Dan switched back to Chris. "Okay, Raven, let's drop the landing gear. Can you feel for the handle?"

"Yeah...there. Let me know when it's down, Dan."

He watched as the tricycle landing gear slowly lowered. "It's down. Can you see anything?" he urged, hoping she might see the light indicator that would confirm the gear was down and locked.

The shearing wind slapped at her exposed face and she cringed, trying to ignore the pain. N—no... blind...damn, the blood...nothing, I can't see anything anymore...."

Dan fought down his rising panic. "It's okay," he crooned. "Your nose is level. You've got what it takes to get the bird down. Let's lower slats and flaps now. Speed is the same. You're holding nicely."

The Phantom's flaps slowly lowered, pulling up the nose. Chris automatically made the correction using her incredible sensory perceptions as never before. Her eyesight was gone; she was no longer able to steal momentary glances at the needles and gauges. She could feel the bird trembling around her, hear the huge engines just this side of stall speed, feel the buffeting as the plane hit the up and down drafts that plagued the desert region. Dan's calming voice washed over her and Chris steadied herself, listening because her life depended upon it.

"Okay, Raven, roll into a left bank...stop...roll right...stop. Good. Bring the nose down just a hair. Great. You're now right on the button for the landing strip."

Chris grimaced, needing the comfort of his husky voice.

"How are you doing?" Dan asked, some of the official tone leaving his voice.

"I'm afraid to answer that one right now," she returned. "Tough keeping my head from getting banged around by the wind gusts."

Dan's mouth tightened, his eyes never leaving her. "You're doing great, honey. Just hang in there. We'll get you down. Bump in a bit of trim, and it will help keep the jet level. I'll slow you down to landing speed in about a minute."

"Ten miles out," Rondo said tensely, carefully watching the distance between the two fighters as they stayed in tight formation.

"Roger," Dan murmured.

"Ten miles, Raven. Put the nose down slightly, and we'll start down to the lake bed. Good. Okay, the bird's drifting slightly to the right. Roll left now...okay, stop...good."

Her pulse pounded without relief in her dry, constricted throat. Chris gulped oxygen, her breathing erratic, the adrenaline surging through her tense, bruised body. A mile to go...half a mile.... Her fingers became a living extension of the metal of the jet around her. She felt each air pocket, each imperceptible move of the jet, anticipating, correcting, listening to Dan's welcoming voice guiding her down...ever closer to a lake bed she could not see through the red haze.

Rondo played his jet carefully, his mouth set in a grim line. "Landing both Phantoms wing tip to wing tip in bumpy air like this is dangerous even when both pilots have good vision," he told Dan.

"I know," Dan responded. He frowned. Could Rondo hold their bird steady enough? What if Chris's plane sheared right or left at the last seconds above the runway? Dan felt the cold drench of sweat wash over his body. They'd all die in the crash. Somehow, her courage under the circumstances minimized the fear in him. Chris was holding the jet steady as a rock, taking each updraft and ironing the plane out levelly as if nothing had happened. Rondo broke into his thoughts.

"I'm more worried about my ability rather than Chris's." And then Rondo grinned, thumbing the button. "Damned if I don't feel like we're the Thunderbirds."

The momentary joke broke the silent strain between the three of them. The Thunderbirds were the

Air Force's precision flight team who did aerobatic tricks such as this with skill.

"We're approaching the end of the lake-bed runway, Raven," Dan told her quietly. "You're on glide path, one hundred sixty knots, looking good. Don't worry about flare...we'll drive it on in. We're fifty feet off your starboard wing tip. When I tell you to sit it down, do it. The instant you feel the wheels touch, drop the nose and pop the drag chute. I'll tell you whether you're going to the right or left as we go down the runway."

"Roger," she answered hoarsely, her voice scratchy, her breathing chaotic.

To the firefighters who manned the large lime-green trucks speeding to assigned positions on the lake-bed surface, the two Phantoms looked like a mirage appearing out of the wavering curtains of heat rising off the parched earth.

"Over runway," Dan reported, his voice devoid of emotion. "One hundred sixty knots, Raven. Ease the nose up a little more...." His breath jammed in his throat. If she hit a thermal— He watched the wheels lightly kiss the lake bed. "You're down! Drop the nose! Throttles idle! Pop the chute!"

At the same instant Rondo touched down. Both Phantoms roared down the lake bed; the earth kicked up behind them in billowing, yellow clouds. Dan sucked in air between his teeth, watching Chris's Phantom slow, drifting out again to the left.

"Right rudder, you're drifting left!" he snapped. "Chris!"

Chris sobbed, fighting a losing battle against the pain she felt in her face, pressing her booted foot against the right rudder. Her sense of equilibrium was off due to not being able to see. She felt the tremor of the jet's tires on the lake bed, the roar of the engines behind her as she held the throttles to idle.

"Okay, you're fine, now," Dan reported, an edge of terror leaking through his voice. "One hundred knots...fifty...apply more brake...a little left rudder...fine, fine...we made it, Raven. You did it. God, I love you. You're going to be all right. Shut down. Shut the engines down, and just sit there until I can get to you. There're fire trucks coming from all directions, but it's okay. Your bird's not on fire. Just sit there...."

Weakly, Chris did as she was instructed, allowing her tired, aching arms to drop from the throttle and stick. The jet was oddly quiet, and all she could hear was a roar in her ears. Suddenly the entire dangerous episode overwhelmed her. She tried to lift her hand to halt the pain lancing like shards of glass into the region of her eyes, but she was too exhausted, unable to see anything except a cottony color. She wanted to pull the oxygen mask off, but she was in shock and going deeper every moment. She just didn't have the strength. Instead, Chris dropped her head forward, allowing the blackness to finally claim her.

Dan threw off the confining harness, climbing out of the seat. He dropped his helmet into the cockpit and leaped the last six feet to the lake bed. His hair was wet, gleaming darkly in the hot sun overhead. He loped across the desert, his mouth set in a grim line, his eyes narrowed without display of emotion. He raced around the front of the aircraft, jerking his head up to catch sight of her.

"Chris!" he shouted. Fire trucks and an ambulance were screaming, coming toward them at high speed, their red lights flashing. Dan swore softly, unable to see anything except the top of her camouflaged helmet as he hitched his foot up into the first instep on the jet fuselage. "Chris!" His heart rate soared with fear as he grabbed the handhold, hoisting himself upward. One more step and he would be there....

Dan froze momentarily at the top of the cockpit. Blood was splattered everywhere. For one horrible, annihilating second, scenes of Vietnam flashed vividly before him. She was slumped forward in the harness, unconscious. "Chris..." he whispered harshly, leaning over, gently pulling her back against the seat. His heart plummeted. Dan felt as if someone had struck him in the chest. "Oh, God, no. ...." He reached forward, unsnapping the oxygen mask and allowing it to drop to the floor of the cockpit. He rapidly examined her. Anguish rose with bile, a bitter taste coating his mouth as he surveyed her injuries. The visors had split and shattered, making several small but bloody lacerations on her temple and forehead. Dan gently loosened the harness, keeping one arm around her to prevent Chris from falling forward. His heart hammered in his chest as he again looked at her face. Her eyes were swollen closed, bruises beginning to discolor her skin due to the ferocity of the wind across the open cockpit.

The first fire truck pulled to a halt. Dan looked up. "Get the flight surgeon!" he yelled hoarsely. "Hurry up, damn it!"

He worked like a madman to unsnap all the confining buckles on the harness, his hands trembling badly. Dan became aware of someone climbing up on the other side of the fuselage. It was Rondo.

"You looked like you needed help," he said, panting as he came up the final step. Rondo's eyes widened and he stared at her. "Oh, God..." he muttered. "Is she—"

"I don't know," Dan snapped. "Get down on the other side. I'll lift her free and lower her to you."

Rondo nodded, heeding his directions immediately. He ran under the Phantom, stopping at the foothold, arms held upward. "I'm ready," he called. Several firefighters joined Rondo below.

Dan couldn't stop the fear choking off his breathing as he lowered Chris to the men. She had kept saying calmly she couldn't see...that she was blind.... Were her eyes damaged? Was she truly blinded? Dan climbed down off the bird, kneeling beside Chris as they carefully eased her down to the yellow-ocher earth. Gently he worked the helmet off her head. The blackness of Chris's hair made them all realize how pale she had become. Dan's trembling fingers immediately went to her carotid artery at the base of her throat. Her flesh was cool and damp, a bad sign indicating severe shock. Rondo hunched over them.

"Well?"

"Her pulse is hard and erratic," Dan replied shakily.

Rondo ran his fingers through his hair, staring down at her. "God, I don't know how she landed that bird. She's in bad shape."

Dan twisted his head, glaring up at the pilot. "Shut up!"

Rondo straightened up, surprise written in his tense features. He opened his mouth to say something and then shrugged. "I'm sorry, Dan. I didn't mean—"

Dan gripped Chris's arm, fighting back tears that shouldn't fall, that shouldn't be seen by anyone else standing there. "It's okay," he whispered tautly. He glared up at the gathering crowd. "Where the hell is that flight surgeon!" he roared.

11

DAN ENDLESSLY PACED the long tiled halls, head sunk against his chest, hands behind his back. He glanced at his watch again for the hundredth time. It had been over an hour since they had gotten Chris to the base hospital. He had ridden over in the ambulance with her, pressing her hand tightly within his own. Alarm had given way to stark fear as he listened to the attendant and the flight surgeon as they worked over her unconscious form. As they wiped away the blood, he had seen that a small piece of plastic was deeply embedded dangerously close to her left eye. Dan tried to talk himself out of the panic he was feeling for Chris's sake, but it was impossible.

He replayed the sequence of events in his mind one more time: the T-handle was located in Brodie's rear cockpit. If he was going to bail out by himself, he shouldn't have twisted that handle ninety degrees. By twisting it, he had deliberately popped Chris's canopy against her express orders. Anger, dark and murderous, raged within Dan. If he could only know how Chris was, he could hunt down Brodie....

"Dan! Dan!"

He turned, snapping up his head. He recognized Karen Barber and Mark Hoffman rapidly approaching him. Karen began to run, and arrived breathless at Dan's side.

"What happened? How is she?"

He patiently told them the entire story, unable to

keep the emotion out of his voice. Karen's face went ashen.

"Brodie!" she breathed. "He said he was going to get her." She looked up at him. "Oh, Dan! How could this happen? Who would think that Brodie really hated her enough to cause her to crash?" Karen sobbed and Mark came up, placing his arm around her.

"This isn't the first time pilots have played tricks on one another," Mark said. "I don't think Brodie had planned for this to happen. Is there anything we can do?" he asked Dan.

"No...pray, maybe." He swallowed hard, turning away so they wouldn't see the tears threatening to spill from his eyes. "She might be blind. Nobody seems to know for sure. Blind..." he croaked.

"Where is Captain Brodie now?" Hoffman inquired coolly.

Dan shrugged. "They were sending out a rescue helicopter to pick him up. Other than that, I don't want to know." His voice hardened. "At least not now. I'll deal with him later."

"Major McCord?" Dr. Hunter asked, coming up to the three of them.

Dan turned quickly in the direction of the voice. "Yes? How is she?"

Hunter was a man in his early fifties and balding. The doctor's lined face gave no indication of an answer. "Captain Mallory is semiconscious, and she's asking for you, major. If you'll follow me...."

Dan walked quickly beside him, leaving Karen and Mark waiting in the hall. "How is she, doctor?"

"We've got her on a pretty powerful tranquilizer right now and a painkiller, major. She's in a great deal of pain because of the damage sustained to the eyes and that region of her face," he answered quietly. He glanced over at Dan. "I'm not allowing her any visitors for now. And I don't want you or any

Board of Inquiry questioning her. She's in shock from the incident and needs to rest."

Gripping the doctor's arm and pulling him to halt, Dan's face mirrored his anguish. "What about her eyes? Is she—is she blind?"

"There has been damage to her eyes, major. I won't try and tell you there hasn't." He shook his head. "It's incredible to believe that she could land that plane with so much wind tearing at her face." Sighing, he watched the major intently. "We don't have an ophthalmic specialist here at Edwards. I can only tell you that the eyes are bruised, the skin around them badly swollen with some deep and mild lacerations caused by the visor being broken off under the force of the wind."

"But is she blind?" Dan demanded tautly.

"It's too early to tell, major. Her eyes won't dilate when light is put upon them, but that may be due to the fact that the injury just occurred. Given a couple of days' rest, she might be perfectly fine. But I doubt it," he added in warning.

"So what are you going to do about it?"

"First we're trying to get her records from personnel to contact her family and—"

Dan's eyes narrowed. "She was an orphan, doctor. I'm all the family she has. She's going to be my wife."

"I see..." he said slowly, giving Dan a more compassionate glance. "Well, as I was going to say, I'm putting a call into Carswell to get Captain Mallory transferred up there after she's stabilized. The ophthalmic specialist, Dr. Chen, will be able to diagnose her condition much better than we can."

Dan wrestled with the explosion of anger and grief. "Let me see her now, doctor," he ordered tightly.

Dan stepped into the silent room. Chris lay on the bed, her black hair a stark contrast to the whiteness of the sterile room. A heavy gauze bandage encircled her head, protecting her injured eyes. An IV was suspended above her, the needle in her left arm. She must have heard the door open because she slowly turned her head in his direction.

"Dan?" she called, her voice tremulous.

He crossed the room in three strides, gripping her right hand. "Here," he returned softly. He stared down at her, an avalanche of dammed emotions breaking loose within him. "You know something, Raven," he whispered thickly, "you're the bravest woman I know. And I love the hell out of you."

He leaned down, gently touching her lips. Her lips were cool and chapped beneath his mouth. He felt her weakly respond. It was enough. Continuing to grip her hand, he straightened up, remaining at her side, watching her closely. "How do you feel?"

Chris ran her tongue across her lips. "Like hell. I hurt all over. My eyes, Dan...." Her speech was slurred from the drugs, her movements jerky and uncoordinated.

"Just a precaution, Raven," he soothed her, hearing the fear in her torn voice.

She moaned softly. "No, they hurt. God, they hurt so much...the wind...." And she babbled on for a moment, finally quieting when he placed his hand on her hair, stroking her head gently.

"Ssh, Raven, everything is going to be all right," he crooned. "I'm here and you're safe."

"Don't—don't leave...."

His heart wrung in anguish over her words. "No, honey, I won't leave you for a moment. Not even a second." He stroked her damp hair. "Go to sleep, Raven. You're tired and you need to rest."

"My eyes...hurt...."

"I know, I know. But soon they'll stop hurting, Raven. Sleep, honey. I'll be here when you wake up."

A small sob escaped from her. "Promise, Dan?"

He shut his eyes tightly, fighting back his own need to weep. "Yes, I promise, Raven. I'll be here for the rest of your life."

As soon as Dan was convinced she was sleeping, he strode out of the room, finding the nearest phone. When he called Operations, his face became set with tension and anger. Settling the flight cap on his head, he stopped just long enough at the desk to tell the nurse where he could be reached in case Chris awoke. Then he told Karen and Mark what the doctor had said.

"Where are you going now?" Karen asked, tears staining her cheeks.

"Over to Ops. They just brought Brodie in," he snarled softly.

Karen gripped his arm. "Do you want me to stay with Chris until you come back?"

Dan nodded, his features softening for a moment. "Yes, I promised I'd be there when she woke up. This won't take long. I'll be back."

DAN JERKED OPEN THE DOOR that led to the commandant's office. Peggy, the secretary leaped to her feet, ready to say something and then wisely decided not to. Dan glared over at her.

"Where's Brodie?"

"In there. Dan...the colonel is on his way over here. Why don't you wait—"

His nostrils flared. "Peg, you keep this door shut. Whatever you hear in there, you ignore, understand?"

Peg nodded jerkily, never having seen Dan Mc-Cord angry. "I—ah, sure."

Brodie was sitting on one of the leather chairs, a paper cup filled with coffee balanced in both of his trembling hands. The captain's face drained of what little color had returned as he saw McCord silently enter the room. The stillness became brittle between them as the captain shakily put down the coffee on the desk.

"You'd better stand up," Dan snarled, advancing.

Brodie stood, his fists clenched at his sides. He looked exhausted, his green flight uniform still retaining marks of his recent ejection. "Look, McCord, I didn't mean for the situation to get out of hand. I just wanted to shake her up a little. That's all. Nobody in their right mind would want to have to eject in a situation like that. Use your head. It was a—"

Dan grabbed him by the collar of his flight suit. "You son of a bitch," he breathed harshly, "you damn near killed her."

Brodie threw up his arms, trying to push McCord away. It was useless. Both men were lean, but McCord had the height, and an anger that wouldn't be stilled.

"It—it was just a joke, damn it!" Brodie pleaded, his eyes widening. "It got out of hand!"

The roar of rage filled Dan's ears. "A joke! You call twisting that T-handle a joke? An accident? You lying bastard. Do you know she's over there in the hospital right now because of you? She could be blind!" he roared at Brodie. "Do you hear me? Blind because of your lousy hatred of a woman being a test pilot!"

"But I didn't mean—"

Dan muttered a snarl, doubling his fist and landing it squarely against Brodie's jaw. The pilot slammed backward into the wall, holding his bloodied mouth.

"McCord!"

Dan turned, straightening up from his hunched posture.

Colonel Martin glared at both of them. "Captain Brodie! Sit down!" he snapped. He swung sharply. "Dan, why don't you go back to the hospital?"

Shakily Dan turned toward the captain. "You're

going to pay for this," he breathed harshly. He glared back at the colonel. As much in warning to his commanding officer, Dan spat out, "He damned near killed Chris. She could be blind for life because of him. I'm not letting him get away with this!"

Brodie edged toward the chair closest to the colonel, seeking an ally in the commandant. Blood trickled through his fingers as he tried to stem the flow from the cut at the corner of his mouth. "You can't prove a goddamn thing, major," he growled. "Colonel, it was just a little joke. That's all. I didn't plan to eject or put her in a dangerous situation. Hell, the way McCord's acting, you'd think she's something special. She's just an officer like the rest of us. Everyone plays tricks on someone else. It's common."

Dan took a deep, unsteady breath, his blue eyes black with anger. "You sick bastard," he growled ominously, "she's going to be my wife. And there's no way in hell that I'll let any court-martial get away with not taking your wings and kicking you out of the Air Force." He pointed his finger at Brodie's stunned features. "And that's a promise, mister. And if the Air Force doesn't back me on this, I'll haul your ass into civil court and see you behind bars where you really belong." McCord trembled violently, throwing off the hatred and murder that seethed inside him. He looked over at the colonel. "I'm going back to the hospital. If you want me, I'll be there."

Martin nodded grimly. "Go ahead," he answered, his voice losing an edge of its hardness. "And tell Dr. Hunter I want a full report on Chris's condition as soon as possible.

Anger drained from Dan, making him feel suddenly weak and shaky. "Yes, sir. They'll probably be transporting her on a MATS flight to Carswell," he said slowly, "they have an ophthalmic specialist there."

"On your way out, Dan, tell Peggy to get those details. I'll personally make sure we have a C-130 standing by to transport her there."

Gratefully, Dan nodded. "Thank you, sir."

"Get going. I'll talk to you later, Dan."

LATER, AS DAN SAT ON A CHAIR next to Chris's bed, he realized just how much he had lost control at the commandant's office. Martin could have had him up on charges for hitting a fellow officer. But he hadn't. He rubbed his face tiredly, keeping a firm grip on Chris's right hand. Several times she had become conscious, only to be pulled back under by the powerful sedative. And each time, he would talk soothingly to Chris, watching her immediately relax and stop fighting the effects of the drugs. Colonel Martin had made a visit, and arrangements had been made for Chris to be flown to Carswell tomorrow morning. By the grim look on Dr. Hunter's face, Dan tried to prepare himself for the worst possible diagnosis.

He stroked Chris's limp hand, trying to pass some of his own body warmth to her cool fingers. Not only did he have to now control his own emotional state, he also had to help Chris realize that she could be blind for the rest of her life. With a deep sigh, Dan leaned back, resting as best he could in the uncomfortable chair, the world closing in on him.

CHRIS AWOKE SLOWLY, aware of a dull ache pounding in her head. Her mouth felt dry, as if cotton balls were lodged inside. She tried to lick her chapped lips. The drugs were wearing off, leaving her in a hazy in-between state. With her keen hearing she picked up the sound of jets taking off from not too far away. Blinking, she gradually realized that she wasn't seeing anything. She was only aware of the fact that there was light. Weakly she raised her arm to touch her eyes.

"Don't do that," Dan instructed softly, catching her hand in midair.

"Dan?"

"Better believe it. How do you feel, honey?"

Chris responded to the gentle quality in his tone. His voice was soft, providing a balm to her shattered senses and disorientation. She frowned. "Where am I?"

"You're at the hospital on Carswell Air Force Base. We had you flown in here yesterday."

Bits and pieces of the entire jigsaw puzzle of events began filtering into her questioning, groping mind. Slowly Dan reconstructed the series of events, answering her questions. Between explanations, he poured some orange juice into a cup, guiding it to her lips. She drank thirstily, asking for more.

"Help me sit up, will you? I hate feeling like such a weak sister," she said, holding out her arms in his direction.

Dan smiled, loving her courage. "For you, lady, anything."

She managed a sliver of a smile for the first time and it buoyed his spirits. "There's that McCord b.s. again."

He brought her into a sitting position, stuffing several pillows behind her back and head. "That's okay, you're going to be a McCord real soon yourself, so don't be making too much fun of the name."

Chris tilted her head. "You're right," she murmured. She grimaced, feeling the threads of panic rising in her throat as the effect of the drugs continued to abate. "My eyes, Dan. What about my eyes?" She touched the bandages carefully. "Is this temporary? I know I took a lot of wind coming down."

"Yes," he hedged forcing his voice to remain neutral. Dan gathered her hands, cradling them within his own.

Chris became quiet, her head tilted toward him.

Only the tension at the corners of her mouth was evidence of her anxiety. "What's wrong with my eyes?" she asked, pain etched in her voice.

Dan cleared his throat, taking a better grip on her hands. "We don't know the extent of the damage yet, Raven."

Her heart began to pound in her chest. "Damage?" she whispered. "Am I—I—"

"We don't know, honey," he reassured her quickly. "It's too soon—"

Chris gave a small cry, pressing her hands against her mouth. "No! Oh, God, no!" The strangled sounds filled the painful silence seconds afterward.

Dan's heart wrenched in anguish as he sat there watching her struggle with the reality. He felt her utter helplessness and wanted to console Chris. But there were no words to assuage the terrible anguish apparent on her face and in her voice. He gently captured one hand, squeezing it tenderly.

"Listen," he began, "it's too soon to tell, Raven. No matter what happens, I'll be here. You aren't alone this time. Do you hear me?" His voice cracked and he compressed his mouth, fighting back his own tears. "I love you, lady. Enough to see us both through this...together."

"At least I didn't punch out," she said hoarsely.

"No, lady. You rode the bird down like a true champ."

Chris fretted over the bandage on her eyes. "Brodie did it on purpose, Dan. He pulled the T-handle. I didn't give him permission to eject."

"He's being taken care of," he reassured her tightly. "Right now all I want to do is have you concentrate on regaining your strength. Dr. Chen says you can go home in another day or two."

"Home?" she questioned, rawness evident in her voice.

Dan rose, sitting on the edge of the bed, caressing

her cheek. "Yes, home. To Howard and Melvina's ranch. The doctor felt since it was going to take another ten days before we knew the extent of your injuries, you would do better in a home environment." He searched her face, now glistening with tears. "Are you game, Raven? Will you come home with me?"

Chris sobbed, nodding her head. Blindly she reached outward, seeking the safe haven of Dan's embrace. His strong, protective arms slid around her body, holding her close, assuaging her grief, pain and terror.

He held her for a long, long time, trying to give her the renewed strength and courage that she would need. Kissing her hair, he finally released her from his tight grip. She raised her hand, groping, finding his face. Her fingertips were cool against his jaw.

"I—" she floundered "—I hate not being able to see you, Dan."

He winced, trying to keep his voice neutral despite the horror he was feeling. "I know, Raven. Now quit fretting like a young filly who's had a saddle on for the first time."

"I make a lousy patient, don't I?" And then Chris raised her head toward him. She extended her hand, caressing his cheek. "I love you, Dan McCord. Kiss me. Please?"

It took every fiber to remain in control of his emotions as he leaned forward, holding her pliant body against his. He brushed her lips with a feathery kiss. "I love you, lady. More than I'll ever be able to tell or show you," he whispered against her mouth. The second time he claimed her he imprinted the burgeoning love he had held in until this moment. Hungrily he drank in the warmth of her, tasting the honeylike depths of her mouth. Fire sang through his body as he captured her in a kiss that melded them like hot, tempered steel—steel that would be tested to the limits of their love.

DAN STOOD tensely at the end of the hospital bed as Dr. Chen slowly unwrapped the bandage from Chris's face. It had been two harrowing days since they had come to Carswell, and she was showing her impatience at being bedridden. Wisely, the doctor had decided it was time to release her to Dan's care.

Chris was aware that her palms were growing more sweaty as each layer of gauze fell away. She couldn't get a straight answer out of Dan or the doctors about her eyesight, adding to her tightly leashed fear and frustration. The only time Dr. Chen would come to check her eyes was at night. And then he would fastidiously use his small flashlight and ask her the same questions again and again. "Is my flashlight on, Captain Mallory?" he would ask.

"Yes."

"What do you see?"

"Light."

"Hmm, very good. How about now?"

She frowned, blinking away the tears that always fell when her injured eyes were exposed to the open air. "It's dark again."

"And now?"

"Light."

"Good. Very good."

She wondered if he was going to go through the same thing today. It was so dark when he would check her that she couldn't see anything beyond the scope of the light being flashed into her eyes. Today was the first time she would be able to see Dan...to see his smiling face once again. Excitement wound through her, and she could barely keep herself under control. "It will be so *good* to get this bandage off," she confided huskily, clasping her hands in her lap.

Dan watched her mobile, expressive face, searching for the marks of the crash that had occurred five days earlier. As the last of the gauze fell away, Dan saw the yellowing of the bruised flesh around her cheekbones and on her brow. Dr. Chen asked her to lean back while he removed the protective pads from her eyes. Dan walked quietly around to the other side of the bed, slipping his hand into hers. She gave him a game smile.

"I bet I look awful. Black eyes and all," she managed.

"You look absolutely gorgeous," Dan parried.

"If you like women with black eyes," she retorted, hardly able to wait until the last pad was removed. Dr. Chen had warned her sternly to keep her eyes closed until he told her to open them.

"I happen to love you with or without black eyes," Dan said.

Chris wrinkled her nose. "Masochist."

"No, just lucky. Now be still while Dr. Chen works on you," he admonished gently. Dan knew it was her way of showing her nervousness. He saw the four hairline cuts that had been caused by the broken visor, relieved that none had required stitches or plastic surgery. The swelling around her eyes that had frightened him so much was nearly gone. Chen gently placed his thumbs below her eyebrows.

"Hmm, still some fluid retention. But that's to be expected under the circumstances." He deftly continued to press around the bones of the upper face until he was satisfied. "Much better, Captain Mallory, much better."

"Great, can I open my eyes now?"

Chen took out his small flashlight. "Not quite yet.

Tell me, do you see a difference of light now?'' He pointed the light at her closed lids.

Chris frowned. "I—no...should I?" There was a trace of fear in her voice. She felt Dan grip her hand more solidly.

"Hmm, it may be too soon. All right, I want you to slowly open your eyes, captain, and focus them straight ahead."

Dan inhaled softly as her beautiful violet eyes opened. They were still the most unearthly color he had ever seen. But he noticed the bloodshot quality to the white portion of her eyes as her thick ebony lashes opened. Chen leaned forward with another instrument, intently studying them.

"Tell me what you see, captain."

Chris blinked several times, aware of tears surging into her eyes. Embarrassed, she raised her hand.

"No, captain, let them tear. Remember, you've been kept in the dark for five days now and they will need time to adjust. Now, tell me what you see."

Her heart contracted. Her mouth went dry. "Nothing..." she whispered tautly.

Dan scowled, responding to the anguish in her voice. He glanced sharply over at Chen. The doctor didn't seem overly perturbed by the development.

"Light? Darkness, captain? Describe it to me?" he ordered.

Tears fell down her cheeks and she blinked rapidly. "I see...like a white wall. Is the opposite wall a white color?"

"No, it's green, captain. Now just relax and lay back down. I'll be looking at your cornea and pupil with an instrument for a moment. It will be painless," he assured her.

Dejected, Chris remained motionless as the nurse completed putting on a new dressing. Dr. Chen jotted down several notations on his ever-present clipboard. He patted Chris's arm. "Don't be too upset at this point, Captain Mallory. Your eyeballs sustained bruising from the wind force. They are still quite red and bloodshot. Many small capillaries were broken. And until they heal themselves, your vision will be impaired. At least your pupils dilate properly, and you can tell the difference between dark and light.''

"Is that good?'' she demanded bitterly.

Chen nodded. "Yes, it is.'' He looked over at Dan. "You may take her home, major. Bring her back in ten days. By then, the swelling will be gone, the capillaries healed, and we'll know better what we're dealing with.''

"Does that mean I'll be able to see, then?'' Chris asked hopefully, touching her bandages once more.

"I don't know, captain. Each case is dependent upon the individual body and its own healing mechanisms. Until then, I'm going to give Major McCord a short course on how to change your bandage daily.'' He gave Dan a brief smile. "I think she'll be happier at your home, major.''

"I think so, too,'' he responded, reaching out and laying his hand on Chris's shoulder, trying in some way to console her.

CHRIS WANTED TO BE LEFT ALONE in her bedroom at Howard and Melvina McCord's ranch. She had endured the embarrassment of stumbling up the steps despite Dan's guiding hand and helpful instructions. She had blushed, her face burning as if on fire, and she'd plunged more deeply into depression. Sitting on the edge of the bed, Chris clenched her hands together until her knuckles whitened. Anger raged with anxiety within her breast.

Blind? Dr. Chen had matter-of-factly said that he didn't know if she would ever see again. Her mouth went dry as Chris thought of no longer being able to do the one thing that had helped her escape from the misery of her childhood and a lifetime of loneliness:

flying. Her heart wrenched in further agony as she acknowledged another fact: how could Dan love her if she was blind? Would his love turn to pity? Oh, God, she couldn't stand pity! Unable to sit still any longer, she got up and took halting steps forward, both hands outstretched. The frustration of not being able to see intensified. Finally she made contact with the lace curtains at the window, running her fingers down them, aware of their texture as never before.

How long she stood there mulling over the possible end of her flying career and the loss of the man she loved so fiercely, Chris did not know. As she turned and carefully traced her steps back to the bed, she was only aware of a heavy weight in her heart and in her anguished soul. Some time later, she lay on the bed and willed herself into sleep to escape a reality she no longer wanted to be part of....

Dan quietly closed the door to the bedroom after checking on Chris. It was nearly eight in the evening. He had let her sleep through supper, realizing she was exhausted from the entire incident. Howard came over, putting his large gnarled hand on his shoulder.

"How is she, son?"

Dan frowned and walked with his uncle to the living room. "Sleeping pretty soundly."

Howard grunted, nodding his head. "Come on, let's go sit on the back porch with some good whiskey and watch the sunset."

Dan nursed the mellow whiskey. He sat in the ancient, hand-carved chair that had been a fixture on the porch since he was a boy. Howard had taken another chair, leaning back on it, resting it against the frame of the house, tasting his whiskey with obvious pleasure. Raising one eyebrow, Howard fixed his gaze on Dan. "I can hear you worrying clear over here, son. What's eating at you?"

Dan turned the heavy tumbler slowly around in his hands. "It's Chris," he admitted softly. "She's slipping away from me, dad. She's retreating inside those walls she erected when she was growing up." Dan pursed his lips, fighting back a wave of fear.

"You afraid for her or yourself?"

Dan grimaced. "Both of us. I'm afraid of losing her if she doesn't regain her eyesight."

"You mean you don't love her enough to marry her, even if she does turn out to be blind?"

Dan lifted his chin, studying his uncle in the twilight. That was a true McCord trait: straight-as-an-arrow questions. "I'd marry her even if she were a quadriplegic," he answered fervently.

Howard nodded sagely. "Kind'a figured that, son. But I wanted to hear it from you. So you think Chris might not marry you because of this?"

Dan felt as if a knife had slashed through his heart. "She's proud, dad. If she goes blind I think she'll revert to what she was before: a loner who survives at any cost."

"I don't think so," Howard countered gently, rocking forward, the chair coming down with a "thunk" on the wooden porch. "Look here, boy. That gal has heart. Look what she did with that plane when she couldn't see a thing! That's spirit. That's all heart. And you think she won't fight back once she knows which side of the street she has to live on? Come on! You be there for her and she'll rally. Just like she rallied when you talked her down to landing on the lake bed."

Howard shook his craggy head, a grin pulling at one corner of his mouth. "She's just like that gray filly you tamed when you were sixteen. You remember Nell? She was a headstrong young horse with plenty of heart, bucking you every inch of the way until you stayed on her. How many times did she throw you, boy? And finally, when you were both ready to keel over out there in that corral, you crawled up on her one final time. Remember how Nell just stood there panting, all four feet planted apart, finally accepting you?"

Dan vividly recalled that event. There wasn't a hand on the ranch who didn't want the three-year-old gray filly they called Nell, for a cow horse. She came from the best of King quarter-horse breeding. Howard had promised Nell to Dan providing he could break and train her. It had taken five hours out in the hot Texas sun in one-hundred-ten-degree heat to finally get Nell to accept him in the saddle. "Yeah," he said fondly, "I remember."

Howard nodded. "Chris ain't no different, son. She's a proud filly herself. She's done it all. And now, she may be faced with the greatest test of her life. Despite what she thinks, she's going to need you. And not out of pity, but because she loves you just as much as you love her." He jabbed his finger in Dan's direction. "Chris is gonna be a Texas thunderstorm for the next ten days. She's gonna go up and down, creating emotional whirlwinds around herself. You be there to steady her out, whether she likes it or not." Howard slowly rose. "She's fearful, son. And she'll be taking it out on those who love her the most."

Dan nodded firmly in agreement. "I love her enough to weather it," he answered simply. "We'll do it together. She's not going to have any other choice."

"GOOD MORNING, SLEEPYHEAD," Dan called, sitting on the edge of the bed next to Chris. He watched as she roused herself, the whiteness of the gauze surrounding her black hair a startling contrast. He leaned down, gently brushing her cheek. He had risen earlier that morning, showered and shaved. Chris had tossed and turned all night, moving in and out of nightmare states until dawn. Dan had simply held

her, soothed her with words, caresses and a steadying voice. As dawn approached, Chris finally slept
deeply and so did he. The crowing of a rooster near
the window had awakened him at nine.

Chris raised her hand, briefly touching her ban-
daged eyes. "What time is it?" she asked.

"Almost ten-thirty. Thought you might like to get
a bath and maybe a late breakfast."

She frowned, unsettled by Dan's pleasant voice.
She felt peevish and irritated. "I just want to sleep."

Dan gauged her grumpy voice. "No way, lady.
You've slept a good twelve hours. It's time to get up.
Now, do you want to get up under your own power
or do I carry you?"

"I'll get up!" She pulled herself into an upright
position, feeling suddenly light-headed. Touching
her brow, she frowned.

"What is it?"

"Nothing," she snapped.

"You wait here, and I'll get the water ready for
you," he said, rising.

As Chris felt him get off the bed, she experienced a
rush of guilt. "Dan..." she called, suddenly thrusting out her hand in his general direction.

He caught her hand. "I'm here," he said gently.

Chris wet her dry lips. "I'm sorry. I shouldn't
have snapped. I guess I'm kind of grouchy."

Leaning over, he kissed her cheek. "I understand,
Raven. Feel like walking to the bathroom or do I get
to carry you?"

A slight smile pulled at her full lips as she raised
her head in the direction of his voice. "I'll make it
under my own power. Just give me your hand."

Dan smiled, throwing off her covers. She looked
incredibly sensual in the black silk nightgown. Fighting back the urge to caress her, he murmured, "You
look so damn sexy that I might keep you here the rest
of the day." He offered a hand, allowing her to rise.

Conflicting emotions warmed within Chris. Since the accident he had made no move to make love to her. Was she that disfigured by the accident? Was she no longer desirable to Dan? Her heart sank. It didn't matter anymore. She would not hold him to his promise to marry her. No one would want a blind ex-pilot for a wife. She would only be an increased burden on Dan's incredibly busy and stressful life-style.

She forced a sliver of a smile over his teasing remark. "It would be rather boring, believe me."

Dan frowned, forcing her to halt, taking her into his arms. He felt Chris tense as she rested lightly against his body. He was aware of the fullness of her breasts against his chest and the soft curve of her thighs. He pulled a stray strand of hair from her cheek, tucking it behind her ear. His eyes darkened. "You can make even the gloomiest day look bright to me," he whispered. Dan gripped her tightly, loving her nearness. "Honey, you are the sunshine of my life," he returned, his voice sounding choked. "Always. Just remember that, my raven-haired beauty. Nothing is ever boring about you."

Chris turned her head to one side, aware of the intensity of his feeling toward her. "Even when I'm blind?" she forced out bitterly. "Don't fool yourself, Dan."

His mouth compressed as he gazed down at her contorted features. His voice grew quiet with conviction. "I'm very clear about you and me, Chris. In fact, I've never been as realistic about myself and my feelings as I am now." He gave her a small shake. "I love you, lady. And it doesn't make a damn bit of difference to me whether you can see or if you're blind. Do you understand that?"

The first three days of her convalescence at the ranch were nerve-racking. At times Chris was grateful for Dan's presence. He refused to allow her to sit in the bedroom or in the living room listening to the television set. Despite her fear and protests, he had taken her riding with him for the first day. On the second day, the temperature soared to over a hundred, and Aunt Melvina decided Chris shouldn't be outside in that kind of heat. Melvina had invited Chris to assist her in simple preparations for meals for the ranch crews. On the third day Howard drove them in the Jeep to various pastures to check on herds that were being readied to ship back to eastern markets.

CHRIS AWOKE to the sound of roosters crowing. *It must be close to dawn,* she thought. She lay beside Dan, her head resting in the hollow of his shoulder. Just the sound of his soft breathing steadied her tumultuous feelings. In six more days she would know whether or not she was permanently blind. And if she was? Fear twisted in her heart. Dan had treated her as if nothing was wrong. But there was! She was blind! He would always be waiting on her hand and foot. She couldn't have that. But she loved him, and despite what she tried to tell herself, she wouldn't kill those powerful feelings of love that persisted toward him.

Carefully Chris slipped out of bed, locating her cotton robe and pulling it on. By now, she had counted the steps from the bed to the door and mentally called them off in her mind. She hesitated, hearing no one up and about. It meant that it was around five-thirty. Quietly opening the door, Chris slowly made her way to the back porch. She had come to love the old, creaky porch with the chairs and the swing. The screen door protested noisily as she opened it and made her way to the swing. Sitting down, Chris tried to pull her thoughts together. Her head was screaming with all her deeply hidden fears of the future. Her heart wrenched with anguish.

Burying her head in her hands, Chris began to sob softly, unable to sort out the nightmarish mixture of anxiety, fear and insecurity.

"Raven?"

Chris jerked her head up, a gasp escaping her. It was Dan. She sat tensely, listening in the direction of the voice. "Dan?"

He moved noiselessly across the porch. He was clad only in a pair of jeans. "Right here," he answered, holding out his hand, sliding it down her shoulder. He sat down next to her. "You were crying."

Chris hung her head, emotions warring mightily within her. "I—yes—"

"Want to talk about it?"

She pursed her lips. "No."

"Afraid you'll sound like the rest of us human beings when we're caught in a cross fire?" he ventured.

Anger roared through her, and Chris snapped her head to the left. "Just what does that mean?"

"You're not going to fight this alone, Raven." The note of finality was deep in his voice. "You can't."

Suddenly Chris wanted to escape. She bolted to her feet and made a half turn to where Dan was sitting, her hands clenched. "Leave me alone!" she cried hoarsely.

Dan got to his feet, gripping her shoulders strongly. "I have been leaving you to your own thoughts, Chris," he growled. "And it isn't working. You're retreating and trying to fight your way through this whole damn thing by yourself."

Chris sobbed, trying to throw off his grip. It was impossible. "Damn you!" she shouted. "It *is* my problem! Not yours."

"You're wrong. It's mine because I love you," he breathed.

Her lips parted, glistening with tears. She was trembling visibly. "No! No, I don't want your pity or guilt, Dan," she said, sobbing as she threw her hands against his chest, trying to struggle and free herself.

"Quit fighting me!" he ordered angrily, giving her a small shake. "Just what does that mean: my pity or guilt? Is that why you think I brought you here? Or why I stay with you?"

Chris raised her hands, burying her face in them. She didn't want to cry like this in front of Dan. He didn't deserve to know the nameless horrors that stalked her twenty-four hours a day because of the blindness. "I don't know!"

"Well, I do know," he ground out. "You're so used to having no one that it's easy for you to escape inside yourself, Chris. But this is one time when you need other people." His voice softened and became coaxing. "I'm here because I love you. I wouldn't hurt you by pretending to do it out of guilt or pity. Listen to me!" He drew in a sharp breath, watching her facial features contort. Chris was going to fight him every step of the way. "I don't care how much you think you're going to battle this by yourself, you must know I'll be here to help. Do you understand me, Chris? Come on, dammit, say yes or no!"

She froze in his grip. Suddenly, she cried in anguish. "Yes! Is that what you want to hear? That I can't make it on my own anymore? Is that what you want me to admit, Dan?"

Dan winced at the rawness in her voice. "Oh, honey," he whispered thickly, pulling her against him. He held her tightly for a long, long time until her sobs subsided, until her body stopped trembling. He gently lifted her into his arms, carrying her back through the ranch house to their bedroom. If Howard had heard them, he was remaining out of the

way because it was well past time for him to get up.
Dan gave the door a push shut with his foot and
carried Chris to the bed.

Depositing her on it, Dan lay down, bringing
Chris beside him. Stroking her silken hair he said
softly, "I want you to know, Raven, that you *are*
someone. Whether you're blind or you get full use of
your eyesight back, you are someone very special to
me, honey. Maybe in your past no one cared what
happened to you or how many times you cried
alone. But I care from here on out. And it doesn't
matter how big a storm we have to go through, we'll
do it together. Do you understand me?"

Dan felt her heart beating like a snared rabbit. She
was damp from perspiration, her face wet with tears
of agony. He cupped her chin, forcing it upward,
leaning over and caressing her trembling lips. The
bitter taste of salt melded them together, but it was
the sweetness of her mouth that flooded his senses,
blinding him, sending them on a spiraling level of
ecstasy in each other's arms. Since the accident, he
had deliberately not made love to her, sensing that
she wasn't ready. Now, the urgency to show Chris
how much he loved and needed her overrode that
concern.

Chris moaned, calling his name, pressing her
body against Dan. His mouth moved masterfully
across her parted lips, coaxing her with his tongue
to join him in the celebration of life . . . of his love for
her alone. Her breasts became taut beneath his urging, the nipples hardening against the silk barrier of
her nightgown. The violence of her emotional up-
heaval left her hungry for his embrace and the natural strength that seemed to flow from his hands,
mouth and body into hers. She was lost, thirsting for
his steadiness, needing the stability Dan gave effortlessly. Suddenly the blindness didn't matter. She
reached out with her long, beautifully tapered fin-

gers, sliding them in joyous abandon over his aroused male body, glorying in his returning ardor.

Dan slowly removed the black nightgown from her body. "You're beautiful," he said thickly, shedding his jeans and joining her on the bed once again. "So beautiful." Leaning down, he claimed the thrusting peak of the nipple, tasting their hardness with his tongue and then his teeth. He felt her tremble violently, pressing insistently against him. A powerful wave of emotion nearly overwhelmed him as he sought to bring her to the brink of euphoria with him. Shaken by the fact he had nearly lost her in an aircraft accident, Dan wanted to brand her with the fiery knowledge that he loved her more than life itself. Without her, there would be no dawn, no dusk. Without Chris, life would be a pallet of gray colors instead of the myriad of rainbows that she shared with him by simply being herself.

Chris gasped with pleasure as she felt his hand sliding down her long torso, coming to rest on her silken triangle before parting her thighs. A sigh of delirious desire escaped her lips as she responded to the touch of his hand, her fingers sinking deeply into his shoulders. "Please..." she said, sobbing, "love me, Dan...love me...please...." Raising her hips, she met his deeply plunging thrust, a cry of joy on her parted lips. The insatiable need to be one with Dan was a driving, throbbing force. She had nearly died. She had nearly lost him and he had saved her life. Each movement together, each rhythmic dance they performed to the other's silent command brought her higher and higher into the glory of a euphoria she had never before entered. Her heart threatened to explode with a fierce and boundless love for Dan. Her body became a molten volcano unleashing a reservoir of pleasure, pleasure that took her breath away. *I love you*, she cried silently. *I love you over life and above death, Dan. I'll love you forever....*

Chris collapsed against him, gasping and spent by the avalanche of love and pleasure she had never known until then. Dan drew her close, rolling on his side, bringing her next to him. Gently he tamed the damp tendrils from her cheek and brow, kissing away the light film of perspiration. She clung mutely to him, aware of the solid drumlike beat of his heart in his magnificent chest. Was there anything unstable about Dan McCord? Nothing. Nothing except her and her explosive emotionalism. Chris nuzzled beneath his chin, needing Dan's embrace badly. "Hold me," she begged softly, on the edge of tears.

"Forever," he husked next to her ear. "Forever and one day after that, Chris."

"Promise?"

Dan closed his eyes. "Promise, my beautiful, brave love."

THE ROOSTER CROWING IN THE BACKGROUND slowly pulled Chris out of her rapture. She inhaled Dan's masculine scent, a heady aphrodisiac to her sensitive nostrils. The dampened hair on his chest became her pillow as she rested contentedly on him. "It was beautiful," she confided a long time afterward in a hushed voice.

"The best," he agreed quietly, stroking her hair. "But then, we love each other. And when you share a love like ours, its bound to be good."

Chris smiled softly. "Not only are you a warrior, but you're also a romantic, Dan McCord."

"Just another little extra you get by marrying me," he reminded her.

Her heart stopped momentarily and she tensed. Dan stopped making lazy circles on her naked back with his hand.

"You are going to marry me, you know," he said, his voice becoming more firm and less teasing.

Chris didn't answer, the same old quandry of feelings rushing upward, dashing her happiness, tearing the gauzy screen of love to shreds before the blackness that met her eyes. "We'll see," she mouthed in a whisper.

Dan deposited her beside him, raising himself up on one elbow. "No, you don't," he warned. "That's one promise to me you'll keep, Chris."

Her lips drew into a petulant line, indicating her fear. "Have you forgotten about this?" she demanded, pointing at her bandages. Her voice dropped to an aching whisper. "I worry about being just another burden on you. I mean, your job in the Air Force is so demanding that I—"

Dan's face grew tense as he observed the parade of negative emotions crossing her lovely face. "If you think your reasoning will scare me off, you're mistaken. And frankly, I don't give a damn what the Air Force thinks. They pay me to provide certain professional services. They don't run my private life. And I'll make sure we have the necessary time with each other."

Chris put her hands over her eyes, fighting back a sob. "Oh, Dan! I'm so scared! I'm—"

"Ssh," he commanded, gently pulling her hands away from her eyes. "You can be scared, frightened silly, depressed or whatever you feel around me, Raven. Just don't shut me out from those feelings. Let me share your pain and fear. That's why I'm here. Listen to me," he coaxed, holding her tightly. "What you give me in the way of emotional nurturing, of love, care and unselfishness is one of a kind, honey. And whether you get your eyesight back or—" he choked back his own tears "—if you end up blind for life, it doesn't stop you from feeling with your heart and soul, Chris. We just made the most wonderful love either of us has ever experienced. Did darkness stop you from sensing, feeling, knowing that I love you? No. And it never will."

Chris clung to him, her emotions still raw. Dan's strength for both of them lay in his firm convictions. The trembling note she heard in his husky voice only served to heighten the knowledge that he did love her, regardless. Reaching upward, she placed her fingers on his bearded, stubbled face, feeling the wetness of his tears. "I believe you," she whispered achingly. "And from now on, I'll share everything with you, darling." She choked back another sob. "It won't be pleasant."

Dan nuzzled her cheek, kissing her fiercely. "You're worth it," he said, his voice shaking with emotion.

12

"YOU ABOUT READY?" Dan called, poking his head into the bedroom.

Chris groped for her belt, which Dan had placed earlier on the left side of the bed. "Yes... just a moment." There. Her fingers wrapped around the slender leather belt, and she fumbled to slip it through the loopholes on the jeans. Had nine days gone by? It had passed quickly since that early-morning confrontation on the back porch with Dan. And every day since then had been filled with moments of agony and moments of rapture. For the first time in her life Chris found that confiding her fears and worries to someone else relieved her of the load she had carried constantly. She heard Dan approaching and turned.

"I'm not too swift with this belt," she apologized.

Dan grinned, taking her into his arms, placing a tender kiss on her parted lips. "Want some help? I'd rather undress you anyway...."

Chris grinned, smacking at his hand as he tugged playfully at the belt. "Dan McCord!"

He laughed gently, drawing her back into his arms, nuzzling her slender neck with a series of small kisses. "I love you, Raven," he murmured. Her laughter was clear as she swung her arms up, finding his shoulders and then pressing herself against him.

"You're impossible."

"Does that still mean you love me?" he demanded, growling.

Chris became more serious. "I never realized how much love could make you feel like you could beat the world," she confided softly, becoming serious. It had proved impossible to put into words how much Dan's support had given her the courage to fight back despite the threat of blindness. She was learning to cope. Chris had insisted on learning the layout of the house and each of the rooms. Counting steps to and from the barn, she asked Dan to teach her to saddle and bridle the horse she rode each day. With Howard and Melvina's loving encouragement, she discovered the blindness was less of a threat to her independence, realizing that she wasn't a burden to the people who cared.

Dan gazed down at her thoughtful features. "Love can challenge the very depths of hell," he returned, "and win. It brought you back, and look how much progress you've made in nine short days. I'm proud of you, Chris. Everyone is."

She felt the heat of a blush sweeping into her face and gave a shy laugh, breaking free of his grip. "I get maudlin often enough as it is," she muttered, finally buckling the belt.

Dan smiled benignly. "It becomes you, believe me."

Chris shrugged, embarrassed. "After bottling up all my emotions for years, suddenly just letting go is hard," she admitted. Reaching out, she sought contact with him. "But you've made it easy."

He leaned over, kissing her soundly. "That's because I love you. And I don't mind you getting maudlin on me." A grin edged his mouth. "Come on, I'm starved, and we have at least an hour's ride to the creek."

"Lead the way, major," Chris urged, caught up in his infectious mood of happiness.

As always, the small gray quarter-horse mare that Chris rode automatically stayed close to Dan's black gelding as they traversed the flat grasslands. The sun was high and hot, the temperature hovering in the nineties. Dan looked over at Chris, mesmerized by her natural beauty. She had disdained a cowboy hat, her black hair shining with a bluish sheen in the strong sunlight. Her skin was a healthy golden color now, the pallor chased away by the fact that she had been outdoors and close to nature for the past week.

He admired the movement of her body as she rode the gray mare: most beginners never picked up the natural rhythm of a horse's gait, but she had. That same sureness of guiding the mare was there as it had been when she piloted the mighty Phantom. Whether she had the firm grip of a stick of a jet in her hands or the reins of a horse—Chris exuded confidence. And it was that confidence and courage that had helped her come to terms with the blindness.

"Come on," he urged, "there's a nice two mile straightaway ahead. Let's gallop the horses."

Chris turned her head toward Dan's voice, smiling. "Okay, let's!"

Dan squeezed the gelding with his calves, the animal immediately breaking into a long, loping stride. Dan was careful to watch for any holes or debris that might be in the path of the gray mare, acting as her eyes.

Chris's hair flew back across her proudly drawn shoulders, her head held high, face to the wind. Her body slid effortlessly into the three-beat rhythm of the mare, her legs firmly clamped along the horse's barrel, flowing into each movement. The staccato of hooves hitting the dry, hard Texas soil became a repetitive drumbeat to Chris. Her spirits rose skyward as she felt as one with the quarter mare, enjoying each swinging, graceful stride. There was a beauty in being in sync with an animal or aircraft. She heard the soft snort of each exhaled breath of the mare, smelled the sweat, felt the dampness of the skin, the flick of the coarse mane as it whipped across her hand holding the reins. Suddenly Chris realized that although her sight had been taken from her, she still had her senses of smell, taste, touch and hearing. It was a joyful revelation, enabling her to put her blindness into even better perspective than before. Inwardly Chris thanked Dan for his idea of galloping the horses. It had been the first time that he had allowed her that freedom, and she loved him fiercely for his courage. There weren't many things she couldn't do, she realized.

After the exhilarating gallop, they arrived at the stream bordered by cottonwoods fifteen minutes earlier than expected. Chris helped to spread the tablecloth and retrieved the chicken sandwiches from the leather saddlebags while Dan hobbled the horses. The air was alive with sounds she had never been aware of before. She had always prided herself on her acute hearing, but now it was even sharper. She could distinguish between the chirp of a cricket, a katydid and the humming of a honeybee. Smiling to herself, Chris pulled the wine from the plastic bag Dan had wrapped it in. It was cool to her touch, and she ran her fingers along the sweating surface, enjoying the sensation. She heard Dan approach.

"I wish we could go swimming," she lamented.

Dan knelt down beside her, taking the bottle from her hands. "We can."

"Really? I thought this was only a stream?"

"No, it empties into a small lake on the other side of this hill." He popped the cork, placing a plastic glass in her hands. "How about if we eat, rest awhile afterward and then take a swim?"

Chris lifted the plastic glass to her lips, tasting the full-bodied sweetness of what must have been a white wine. "Sounds great. Hey, is this a Moselle by any chance?" She sniffed the bouquet, allowing the aroma to touch her senses.

Dan looked up, smiling. "Right on the money."

The afternoon lulled time to a peaceful halt. It was nearly four when she awoke from a small nap in Dan's arms. A feeling of joy enveloped her heart as she snuggled close to him for a moment before sitting up. The lowing of cattle was now present, and she cocked her head in the direction of that new sound.

"I thought Howard said all the cattle were on the southern range?" she said, reaching out and touching Dan's arm as he sat up.

Dan ran his fingers through his hair, glancing over at the hill across the stream. "There's about twenty Hereford cows on the rise. Looks like we'll have some company when we swim. Do you mind?"

Chris yawned, putting her hand across her mouth. The gauze bandage that held the protective pads against each of her eyes had loosened during her nap. She had a wild urge to tear them off, hating the band around her head. One more day...tomorrow morning Dr. Chen would unwrap the gauze and—

"You're nose-diving," Dan murmured, reaching out and caressing her chin.

"I'm sorry," she stumbled. "I was just thinking of tomorrow and...."

"Everything will turn out okay," Dan reassured her, getting to his feet and pulling her upright. He held her lightly in his arms, the afternoon too hot to promote closeness. "We'll drive in early tomorrow in time for the 10:00 A.M. appointment."

Chris frowned. "And then?"

"One way or another you're flying back with me to Edwards."

Relief washed through her at that thought. "Good, because I don't want to be stuck alone in a hospital,

Dan. Especially if—if I'm blind. I couldn't take it. I need—"

He leaned down, claiming her lips in a gentle kiss meant to reassure her and neutralize the fear he heard in her voice. "Raven, you're not going to be left alone. Ever. Just know that. I'll always be here. And by tomorrow afternoon, you'll be flying in that T-38 with me." His blue eyes darkened with love as he surveyed her upturned face. "Besides, I know Karen Barber, Mark and a whole lot of other people will want to visit you. Hell, the first day you were in the hospital recuperating at Carswell I must have handled at least twenty different phone calls from people who were concerned about you." He gave her a squeeze. "So you see, you have plenty of friends waiting for you back at Edwards."

Chris sobered even more. "And Brodie? You haven't said anything about him, Dan."

He reached up, coaxing several black strands of hair behind her small, delicate ear. "You're right," he admitted. "But only because you didn't need to be bothered by those details while you were healing."

A sigh escaped from her as she leaned against his strong, steadying body. "I can't help but wonder what kind of publicity this whole fiasco brought the test-pilot school and the Air Force. I was trying so hard to be the perfect student, Dan, so that other women would have an easier acceptance. I wanted things to go smoothly so there wouldn't be a blotch or stigma attached to women as test pilots." Frustration laced her voice. "And I blew it. Right in front of everybody. You must have seen the television news. What did they say?"

Dan compressed his lips. "You didn't do a thing, Chris. Get that through your defensive head. Brodie is the one who was wrong."

"And the school? What about its image?"

"Colonel Martin and the public-affairs people

have done a credible job of salvaging the Air Force's image. Although allowing Brodie to resign for the good of the service didn't make me very happy." He frowned. Dan had preferred to see charges leveled against Brodie for his actions. He forced himself back to the present, regarding her upturned face with renewed pleasure. He would never tire of gazing at her mobile, expressive features.

A slight grin edged his mouth. "You came out of this looking like the heroine you are, honey. And nothing short of that."

She shrugged. "I didn't do anything anyone else wouldn't have done in my place," she groused. "We're paid to save aircraft, not destroy twenty million just because of extraneous circumstances."

Dan gave her a fierce embrace. "I don't call being blinded an extraneous circumstance, Raven. I know I would have punched out and let the bird go." He sobered, his blue eyes wide with admiration. "Hey, what do you say we leave this serious talk for tonight? There's a number of things I've got to discuss with you before we go back to Edwards. There is liable to be some press there when we arrive."

"No, Dan," she groaned. "What if I'm blind?" her voice cracked. "Please don't let them embarrass me like that! Can you see me trying to get out of the cockpit without seeing what I'm doing?"

He placed a finger on her lips. "Ssh," he commanded. "I didn't say they would meet us on the ramp. After we land and file our report and get settled, we'll get briefed. There won't be any damn cameras on the ramp, I can promise you that. Now, come on. We've got a date with a small lake over that rise. A careless grin came to his mouth. "Bring a bathing suit?" he teased.

Chris grudgingly allowed the worries that plagued her to recede. She rallied at Dan's teasing tone. "No. But I don't dare get these bandages wet. I'll just wade along the shore and cool my feet off. How about you?"

"I'm not going to wade. Too bad you can't go swimming." Dan grinned. "I'd dunk you."

She gave him a game smile. "There will be other times," she warned, picking up his challenge.

"Will anyone be around to see us?"

"Just a few Herefords and they're all females. I don't think they'll mind."

She smiled. "Okay, hotshot jet jockey, let's go. I'm ready to cool down!"

In no time they had approached the fenced in area that held the lake. Dan dismounted, disregarded the Keep Out sign, and opened the gate. Leading the horses around it, he shut the gate and remounted, guiding them over the rise. At least thirty Hereford cows with newly born calves remained on the shore at one end of the small, beautiful lake. One third of the area was surrounded by a steeply sloped region covered with brush and thickets. A large stand of cottonwood graced the opposite end where most of the animals stood beneath their shade trying to escape the burning sun.

Dan took the time to explain the layout to Chris as they rode their horses toward the grassy bank. She turned toward him, puzzlement written on her face.

"I thought Howard moved all the herds to the southern pastures? Didn't he say he was going to allow the grass to grow up here?"

Dan nodded. "You've got a razor-sharp memory," he congratulated her. "For some reason I guess he wants this herd to remain."

"And they won't bother us while we swim?"

He reached over, catching her hand and giving it a quick kiss. "No, city girl. Cows and calves are much more frightened of you than you are of them. They'll probably just stare a lot."

Chris grinned. The consistency of the earth changed

beneath the mare's hoofs, and Chris could feel the horse sinking down into what she was sure was grass. She inhaled the changing scents, the smell of the lake nearby. "How close are we?" she asked, excitement in her voice.

"Just another few feet," Dan cautioned. "There's a bank with about a one-foot drop-off. The water is pretty deep at this end, and muddy at the edge. Most of the cattle come here to drink, and it's pretty torn up. I used to swim here when I was a kid." Dan watched her carefully.

"You'll have to get out about a yard from shore before you hit a steeply sloped sandy bottom. It's only a couple of feet deep and perfect for wading. Matter of fact, you can use the mare and have her go through the mud. Then you can slide off the saddle into the water."

Chris dismounted and sat down, taking off her cowboy boots and rolling up her jeans to her knees. Groping for the reins, she remounted by herself. "Which way, Dan?" she called.

He had just taken off his shirt, throwing it on the ground beside his boots and socks. "This way," he said leading the mare to the edge of the water. "Okay, just nudge her forward about five feet. Then you can slide off the saddle onto the sand instead of the mud."

Giving Dan an eager smile, Chris clucked to the mare. "Meet you in the water," she called, waving to him.

Dan smiled, watching her for a few seconds while the quarter horse negotiated the sticky mud along the shore. Then he turned his back to finish undressing.

Suddenly Chris felt her mare tense and slip. She grabbed for the saddle horn, but in doing so, her heel sank deeply into the horse's flank. Instantly, the gray took a huge lunge forward, sinking heavily in chest-deep water. Chris clawed at the horn, completely unbalanced. She was jerked free of the saddle midair by the mare's frantic jump. Suddenly, she was airborne. She screamed for Dan just as she slammed into the water, landing heavily on her back. Icy coldness closed about Chris's head and she fought down the panic. Water surged up into her nostrils flowing down her throat, suffocating her. She fought her way to the surface. Her feet weren't touching bottom! What had happened? She heard Dan shout in the distance. A whinney of a horse pierced the air. Floundering, panic eating away at her normal calm, Chris vomited up the water, choking.

Out of survival instinct, Chris jerked the bandages off. Light pierced her widened, frightened eyes. The world was a blur, water trickling down into her eyes. The gray mare swam past her, causing turbulence and throwing Chris below the surface.She felt lancing pain through her head, momentarily dizzied.

Suddenly she felt strong arms wrapping around her waist and pulling her upwards. Breaking the surface, she gasped as Dan swam toward the shore. Desperately Chris clung to him until her feet finally hit bottom.

"Chris," Dan rasped. "Are you all right?" He steadied her in his arms, holding her trembling body close to him.

"Fine . . . the mare . . . I kicked her accidentally. . . ."

He shoved the wet strands of hair off his forehead, tightening his grip as she swayed unsteadily. "It's okay," he gasped. "Come on, just a few more feet and we'll be out of this mud."

They wove drunkenly to the water's edge. Trying to shield her ailing eyes, Chris put her hand up to cut the sun's blinding rays. Her breath was coming in short sobs as she squinted up at him.

"Oh, my God...Dan!" Chris halted abruptly, staring wildly up at him.

He scowled, swinging his attention to her. She looked like a drowned puppy, her black hair limp and plastered to her skull and face. Mud clung to her lower legs and knees. "You okay?" he asked quickly, pulling her away from him, anxiously perusing her. "Your bandage," he began and his breath lodged in his throat. "Your eyes...."

Chris sobbed and then laughed. "I can see! Dan, I can see! I—everything happened so fast!"

It was true. Dan looked into her beautifully violet eyes and felt his heart constrict with relief. He breathed in sharply, watching her black pupils dilate and contract. The same lovely golden flecks rested in their mauve depths. The dancing, intelligent quality was back in her eyes. Tears came to his eyes. "You can see! You can see," he repeated reverently.

Shaken, Chris could only grip his arms, hungrily drinking in his sweaty, dirt-encrusted features. "Oh, Dan, you look so good!" she cried, throwing her arms around him in utter abandon.

He laughed solidly, holding her until he thought he might break her in two. Gradually he released her, anxiety giving way to his joy. "You shouldn't be out in this sunlight. Come on, let's get you into some shade."

CHRIS TOOK ANOTHER LONG LOOK at the blue that surrounded them. She couldn't remember ever being so happy. Dan was in the rear cockpit, she had the stick of the T-38 in her hand, and they were flying together in the arms of the welcoming sky. She smiled. "I never thought anything could ever look so good," she whispered. "God, it feels wonderful to be flying."

"I know what you mean, Raven. And it feels great having you at the stick again. You haven't lost your touch."

Chris warmed to the intimacy in Dan's voice. The soft smile continued to touch her lips beneath the oxygen mask she had to wear. "And you haven't lost your touch, either." Warming memories swam back to her of last night. The fact that Chris could see once again was overwhelming news, and everyone had celebrated it. Dan had taken her into the hospital immediately afterward. By nine that night, Dr. Chen had given Chris permission to fly once again.

Her eyes had been severely bruised by the buffeting that had taken place in the open cockpit. The capillaries had healed, the swelling reduced. By the time she had ripped the gauze off her head, her eyes had been ready for use once again. Chris took a deep breath, thankful for her sight as never before. They arrived back at the ranch by eleven. Howard and Melvina rejoiced with them. By midnight Chris had fallen into Dan's arms, exhausted but happy.

Her body still tingled from Dan's exquisite lovemaking. To be able to see his face, the changing color of his eyes as she adoringly loved him made it more poignantly special. Dan had more than a few bruises from his rescue of her. And so did she. Chris grinned, touching her right thigh that held a spectacular bruise she must have gotten when flying off the gray mare and landing in the water.

"Well, nobody can say you lead a quiet, sedate life," Dan teased.

She laughed. "Listen, hotshot, it's all your fault, you know. As if I don't get enough excitement being in the Air Force, you have to drag me to a Texas ranch and damn near get me drowned."

"The mare was a little upset, wasn't she?"

Chuckling, Chris shook her helmeted head. "I was never so frightened."

"Think you want to sign on at the ranch as a hand?" Dan teased.

Her violet eyes darkened with silent laughter.

"You damn Texas cowboy. As if it isn't enough you're a fine test pilot, you also have to have a second career as a rancher. Do the two images fit?"

"Sure they do, Raven. Both require strength, special skills and the ability to ride out the situation."

"Give me a helmet anytime."

"No cowboy hat?"

"I won't take the hat, but I'll take the cowboy," she teased gently.

"Raven, you're all heart. I promise not to wear my cowboy hat or spurs to bed."

She laughed solidly. "McCord, you're so full of b.s.—"

"There she goes again," he teased. "Being her normal, nasty test-pilot self."

"And you love it!"

"Every beautiful inch of you, I do," he promised huskily. "Hey, you realize in another hour we'll be home?"

Home. It sounded good to Chris. Back to their air base and back to flying once again. The incident with Brodie now seemed like a bad dream. She lifted her chin, looking through the dark, protective visor drawn down to fit against her mask. The sky was clear with the exception of a few mare's tail cirrus clouds. Up there, everything looked so peaceful and quiet. The ranch had given her a similar feeling. Chris could understand why Dan could move so easily between two seemingly very different environments.

As she taxied the T-38 up to the ramp after landing at Edwards, Chris could see a knot of people waiting with the ground crew. "What is this, our welcome-home party?" she asked, trying to make out the faces.

"Yeah. I know Karen and Mark wanted to see you. I think I recognize Julio. Hey, there's Rondo!" Dan's voice took on an edge of admiration. "Rondo did one hell of a fine job of landing at your wing tip. It was a fine piece of flying by both of you."

Chris hit hard left rudder, revving up the engine to turn the T-38 around and guiding it forward until the ground crewman gave the arm signal to stop.

"I'm going to pop the canopies," Dan said. "Looks like you've got one hell of a welcoming committee that can hardly wait to greet you, lady."

Chris was overwhelmed by the fact that at least forty of her schoolmates had come out to meet them on the ramp. Clambering down the ladder, Chris was immediately engulfed by her fellow test-pilot students. Karen managed to wriggle through, hugging her and crying at the same time.

Dan stood on the ramp, helmet beneath his arm, a wide grin on his handsome features as he watched the scenario. Chris was crying openly. But then, so were a few others, including Karen and Julio. Dan saw Rondo walk up to Chris and pump her hand in welcome. His eyes weren't exactly dry, either, Dan noted, suppressing a warming smile. Colonel Martin finally made his way through the milling crowd to shake Chris's hand and welcome her back. A shout went up as Rondo and Julio lifted Chris off the ground, resting her precariously on their shoulders. Chris glanced around, her eyes wide with surprise and happiness. Karen grabbed Chris's helmet, shouting along with all the others.

Dan followed the crowd, his blue eyes dancing with pride. _You deserve this, Captain Chris Mallory._ No longer was she a woman who hid behind walls to protect her vulnerability. There wasn't a person present who wasn't touched by Chris when she simply allowed those walls to melt away. And this was the result. He studied the other students' faces and knew without a doubt that they all respected her flight abilities. More than that, they liked her as a person. Picking up Chris's duffel bag, Dan happily followed the crowd, which he was sure was headed to the O'Club for some mighty celebrating.

Karen joined Chris and Dan at the bar, one foot hoisted up on the brass rail. She raised her glass of beer in Chris's direction. The music, laughter and cheering never completely ceased, and the club literally rang from wall to wall with celebration. The partying went on until midnight when everyone decided they'd better hit the bunk because tomorrow was another school day. Chris slowly walked out to the parking lot with Dan. The stars overhead were bright, blinking and diamondlike. Dan slipped his arm around her waist, drawing her near.

"Tired?" he asked.

She leaned her head against his shoulder. "Tired but so very happy. I never expected all of this, Dan."

He opened the door of the Corvette for her. "Get used to it, Raven. See what happens when you throw those walls away? People get a chance to see the real you. And it's a hell of a nice lady inside there."

Chris gave Dan a grateful look when he entered the car. "I owe you."

He shook his head. "No you don't. I was only a part of it. Give yourself credit, too."

On the way over to the BOQ, Chris rested, thinking about the day and those who supported her. She had never expected the entire two classes to turn out to meet her on the ramp. She was going to have to adjust her view of others, as well as herself. No longer was she the lone wolf struggling to survive, not anymore. Chris glanced over at Dan. Looking at him, with the shadows and light playing off his strong, composed features, gave her a feeling of incredible joy.

She turned her head toward him, tears glittering in her large violet eyes. "As you always have been, darling. All I know is that I love you with my life, Dan," she murmured.

He gravely met her gaze. "And it's just beginning,
Raven. You'll finish and graduate from TPS. From
there, you'll be known as Captain Chris Mallory-
McCord."

A grin edged her lips. "Isn't that a bit of a mouth-
ful?"

Dan returned the smile. "Well, I could have been a
real MCP and said Captain Chris McCord. I figured
I'd give you the choice of names. When things go
right, use your name. When things go wrong, just
tack on McCord and they'll come hunting me."

She couldn't stop laughing. "You're a crazy damn
jet jock, McCord," she accused warmly.

Turning, he smiled broadly. "And you love it."

Chris agreed. "Every minute of it, darling."

Harlequin Announces...

Harlequin Superromance™

(NEW)

IMPROVED EXCELLENCE

Beginning with February releases (titles #150 to #153) each of the four Harlequin Superromances will be 308 pages long and have a regular retail price of $2.75 ($2.95 in Canada).

The new shortened Harlequin Superromance guarantees a faster-paced story filled with the same emotional intensity, character depth and plot complexity you have come to expect from Harlequin Superromance.

The tighter format will heighten drama and excitement, and that, combined with a strong well-written romance, will allow you to become more involved with the story from start to finish.

Available wherever paperback books are sold or through Harlequin Reader Service:

In the U.S.
P.O. Box 52040
Phoenix, AZ 85072-2040

In Canada
P.O. Box 2800, Postal Station A
5170 Yonge Street
Willowdale, Ontario M2N 6J3

Share the joys and sorrows of real-life love with
Harlequin American Romance!™

GET THIS BOOK FREE as your introduction to Harlequin American Romance — an exciting series of romance novels written especially for the American woman of today.

Mail to:
Harlequin Reader Service

In the U.S.	In Canada
2504 West Southern Ave.	P.O. Box 2800, Postal Station A
Tempe, AZ 85282	5170 Yonge St., Willowdale, Ont. M2N 5T5

YES! I want to be one of the first to discover **Harlequin American Romance**. Send me FREE and without obligation *Twice in a Lifetime*. If you do not hear from me after I have examined my FREE book, please send me the 4 new **Harlequin American Romances** each month as soon as they come off the presses. I understand that I will be billed only $2.25 for each book (total $9.00). There are no shipping or handling charges. There is no minimum number of books that I have to purchase. In fact, I may cancel this arrangement at any time. *Twice in a Lifetime* is mine to keep as a FREE gift, even if I do not buy any additional books.

Name   (please print)

Address   Apt. no.

City   State/Prov.   Zip/Postal Code

Signature (If under 18, parent or guardian must sign.)

This offer is limited to one order per household and not valid to current Harlequin American Romance subscribers. We reserve the right to exercise discretion in granting membership. If price changes are necessary, you will be notified.

154-BPA-NAZJ

AMR-SUB-1